# ZONKS

and

The Gate Keepers

Book 1

*Alex,*
*Never stop dreaming!*

*Martin Galba*

MARTIN GALBA

## DEDICATION

This book is dedicated to Steph, Hunter, Slider, Wacky, Cash and our little Zonks, our amazing daughter Cassidy.

Thank you for being my inspiration.

# CHAPTER 1

*Sunt Venire*

George was awoken by a blood curdling scream followed by the sound of heavy footsteps. He shot up in bed, forcing himself alert so he could assess the situation. Even in a semi-conscious state he could make out the sound of doors slamming, furniture being dragged across the floor and glass shattering. He sprung out of bed and rushed for the door, then cautiously cracked it open. A peek out into the dark hallway revealed shadows of cloaked figures swiftly slithering across the tall walls of Chateau Azeri. Figures that he knew were not from this world. It had been a long while since they found themselves face-to-face with their pursuers, as these midnight heists had become much less frequent over the years.

'I can't let them find Molly,' he thought to himself. That was the only thing he forced himself to focus on. He quietly slipped into the hallway and ran towards the East wing across the stairwell landing overlooking the expansive foyer below. At the top of the stairs, he found Madame de la Fleur lying unconscious on the cold stone floor. She was hurt and barely breathing. George placed one hand on her shoulder and the other on the side of her head, releasing a jolt of energy until she slowly started to open her eyes.

"There was thunder...he's here..." she said. He placed his index finger on her lips to keep her from saying anything more, for fear the intruders may hear them.

"Shhh...everything will be alright," he calmly whispered in his usual gentle tone. Ensuring everyone felt safe and reassured, even under the most precarious of circumstances, was his greatest strength. And it was always genuine and without a hint of arrogance. "I'll go find Molly. Alright?" he said as he stood and turned towards Molly's room.

The wind picked up outside forming a small dust storm that temporarily shrouded the mansion and its surroundings in darkness. The trees came alive as they moved from side to side, desperately trying not to give in to the mighty gusts of the west wind. It appeared that the much-needed rain was coming after all. The raindrops started their dance on the windowpane and although Molly was still asleep, she let out a smile as though she recognized the beginning of a familiar tune. Her face soon turned weary. Normally, she welcomed a good rainstorm. She found it comforting in a strange way. She loved the subtle change in the way the sun-warmed pavement smelled once it got wet. But tonight, for some reason the rain did not bring her peace and Molly became restless in her sleep.

Just before George was rudely awakened, he too was having a restless sleep tossing and turning, trying to find a comfortable position. The other side of his bed was always untouched, the linens straight and the pillows perfectly fluffed. For the past fifteen years George never stopped hoping that he would once again wake up to find Clara sleeping peacefully beside him. He missed her dearly. He could handle being a single parent and all the responsibilities that it came with. He got used to that, but what he could never get used to was not having her in their lives.

The crackling thunder was fast approaching and within a split second, its companion struck a nearby tree with such power, it shook the stone walls of this historic landmark.

Before George got two strides towards Molly's room the solid wood front doors below swung open with a thud. They revealed an imposing hooded figure standing almost seven feet tall. Beneath a long, weathered leather coat his body was covered in thick dark armor. With each labored breath, the breastplate and

3

pauldron, each gardbrace and vambrace nearly giving way to the massive amount of energy flowing through the creature's body.

The ornate chandelier towering over the entrance hall flickered, each crystal bead trembling as the creature stepped through the doorsill. Outside, as the rain pounded down with growing intensity, the thunder and lightning continued their rhythmic duel.

Each step he took reverberated menacingly through the halls of the mansion, sending the centuries old paintings of French nobles and royals aflutter on the tapestry covered walls. The moonlight was fighting its way through the heavy storm outside. Spilling through the doorway, it created an eerie halo around the night visitor.

As the creature looked around, clearly searching for something important, the moonlight danced across its hooded face revealing a savageness one would only find in the face of someone who has lost all hope, not only in the world, but in themselves as well. Someone who was done in, worn-out, then brought back to life and rebuilt with the most godawful particles. Someone that wasn't dead or alive, but barely capable of taking a breath. A merciless creature living an impossible existence - incapable of quenching its blood thirst even though its sole purpose in life was to hunt and kill.

"And we meet again, my brother," whispered George to

himself as he caught a whiff of the rancid smell of rotting flesh that accompanied this creature wherever it went. George peeked over the stone railing only to catch a glimpse of the face that was neither human nor animal. A seared face of a one-eyed beast with a mangled left ear...of someone most feared in all of Heartland. The face that belonged to Corcoran.

"Alright, where is it?" growled Corcoran. "I'm out of patience and you are all out...of...time!" He spoke in broken sentences, pausing before saying those the last few words. The quick and shallow breathing caused by diminished lung capacity was evident to George even in his concealed spot.

George looked around and saw three cloaked figures lurking in the darkened library to the right of the entrance hall.

"Now or never," George thought to himself as he took the opportunity to sneak away to the East wing without notice.

"We have turned the entire main floor upside down but have not found it yet, sir," shrieked a hunched cloaked creature as he limped closer to Corcoran.

"That is not...good...enough!" replied Corcoran with a scorn. With his right hand outstretched he sent a black spark towards the ground. It burnt a path in the hardwood as it slithered across the floor, making its way straight towards the hooded creature.

"Why do I keep you around, you... miserable... scum?" he raged, "Must I do everything myself?"

The spark continued to travel on the surface of the floor towards the cloaked creature, as he tried to slowly back away. Inevitably, it caught up with him and backed him straight into a corner.

"Master, please...we are so close, I can feel it...." begged the cloaked man. As he took one last step, his back hit the wall with his peg leg peeking out from underneath his long cloak. The spark travelled up the wooden leg and headed straight towards his right hand, all the while burning a hole into the creature's clothing. He lifted his hand and screamed in agony as he watched the spark eat away at his palm, fingers and nails until the only thing left behind was a shriveled club of a hand.

"That was just a warning, Olds. Do your job, or I'll forget...to be...nice..." sneered Corcoran.

"Thank you, Master, for your mercy," uttered Olds as the two other hooded figures rushed towards their wounded friend. One of them tall and slim, the other slender but slightly shorter.


In the East wing, George found Molly sitting in her bed, drenched in sweat, shaking. She was repeating the same sentence over and over again, as if possessed by demons. She was chanting, "Sunt venire...sunt venire..."

George tried to snap her out of her trance-like state while desperately trying to keep her quiet at the same time,

"Shhh...Zonks wake up. Wake up, Zonks...you have to be very quiet, ok?" Zonks was his nickname for her. He had called her that ever since the day she was born, for she would often fall asleep or "zonk out" while he was feeding her baby formula.

"Daddy, they are coming...they are coming," said Molly, wide-eyed as she emerged from her dream-like state.

# CHAPTER 2

*The night it all changed.*

Downstairs, two women entered through the open main doors. Gorgon and Gundula, warriors from the Shadowland segment of Heartland whose sole purpose was to serve and protect Corcoran. They were both clad in leather armor and long, tattered skirts that accentuated their figures. Dark hoods rested on their shoulders with dreads of raven hair flowing down their backs. Perhaps what was most striking about them was their menacing steel-blue eyes that once seen, could never be forgotten.

"Master, we have visitors," snarled one of them. Corcoran growled, baring his ugly teeth. This minor setback clearly displeased him.

George knew he had to act fast. He needed to calm Molly down and get them both to a safe place. That's all he could think of. He helped her to her feet and they headed straight for the door. Just as they started to step into the hallway, they saw two flickering lights coming towards them. George and Molly abruptly stopped and backed into the room and ran straight towards the open window. He placed Molly onto the windowsill and spun around, ready to face his incoming enemy. Molly now just realized that it was raining outside, but it was like no rain she had ever seen before. It was wild, untamed, and pungent. It was as if they were right in the heart of a raging cyclone that was swallowing everything in its path.

"Not today, demon!" George called out, ready to fight. The two flickering lights flew into the room, where they briefly hovered in midair, as if surveying George and Molly, deciding what to do next. Then suddenly they apparated into two small fairies. It was Fon and Dorn, the Gate Keeper fairies normally stationed at the Far East Gate located in Germany. Even though George was relieved to see them, he instantly felt that life as he knew it was about to change.

"Oh, it's you...you finally made it, huh? What took you so long, anyway?" said George trying to appear calm and not at all frightened, which if he had to admit, he was.

"Hey, guys - I'm so glad you're here," said Molly as she peeked around her father.

"But...how do you know them?" George asked in amazement.

"From my dreams," said Molly plainly. She had heard that when one dreams their soul actually travels to the place they dream about. The fairy breathers had appeared in her dreams numerous times, she had met them before. Molly hopped from the windowsill and ran to her nightstand to grab her diary. She flipped through it until she found the page with a sketch she had done of the fairy brothers. "You see?"

The brothers flew over excitedly to check out Molly's renderings. Molly glanced at them as they engaged in an animated conversation that neither she nor anybody else could hear, for fairies lose their ability to be heard when they cross to this side of the Gates. Especially when they are in the presence of those with no magical powers.

In reality Fon was quite slim. Dorn on the other hand, was a bit on the heavy side. Fon doubled over backwards through the air in silent laughter when he saw the drawing of his brother. Molly was not quite accurate with the size of Dorn's belly. On the contrary, she made him look slightly larger and rounder than he was in reality.

"I'm so sorry, Dorn," she said, "I didn't mean to hurt your feelings." Molly picked up on this slight oversight and blushed.

Meanwhile, downstairs in the entrance hall, a fight was about to erupt.

"Beatrice, Beatrice, Beatrice...we meet again!" snarled Corcoran as Beatrice and her two protectors made their way through the doorway.

"Three of you against five...and a half...of us?" Corcoran snickered towards the mangled creature in the corner. "I like those odds! How did you find me, anyway?" He snarled as he shot a glare towards the tall, hooded figure cowering in the corner with his fellow friends, "I thought we...covered...our tracks." As he spat out the last word, the short minion cast a spell and all three disappeared into thin air.

"Three against three! I like those odds better," said Beatrice with a smile.

Dressed in a long medieval gown with a high collar, she was a very striking woman who seemed as if she had just stepped out of a fairy tale painting. The moonlight flickered off the silk fabric making it impossible to determine its true color. Her long white hair was meticulously tied back creating a fascinating work of art. She was breathtaking, but ready to fight.

Flanking her were Asgoth and Thana, her protectors. With their extraordinary ability to communicate telepathically, these tall, dark-skinned twins from the Skyland region of Heartland were a pair to be reckoned with. Their royal blue dresses cinched tightly around their waist. Silver metal breast plates and tall boots completed their elegant, but fierce look. Wherever Beatrice went, these two never left her side. They both kept a very close eye on Corcoran's two remaining warriors, ready to strike at any second.

"Leave now and no one will get hurt," said Beatrice calmly, as her trio circled Corcoran and his warriors in the center of the room.

"Not before I get… what I came here… for!" he snarled.

With a wave of their hands, Asgoth and Thana's long dresses magically transformed around their legs into form-fitting pants. They braced for battle. With gritted teeth looking at their opponents menacingly, Gorgon and Gundula did the same.

With these odds, Beatrice had a decision to make. If she had half a dozen protectors with her, they could easily take him down.  But she didn't, so she found herself with two possible options. She could either start a nasty fight to try to capture him, all while risking the three of them as well as Molly, George and Madame de la Fleur. Or she could focus her energy on forcing them far enough out of the mansion to give herself time to cast a protective spell and leave the fight for another day.  She opted for the latter and hoped her protectors would follow her lead.

Then the fight began. Corcoran attacked. Sparks were flying as attack and disarming spells were cast. Asgoth and Thana followed Corcoran's warriors up either side of the double grand staircase. Beatrice, with a few swift spells and counter spells, managed to move Corcoran towards the main door. Tapestries caught fire and paintings from high up on the walls smashed to the ground from the energy created by the magic spells. With a few swift countermoves, Asgoth and Thana both managed to overtake their opponents and positioned themselves defensively at the top of the staircases.

Beatrice swung her right arm and cast a spell so powerful that it shattered the glass windowpanes and unhinged centuries-old doors, sending them flying across the hall. Parts of both staircases collapsed to the ground, taking Gorgon and Gundula down with them. The final blast left Corcoran flat on his back on the ground outside the mansion.

Beatrice levitated off the ground and hovered directly above the rubble of the staircases. "Get out!" she ordered, and with a swift motion of both her arms she cast a spell pulling Corcoran's warriors from the rubble and thrust them behind her straight through the front door to join their master, landing on either side of him.

'I would have ended them right then and there,' thought Asgoth to herself. 'I've been waiting for this day for a very long time.'

'No, you wouldn't have,' responded Thana.

'Why did she let them go, then?' Asgoth looked over to her sister as they both flew off the upper landing and joined Beatrice high up in the air just below the chandelier.

'She did the right thing,' Thana thought. 'We will live to fight another day. But today, our main mission is to save Molly and Lord Enderby.'

'Why must you always be right?' thought Asgoth.

'I don't know,' replied Thana with a smile.

The flames started to engulf the walls, swallowing everything in their path as they moved up towards the ceiling. Time was running out.

Beatrice waved her arms casting a protective spell over the mansion. "The place is secure. You two stay here and keep the fire away from the door, while I find the others," she said as she flew up towards the corridor of the East wing.

# CHAPTER 3

*Time to go.*

**M**oments later Beatrice appeared in the doorway of Molly's room.

"Hi, Beatrice," said George and Molly at the very same time. "Jinx," they both said again in unison. George joked, "is there anyone you don't know?" However, in his mind he was wondering how it was possible that Molly could fill an entire journal of experiences of Heartland while never actually having been there. Molly smiled and turned to the page in her diary that showed a beautiful hand-drawn picture of Beatrice. Dorn was visibly upset over the accuracy of this drawing, compared to his own.

"Hello, George. Hello, Molly. It is good to see you," said

Beatrice with a soft tone in her voice. "The time has come. We have to go now."

Molly quickly grabbed her bag and stuffed her diary into it before they all headed for the door.

"Wait, I almost forgot," she said as she ran back and grabbed a little music box off her nightstand.

As they passed through hallways and corridors, Molly noticed that the entire mansion was completely destroyed. There were broken paintings lying in pieces on the floor everywhere. Curtains were torn, furniture broken and turned upside down.

"Who did this?" asked Molly.

"Corcoran did," replied Beatrice. "But don't worry. The house is sealed, they can't come in anymore."

"Where is Madame de la Fleur?" asked Molly worriedly. "Is she alright?"

"She's safe," Beatrice replied as they hurried down the hallway.

They arrived at the upper landing from where the double staircases once descended to the entrance hall. The fire still spreading furiously throughout the main floor made it seem there was absolutely no way out.

"Follow me and mind the fire!" said Beatrice as she leapt off the stone railing and flew down towards the door. "We'll keep the fire away from you," she shouted from below as she, Asgoth and

Thana reached out to keep the flames at bay. Fon and Dorn followed right behind her. George knew very well that Molly did not possess any magical powers, so he leapt up onto the stone railing and extended his hand towards her.

"Come on now, before we both get scorched," George grabbed Molly's hand and swung her up onto the stone railing. With a swift motion of his arm, he cast a spell that sent the chandelier flying across the hall towards them. Molly could not believe her eyes. Her father, a man she thought she knew everything about, was a wizard?

"How did you do that?" she asked in amazement.

"It's nothing. Just a little magic that's all. Piggyback?" asked George with a smile.

"Don't mind if I do? Even if I am too old for it now," said Molly with a half-smile as she hopped on his back. "Will you teach me how to do that?"

"Maybe another time when we aren't in such a rush," he said with a wink. "Now hang on tight and don't let go, okay?"

As they swung across the great entrance hall it felt as though they were moving in slow motion. Molly looked over to her right and gasped, horrified at the sight. None of the books on the library shelves were in their original places. Thousands of books lay in burning heaps, scattered across the floor, tossed around like worthless pieces of rubbish. When Molly and George first arrived at Chateau Azeri, she spent countless days organizing and categorizing these books. She was determined to read all of them. A book is a precious gift that deserves to be read, she always thought. And now here there they were, reduced to fodder for the hungry fire.

Their weight was more than the chandelier could bear and just like a surgeon's scalpel cutting a line on his patient's skin, the cords of the chandelier ripped through the ceiling, making it quickly lower to the ground - inch by inch. Molly hung onto her father for dear life, closing her eyes tighter and tighter. She was terrified. Within a split second the crazy ride, as if something from a haunted Coney Island carnival, was over and the chandelier stopped mid-air eight feet off the ground. George let go and they both landed on the stone floor.

"Are you alright?" asked Asgoth as she and Thana rushed over to help them up. They both nodded and slowly started to get up on their feet.

"Stand right behind me. I'll activate the portal," said Beatrice. They all moved directly in front of the main door - the only thing that still seemed intact amongst all the destruction. Behind them, the cords of the chandelier could no longer hold and snapped. The chandelier smashed to the ground with such impact it caused the fire to swirl away then circle right back in and towards the doorway.

"Get started, we'll hold the fire back," said Asgoth. Beatrice raised her right hand and cast a spell. The massive double door, which Molly knew to be extremely heavy, sprung open with minimal effort. There, outside of the house, stood a furious Corcoran, and slightly confused Gorgon and Gundula. Corcoran lurched for the door but was shot right back. The magical protective shield did not allow him to get through. This made him even more enraged.

A force of light framed the door opening as Beatrice activated the portal. "Alright, this is a free-formed portal, and as such, we don't know which segment we will cross into. Everyone be extremely vigilant."

The light appeared transparent but grew brighter and stronger as Fon and Dorn crossed through, followed by Beatrice. As they went through, they instantly disappeared into the light, leaving behind the invisible membrane of the magical portal. Now it was Molly's turn. She did not know what was about to happen. All she knew was that she had to leave the place she had called home for so many years. She hesitated and just stood there not able to move an inch. The sight of Corcoran paralyzed her.

"Zonks, they can't hold the fire back much longer. We have to go!" said George noticing Asgoth and Thana moving closer and closer to the doorway, desperately keeping the blaze at bay. Molly took a few steps closer to the portal then said, "Dad, I don't know if I can do this."

"Don't worry, Zonks," said George calmly. "He can't hurt you...I won't let him! I promise!"

"I will find you, brother," shouted Corcoran. "I will find you and I'll skin you like a snake! Do you hear?!?"

"Brother?" asked Molly in horror as she turned around to look at George.

"We have to go, Molly. I'll be right behind you," said George as he placed his hands on her shoulders and turned her towards the door.

Molly looked straight at Corcoran standing outside the house. He scared her and the thought of taking even one step closer towards him terrified her. She closed her eyes trying to find the strength. She was not like her father. He was brave, quick on his feet, always there with a joke to make her laugh. Or kind, calming words to talk her off the ledge when she was furiously upset over something. Why could she not find even an ounce of bravery in herself now? In her dreams, she was a fearless warrior. But in real life, she was simply ordinary. Her heart was beating a-mile-a-minute. She was trying to make sense of it all - everything was just happening so fast.

"Master! That's her! That's the girl!" shouted Gorgon just as Molly took a deep breath and disappeared into the light.

Corcoran stood in front of the mansion, relentlessly casting spells and cursing away for nothing, since Beatrice did such a fine job with the protective spells.

Once they all crossed safely through the portal, the doors to the mansion shut with a bang, and the energy from the protective spell transformed the house from a burning ruin back to its former glorious state. Furiously, Corcoran waved his hand and the three of them turned into a black mist, disappearing into the night.

# CHAPTER 4

*Why so angry all the time?*

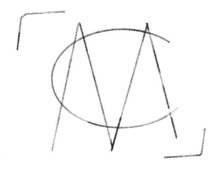

"It's not raining anymore. Why don't you run along? Maeve will be here any minute. And stop arguing. I'm not going to side with either of you this time. You will simply have to learn to disagree," said Dr. Claremore quietly just as the door opened.

"Who were you talking to, Doc?" asked Maeve as she walked into the room, chewing gum with her mouth wide open. Maeve threw herself onto the couch opposite Dr. Claremore's and continued spouting off disrespectfully. "I don't see anyone in here. Who is it this time, Doc?" Dr. Claremore did not respond. Maeve leaned forward and stared at her intently. "Between you and me," she whispered, "if you keep talking to your invisible friends, the next thing you know you'll be lying on this couch, not me."

*Maeve looked like any ordinary seventeen-year-old girl, with a slim figure and long dark brown hair pulled into a ponytail. She was dressed in the urban-chic fashion popular in the year 2132. It consisted of tight grey pants with built-in kneepads, matching grey shoes and a grey sweater top with a wide cowl neck that casually draped on her shoulders. She was troubled, and often referred to as a rotten egg by her parents.*

*"I see we are in a good mood today," said Dr. Claremore, crossing her legs and placing her glass tablet on her lap. "And Maeve, we discussed this on your last visit. My name is Dr. Claremore."*

*"I promise I will remember for next time," Maeve replied with a smirk.*

*"It's only our second session with her and I can already tell she's going to be a tough cookie. I have a feeling we won't get far with her," said Fon as he circled around Maeve. Dr. Claremore was trying to ignore him and focus on the therapy session with her new patient. "Look how smug she looks. Does she remind you of anyone?" he said looking over at the doctor with a sly smile, just as Maeve popped a big bubble with her gum.*

*"I have a good feeling about her," said Dorn as he flew directly in front of Maeve's face. "There is gentleness in her eyes. She tries to act all rough and tough, but deep down there is a good soul inside.*

*Maybe she's the one!"*

*"Let's hope you're right,"* said the doctor with a smile, realizing her answer fit both what Maeve and Dorn just said.

*"Can I ask you something?"* said Maeve.

*"Well, of course, you may,"* Dr. Claremore replied.

*"Do all your patients get the pleasure of listening to you read these outrageous stories or am I just a special case?"* asked Maeve as she straightened, leaning closer with such attitude, she startled Dorn and sent him flying across the room and onto the windowsill.

*"Wow, this early in and she's already throwing in the towel,"* said Fon.

*"The therapy sessions are tailored specifically to each of my patients,"* Dr. Claremore replied.

*"Well, I guess I'm the lucky one then,"* Maeve replied, laying on the sarcasm. *"But, still, I don't see how this is going to help me with my anger issues. I don't care about Molly, George, the French lady or anyone else in your stupid little story!"* replied Maeve.

*"Well, at least she admits she has a problem,"* said Fon as he flew over to the window perch and sat down next to his brother.

*"Look, Maeve. Your parents have asked me to help. That's all I'm trying to do. They are very worried about you."*

*"Well, they sure have an interesting way of showing it. They never leave me alone. They never listen to what I have to say!"*

"What about that time you hit your mother? Do you want to talk about that? Perhaps we can unpack some of the deeply rooted anger that made you go down that path..."

Maeve rolled her eyes and aggressively gnashed away on her chewing gum. This seemed to be her natural defense mechanism, whenever she wanted to avoid talking about something.

"I have not seen any of them do that before!" said Fon in amazement.

"She definitely reminds me of someone I know," said Dorn. "I just don't know who. Pass me the snacks, brother," Fon shook his head then pointed towards Dr. Claremore as if to say 'I know...her! Right here!'

"I know you've been having a difficult time lately," said Dr. Claremore, trying to ignore the comedy act on the windowsill. Maeve was once again quiet. "Allow me to share this story with you. There is a character in it that reminds me very much of you. And I'm hoping, as you get to know her, you and I can talk about her actions - how you might perceive them and what they mean to you."

"Well, you get paid by the hour. As long as I'm here, I don't have to put up with my stupid parents. So, I guess there's that," said Maeve angrily. "Go ahead...continue! But don't get offended if I take a short little nap on this couch." Maeve made herself comfortable and closed her eyes.

"Wow, she's sassy," said Dorn.

"We can do this!" said Dr. Claremore assuredly, as she looked over at Fon and Dorn. "Now, where have we left off..." she said checking her tablet.

"George and Molly barely escaped that burning house," said Maeve, rolling her eyes, even though she kept them closed because she was pretending to sleep.

"You see! She does care!" said Dorn happily.

"We'll see, ok? We will see." said Fon. "Ok, I know you are the one telling the story, but you can't continue without telling her a little bit more about George and Molly."

"You are correct," said Dr. Claremore putting her glasses back on. She winked at the fairy brothers, then gazed over at Maeve and started to read.

# CHAPTER 5

*Let's start at the very beginning!*

**M**olly and George spent a great deal of time moving from one place to another. Her father always told her it was for business reasons. The truth was, they were constantly on the run, trying not to be caught by her father's enemies. One thing sure remained the same. It did not matter where they were, which country or city they lived in, her dreams and crazy wild imagination were always there to help her get through the tough times.

Shortly after Molly turned five years old, their travels took them to an old mansion located in the southern region of France. The mansion belonged to Count Azeri of Avignon. The place was often referred to as Chateau Azeri. The Count, a man of noble descent, was a very close friend of George's family. Although, lately, the Count spent most of his time tending to business in another part of the country, so the mansion was practically empty.

One would not be able to see the house when passing by the property, for it was surrounded by tall trees and meticulously kept gardens. Around the perimeter stood an almost ten foot tall stone wall. It was, in most parts, covered with age-old tendrils of vines that crawled their way up the steep walls in search of the life-giving sunlight. A cast iron gate adorned with a symbol of a winged lion greeted any visitors that stumbled upon it. Through the gate, a small cobblestone road lined with decades old trees stretched ahead. The trees created a wonderful corridor which, to a stranger, may seem uninviting and eerie, but Molly fell in love with it the very first time they drove through it. The cobblestone path looked especially beautiful in the autumn with all the branches bare above and leaves of many shades of red, orange, yellow and brown filling the trenches.

The mansion was probably the biggest in all of Avignon. It had many rooms, hallways, and secret passages that Molly got to explore over time. There must have been about fifty rooms if counting both wings and the servant quarters in the attic.

Due to its immense popularity amongst those of noble birth, the mansion, in its high days, witnessed much activity. It was a sought-after place for leisurely relaxation. These days, there was much less hustle and bustle, so the estate was easily manageable by the handful of staff, which included the tender and caring Madame de la Fleur. She was dark-skinned with thick brown hair pulled into a tight bun. A crisp white apron tied around her short, stout frame with pockets full of whatever nuts were in season. She was known to offer them by the handful to anyone nearby. She did run a tight ship, though, when it came to taking care of the big old mansion. Everything was in tip-top shape. Meals were never late and the rooms were always tidy. A speck of dust was nowhere to be found.

Despite the secluded nature of the property, from the time they arrived, Molly was determined to make the most of every single day. There was never a dull moment if one chose it to be so. She believed that boredom was simply just a symptom of a lack of imagination and if one was to be properly occupied, with little effort, there was always something to discover or learn.

The first night at the mansion, Molly woke from a terrible nightmare screaming the names of three people she had never met. These names were not ordinary modern names. They sounded ancient and threatening. "Gorgon!" "Gundula!" "Corcoran!" The light on her nightstand flickered as Madame de la Fleur and George rushed to her room, not believing what they were hearing. They found her crying on the floor by the side of her bed with her arms wrapped around her knees. She looked terrified, as though she had seen a thousand ghosts. She was shaking so violently she could not even utter a single word to describe what she had just dreamt about. Perhaps she was still dreaming, but then why did the raindrops on the windowpane sound so real to her?

George had never seen her cry so hard. She was gasping for air and her heart was beating fiercely. He knelt beside her and with a calm tone in his voice, he gently said, "It was just a bad dream, Zonks. Just a bad dream."

"This should not be happening!" said Madame de la Fleur as she rushed out of the room in tears.

George was trying to keep his voice from shaking. "I will take care of everything," he said, as he wiped the tears off her cheeks. George kissed her forehead, picked her up off the ground and carried her to his room for he knew she should not be left alone. What scared George the most was not the fact that he recognized those names himself, but rather why these people appeared in Molly's dream in the first place. Why now? Madame de la Fleur was right, something was in fact wrong.

George did not let on to Molly that he knew the names she had cried out. He hoped that as she got older, she would simply forget all about her nightmares and the memory of them would fade away and eventually disappear altogether.

This particular nightmare would not return again until many years later on the night of their unexpected departure from Chateau Azeri of Avignon.

The next morning Molly woke up to an unfamiliar voice coming from downstairs. It was a deep male voice accompanied by a loud, boisterous laugh that echoed throughout the whole house. Was it an expected visitor or someone who got lost and found their way here and needed a place to rest before continuing on their journey? In any case, little Molly felt a rush of excitement as she hurriedly ran down the hallway to the landing at the top of the double staircases in the entrance hall, where she stopped dead in her tracks. A man in a long coat and hat was standing below with his back turned to her, talking to her father and Madame de la Fleur. A strange feeling of comfort came over her. Comfort of being in the presence of someone she knew.

"Ah, there she is," said George.

The mysterious man turned around to face her. "And you must be Molly," said the man. "I have heard a great deal about you, all good things I assure you," he added with a genuine smile. As Molly made her way down the stairs, he continued. "Allow me to introduce myself. My name is Count Azeri, but you can call me Uncle Az, if you'd like."

Before Molly even had a chance to respond, Madame de la Fleur stepped in to protest this informality. She was about to say something to which the Count simply said. "It is quite alright, Madame de la Fleur, we are in France, after all!"

Uncle Az was a tall, slender man with a wavy mane of black hair, dark, deep-set eyes framed by thick, distinct eyebrows, and a permanent shadow of stubble – which seemed to always reappear moments after his morning shave. Madame de la Fleur would often blush when she walked into his study with his afternoon tea, finding him casually sitting behind the desk with his feet up and shirt unbuttoned revealing his manly chest. Just simply walking into the room seeing him like that almost caused her to have heart palpitations. "As you wish, sir," she said as she stepped back.

"I heard you are quite fond of books, Molly," he continued. "I have one for you and I hope you will find use for it." The Count reached into his messenger bag, removed a leather-bound book and handed it to Molly. It looked very old. Molly smiled and politely thanked him for the wonderful gift. She flipped through it only to find plain, ivory pages. Not a single word or a picture to be found anywhere.

"Thank you, Uncle Az, but there is nothing written in it," she said looking up at him with a puzzled look on her face.

"There is a story in every one of us that deserves to be told," he said as he crouched down to be at her height. "You write your own, Molly. I'm sure it will be a great one."

This old diary with a strange symbol of a winged lion embedded into its cover would become her most treasured possession. Molly would spend hours staring at the symbol, imagining how fierce that lion would have been in a battle against evil wizards. Just like the lion that appeared in her dreams on countless occasions.

From that day on, Uncle Az's time away became shorter and shorter and more time was spent at home. Joy and laughter filled the house once again. On numerous occasions he, Molly and George sat around the fireplace into the wee hours of the morning, talking about his latest adventures. Although Molly was quite certain that most of his stories were figments of his imagination. She called him out on that many times. Yet his stories were always so vivid and detailed, it was wonderful to think that maybe he had traveled to all the marvelous places he described, and that the amazing people he spoke of were real.

In addition to enjoying the company of his guests, there was another reason why the Count returned home more often. Not only was he giving updates to George and Madame de la Fleur on the events in Heartland, but also providing invaluable information to Molly without her knowledge, which one day would prepare her for what was to come. Knowledge is power, they say, and one day, Molly would realize that the stories her uncle told her were not merely fictional, but rather extensions of her dreams.

One Sunday morning Molly decided it would be a fun idea to spend five minutes in every single room of the mansion. She set out to imagine what it must have been like having grand balls in the beautifully decorated ballroom, its walls covered in gold trimmed mirrors and crystal chandeliers hanging from the tall ceilings above, or spending an afternoon sipping tea and eating biscuits in the drawing room. Madame de la Fleur always complimented Molly on her ability to stick to the task at hand. Molly was not about to give up. Needless to say, that day she managed to check off every room, cupboard, stairwell and secret passage on her list. That evening, she barely made it to supper on time.

Her most favorite room of all was the library, which was located right next to the entrance hall. She spent more time in the library than in any other room in the mansion. It was an impressively large room that was two stories high with large dark oak shelves on all sides and antique furniture placed directly in front of the massive fireplace, which was the spectacular focal point of the magnificent room. It wasn't long before Molly discovered the mechanism that unlocked the door to a secret room behind the fireplace. She was clever and investigative that way. This little hiding place housed some of the world's rarest volumes. Above the fireplace hung a large oil painting depicting a scene with a lion and a lioness standing on the edge of a cliff overlooking a beautiful, serene valley. Opposite the fireplace were a set of French doors leading out into the entrance hall. On the left wall, a tall arched window let in the afternoon sun. Molly often felt she was in a museum and considered herself very fortunate to live in such a beautiful house.

The library was full of amazing books written by the best writers spanning many centuries and Molly promised herself she would read every single one of them. She had not gotten very far yet, but her seemed to lean towards the fantasy novels that remind her of Heartland. The Harry Potter series, Lord of the Rings, The Chronicles of Narnia and Wizard of Oz were among her favorites. She soon realized it would take a lifetime to read every book in the library, as there were thousands of books in Count Azeri's private collection. This did not bother her. Determined, she certainly was.

Madame de la Fleur would come by the library every afternoon with a cup of tea and some nibbles. She was somewhat of a modern-day governess, as Molly had never been allowed to attend school. George had never fully explained to her why, but over the years Molly had come to accept the fact that all her learning came from George, Madame de la Fleur and her Uncle Az. Despite Molly's lack of formal education, she was smart and very clever, although at times quite stubborn. When she made up her mind, it was hard for her to see other alternatives. And yes, George had many conversations with her about this, with hopes of teaching her to have an open mind and recognize other possibilities. Or possibly even asking for help when the task at hand seemed overwhelming. George found it comforting to know that Molly was very much loved by her Uncle Az and Madame de la Fleur, as if she were their own. He took great consolation in knowing that his little Zonks was loved unconditionally by them.

Molly loved the rainy summer days. The rain eased her mind from all the troubles of her daily life – now, at almost fifteen years old, just like any other teenager, she would agonize over the tiniest things. One of Molly's most favorite pastimes was sitting at her window listening to the raindrops falling on the sill. The sound of the raindrops reminded her of a symphony of music. She would imagine it was a beautiful musical arrangement composed by the Fairies of the North Shore or by the ancient good Wizards from the East whose stories were long forgotten by all, but their melodies would forever live on in the sound of each and every rainstorm.

The gentle rain opened a door that led to worlds conjured only by her imagination. Such worlds in which there would always be stories about kings, both good and bad; handsome princes rescuing beautiful princesses; giant castles nestled in the hearts of mountains surrounded by the tallest trees Molly had ever seen. Or fire breathing dragons; tiny fairies that lived in the forest protecting all the animals and good people in need. Or mischievous goblins; powerful wizards and witches, some of whom were lured to the dark side. This always provided a wonderful canvas of possibilities against which Molly imagined great battles between good and evil. Fortune and misfortune along with evil men who only had their eyes set on taking over the whole world. Molly had quite a vivid imagination, which got her into more trouble than she wanted to admit. She often wondered whether her imagination had any effect on her dreams, for she did dream up some crazy ones.

Unfortunately for Molly, this summer was unusually dry. So much so that some farmers had already given up hope on saving their precious crops. It seemed that tough times were ahead if the weather didn't take a turn for the better. Molly found herself wishing for a break from the heat. Even her long, light brown hair was always a mess – a rat's nest, as Madame de la Fleur would often say.

Night didn't bring relief from the heat either. Molly's vivid dreams would have her waking in the middle of the night drenched in sweat. There is a brief moment, just before one awakes from a dream when one feels like screaming but no sound seems to have the power to break through the deafening silence. Molly always wondered why that was. Perhaps there was an unwritten rule, Molly imagined, where if one breaks the silence in that most crucial moment between the time we are still dreaming and the time we are awake – a place Molly called *the passage of no man's land* - the screams one lets out would awaken our dreams and make them a reality.

Often she would be right in the thick of things, fighting an army of evil goblins when she tried to scream for help, but no sound came out. There was one peculiar thing about her reoccurring dreams. In every single one she seemed older than she was. She only recently stopped thinking about this, as her earthly age seemed to have finally caught up to that of her age in her dreams.

Whenever she woke up in the middle of the night from one of her wild and crazy dreams, she would reach for her diary and write down every single detail. She often wondered why her dreams made complete sense as she was transcribing them in the middle of the night, but when she read her notes the next morning, they sounded absurd. Little did she know that in addition to Uncle Az's stories, the dreams were also preparing her for what lay ahead.

# CHAPTER 6

*This is our last chance.*

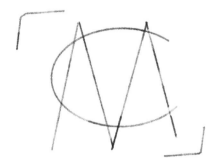

"I need to take a leak, Doc," interrupted Maeve.

"It's Doctor Claremore!" shouted Fon.

"Don't bother, brother," said Dorn. "She can't hear you!"

Dr. Claremore looked up from her tablet but didn't say anything. Maeve rose her eyebrows as to suggest 'and the can is where?'

"Oh...yes, of course. Through that hallway, second door to your right."

Maeve stood up, and slowly sauntered towards the bathroom.

"We are running out of time," said Fon once she was out of the office. "I'm worried!"

"I know Fon, but I'm not about to give up on her. Regina is in there. She was in there in every girl we've treated over the past many decades. I know it," said Dr. Claremore.

"I know, and each one of them took their own life before they turned eighteen," replied Fon. "Leaving us once again at square one with the next one. Maybe she just does not want to change and is happy to live out her existence as Protocol 24601 in the Chambers, while continuing this vicious cycle of her Earthly reincarnations."

"Why are you so negative, brother?" asked Dorn. "Have some faith!"

"It's hard to have faith when you've been given one last chance to fix someone," Fon muttered under his breath.

"I can't hear you when you mumble like that, Fon," said Dr. Claremore.

"I said it's hard to have faith when she obviously doesn't want our help," replied Fon, trying to avoid having to tell her the latest news from the Capital.

"Fon, I understand your frustration," said Dr. Claremore. "It's important to Heartland we give second chances to our convicts through the work we do here. You are absolutely correct in saying that some never actually want their second chance, and so they leave us no choice but to let them continue their Protocol, and through that they simply continue living their cyclical

Earthly reincarnations."

"No wonder they call the Chambers 'The Place of Eternal Doom'," said Fon.

"I'm not prepared to give up. I'm determined to see this through. I know we are taking an unconventional approach to our work with her. With her it's different."

"With her it's personal," replied Fon with a frown. "I was against this from the start, remember? Once an evil witch, always an evil witch and there's nothing any of us can do to change that. Maybe this isn't working with her because it was never meant to work!"

"Don't talk like that, Fon," said his brother. "It has to work!"

"She needs me, Fon," said Dr. Claremore. "But I also need her to experience her story from a different angle. To see, feel and understand why it all went down the way it did. I only hope that she finds some sense of resolution in it. And through it all, I hope she will change."

"Then there's the whole battle against Corcoran. We can't fight it without her. We need her!" added Dorn.

"Okay, okay! I'll admit it. You're both correct," said Fon. "Let's hope Regina will want to 'cooperate' this time around."

Fon knew something the two of them didn't - yet. He knew that this was their last chance. Rules are rules, and he didn't think Clara would give them another extension if they failed yet again.

With *Regina* it was different. Given the severity of Regina's sentence, naturally, Clara was not inclined to have her continue living in any shape or form.

"Can this story move along a bit faster?" groaned Maeve as she walked back into the office. "You are seriously putting me to sleep."

"Bahaha," Fon let out a laugh. "You should pick up a book and read some of the stories by the people of this world. Talk about snoozers. What happens in twenty pages of narrative can be summed up in five...I tell you!"

"Patience...Maeve," said Dr. Claremore looking over at Fon first, then at Maeve. "In order to understand the story, we need to lay down its platform. Laying down the foundation is an important piece of any story telling. You need to get to know the players in order to understand their conflicts, care about them, root for them or against them, cry with them. Some may say laying the foundation of any story successfully is the most critical piece."

Maeve didn't say a word. She threw herself down on the couch, trying to resume the comfortable position she was in earlier, before closing her eyes and raising her hand as if to say 'I'm ready. Resume your stupid story, already'. Dr. Claremore sighed, then continued reading.

# CHAPTER 7

*In Heartland, at last.*

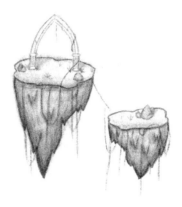

**M**olly found herself flying through a funnel of mad colors. It felt safe, though. She was being carried off in a forward motion by silk-like strings of lights. She looked ahead and saw the rest of the group and was relieved to see her dad as she looked behind her. He was there, just as he promised. Suddenly the mad whirl of colors transitioned into a pool of white light and Molly felt herself stop in mid-air, gently hovering in place with her arms outstretched trying to balance herself. The white light dissipated as she was slowly lowered to the ground.

"Are we in Skyland?" asked Molly in amazement as she looked around, recognizing the magnificent floating islands.

They were standing on top of a smaller one, which was connected by a set of stone steps to one slightly larger. Atop that one stood a stone arch that looked as if it were ripped straight out of some historical building in a medieval European city. This was the Skyland Gate. There were hundreds of floating islands all around, some connected by waterfalls or bridges, some by vines or ropes, and some just floating on their own; a breathtaking view of nature and magical beings living in perfect, suspended harmony. The islands varied in size. Some had villages built on them, some had mountains with trees or just green pastures.

Not far in the distance, Molly could see the largest island of all, the City of Aer, the capital of Skyland, where the royal family and the high court resided. Skyland looked breathtaking from up here. Something did seem odd to Molly though. It was very quiet here. Serene, almost. If it hadn't been for the sound of falling water, or wind blowing, or the occasional bird chirping, the silence would have been unbearable. Molly felt a sudden rush of emptiness in her chest. Something didn't feel right to her.

"Are you alright, Zonks?" asked George. "Isn't Skyland beautiful from up here?"

Molly nodded and responded, "Yes, it is. This is, by far, one of my favorite segments of Heartland."

"We must go on," said Beatrice, sensing the same uneasiness. "Fon, Dorn, fly ahead. But take the low route, just to be safe. And beware of the water falls and the oceans below. The waters are rough this time of day." The fairy brothers flew off.

"Where are we going?" asked Molly.

"Are you ready for an adventure?" replied George with a mysterious smile. Molly stared back with her usual look that suggested she was not buying it. "An adventure? Really?" she replied. "Why do I feel uneasy, all of a sudden?"

"You worry too much," he said with a smile. "We're heading to the Capital."

"The Capital!" said Molly in amazement.

Beatrice turned towards the arch, waved her left arm towards it and said, "Draco Ostendo." Molly found herself staring at five dragons perched up on the top of the gate. They appeared suddenly, as if Beatrice pulled an invisible cloak from over them. Molly didn't have time to think about it. Given her past experiences visiting these lands in her dreams, it was just one of those moments that felt right and didn't seem out of the ordinary at all. The dragons were all saddled up and waiting for their orders.

"Molly, you take the one with the spikes, and George, you take the one next to it," ordered Beatrice. Both of those dragons flew down and landed right next to them. There was no time to waste. They had to leave immediately. They had already been spotted by Corcoran's riders, who were flying from the main island straight towards them.

"I've never flown on the back of a dragon before!" said Molly.

"Don't worry, Zonks," said George, "you'll be fine, just don't let go and don't look down."

If the crazy light tunnel did not scare the daylights out of Molly, flying on the back of a dragon surely would. Molly's dragon followed her every move with its gaze as she walked around to its side. The dragon appeared calm enough, its massive chest moving with deep, even breaths. Molly felt its warmth, sensed the dragon's immense power and energy, and couldn't help but freeze, unable to move an inch closer.

"Her name is Ceara," said Beatrice, standing by Molly's side, "and she is very happy to meet you at last."

The dragon swung her massive head around to her side and gently nudged Molly. This was quite an unexpected gesture of kindness and caring, thought Molly as she turned to face the beautiful round eyes of the creature.

Ceara lowered herself to the ground so Molly could climb onto her back. "Step onto her knee, jump and bring your other leg around," said George from atop his dragon.

Once Molly was securely seated in the saddle, Ceara turned her head to face forward and opened her massive wings. With a couple of swift downward thrusts, they lifted off the ground. Molly closed her eyes tight and grabbed onto the reins even tighter. With every jolt of a wing flap, Molly felt as if she could fall off at any moment.

"Hang on tight!" shouted George, "it can be quite a bumpy ride as she's taking off, but once you are high up in the air, her wings will straighten out."

"We have to fly North, past the islands," said Beatrice. "Asgoth, Thana, fly ahead and distract those riders, then meet us at Junction Manor. Molly, George, your dragons are trained to follow me. Hang on!"

The roller coaster rides in Disneyland were nothing compared to the wild dragon ride they were about to experience. They were flying fast, taking sharp turns, flying around the islands, above and below them. Every turn they took they kept dodging incoming arrows and stones launched from the surrounding islands occupied by Corcoran's army. Molly noticed something terrifying. Hundreds of inhabitants of Skyland were locked in the dungeons located in the bottom half of the main island. Molly saw them all reach through the iron bars, pleading to be rescued. There was nothing they could have done for them, not now. As they flew past the City of Aer, Molly noticed a cloaked figure up on the highest tower of the castle. She instantly recognized this creature. It was Corcoran. He raised his hand and cast a spell that nearly threw Molly off her dragon. At that same moment, Beatrice cast a counter spell and changed the course of their flight.

"We have to get out of here," said Beatrice. "Molly, George! Follow me!"

Corcoran looked furious. With a swift movement of his arm, he summoned his dragon and jumped off the tower straight into its saddle. This dragon, a black-winged, ruby red eyed, fire breathing dragon was easily twice the size of Molly's dragon. Corcoran looked angry as he flew after them. Molly was scared and did not know if they could out-fly Corcoran and his beast of a dragon. Ceara was fiercely flapping her massive wings, dodging the oncoming spells from Corcoran. All Molly knew was that they had to fly faster than ever.

"Go faster, Ceara. Faster!" shouted Molly. She leaned forward and that made Ceara take a deep plunge. "No, not down, Ceara, up and past Beatrice," she continued as she pulled backwards in her saddle, trying to signal the dragon to pull up, just as Corcoran's dragon pulled next to her. She was terrified. Sensing his presence, she forced herself to only focus forward as Ceara breathed fire towards Corcoran's mighty beast. That awful stench she smelled when they left the chateau returned.

"Come with me," he ordered.

"No," she replied, still focusing her gaze forward.

"Stop... fighting... me."

Molly's heart was pounding. She was raging inside. Why does

he want her so desperately? "I'm not scared of you, you know?" she said summoning an ounce of bravery before glancing at him to her left. Her eyes instantly locked on his face, studying it. Even if she had wanted to, she could not turn away. She tried to memorize every imperfection, every minute detailed on his deformed face, trying to find a shred of understanding why he was so obsessively after her.

"I can take you to your mother," he said. "All will be alright, if you...just come...with me."

"Never!" Molly screamed as loud as she could.

"Aaaaargh!" screamed Corcoran. "Don't make this worse than it already is. Come with me and I promise no one will get hurt."

Beatrice hearing this and seeing how Corcoran was moving in on Molly, quickly turned her dragon around and positioned herself between them. She then cast a protective shield to separate them from Corcoran.

"Beatrice, what game are you playing? She belongs to us!" bellowed Corcoran furiously as his dragon let out a blast of fire that engulfed the protective shield.

By this time Asgoth and Thana returned and flanked Corcoran and his dragon.

"I don't wish to fight you or Beatrice!" bellowed Corcoran. "But you give me no choice. Just give me the girl and I will call my...army...off. It's as simple as that!"

"Not today, demon. Not EVER!" George raised his left arm and with strong forward motion cast a spell that pushed Corcoran's dragon back a few feet. Corcoran let out a cry. He was angry. Very angry. He knew he had no choice but to retreat. Knowing very well he was outnumbered in the air, Corcoran flew up and away back towards the castle.

~~~

Upon Corcoran's return to the castle, he was casting spells and causing everything around him to explode in a raging fire. He seemed to have a knack for destroying things. He was an angry, angry wizard. How dare they defy him!

"Master?" a timid voice of a woman came from the shadows. "Where is she, my Lord?" pleaded the woman.

"Destora Contur Sacatar!" he cried furiously. And with a swift motion of his left arm, he conjured an oval shaped pool of light directly in front of him. He looked straight at it. Nothing happened. He was clearly expecting something to happen.

"I need your blood," he said picking up a knife of a table nearby. "Come here, Regina. Are you ready to finally...see your...daughter?"

With an outstretched hand, Regina, a slender, defeated shell of a woman stumbled across the floor towards Corcoran. He punctured the palm of her hand with the knife and flicked a drop of her blood into the oval light. In that instance an image appeared. An image of a frightened girl that quickly morphed into one of five dragons flying across the sky.

"This will get us what we need. We'll be able to watch her every move and see where she keeps that book of hers," he said gleaming. I will take you all down!" seethed Corcoran. He knew exactly where they were heading and had the perfect plan to stop them once and for all.

~~~

This was too close for comfort. Molly was shaking. George noticed she was holding back tears.

"I will never let them hurt you, Zonks. Do you hear me?" he said. Molly did not understand why Corcoran wanted her so badly. She was desperately trying to find the strength, but she was worried that if or when the time came, she wouldn't have the courage to fight against him.

"I'm fine," said Molly, trying to seem brave.

"It will be dark soon," said Beatrice, "but we should have just enough time to reach Junction Manor. We will rest up there before we head out to the Capital at first dawn."

The journey to Junction Manor was uneventfully long. Molly's mind was racing. She had so many questions she wanted to ask. Why does he want her so badly? She dreamt about many battles against evil kings and queens alongside her friends from Heartland, but the battles were never about her. It was never about someone evil wanting to capture her so badly as to cause such chaos and destruction. What purpose did she serve in all of this she wondered? Everyone has a purpose in life. Some teach, some lead, some entertain and some simply guide and nurture, but everyone has a purpose. She could not stop thinking about what hers might be.

After a long flight, they finally arrived at Junction Manor. 'All roads lead to Junction Manor', as they say in Heartland. The dragons landed near a small archway leading into a garden. The archway was connected to a low stone wall surrounding a tiny little cottage that looked like something out of a fairy tale. Once they dismounted their dragons, Beatrice made them disappear with another magical incantation.

Molly noticed a look of worry wash across Beatrice's face. "I just had a vision. They don't happen often, but when they do, they..." she paused, not wanting to say what she wanted to say for fear of scaring Molly. The truth was, whenever Beatrice had a vision, it was not a good thing. "Corcoran is watching us. He is watching us through your eyes," said Beatrice.

"The curse of the invader...I understand," said Molly with a shaky voice, remembering the anti-potion she once took in her dream against the curse. It was certainly not one of her most pleasant memories. She was left incapable of moving for a few hours after taking it while her body fought to protect itself and developed a natural shield against the curse of the invader. She knew exactly what this curse meant and what it did. George was still confused about how it was even possible that Molly knew so much about all of this.

"Corcoran is gaining power..." continued Beatrice. "Clara was worried it may come to this. We have all developed a natural ability to fight against this curse, but those not from our world are most vulnerable against it. She prepared a potion that could temporarily stall the effects of the curse. However, in order for it to take effect, it needs to be administered by someone from the same bloodline. We will have until tomorrow when the sun sets before it wears off."

George also knew very well what else this potion did. The temporary effects of blindness to the invader were no real concern to him. The countless possible side effects to the cursed one were a cause of greater worry for him. The intent of the invader changes these side effects. It's like a lottery. One never knows what they will end up experiencing. Some experience delusions and anxiety, others a slow memory loss of past events or eventually a complete change of personality. He gathered his courage. As much as he hated the idea, he knew he had to administer it to Molly.

"Molly, we have no choice," said George. It may sting a little. Trust me it's for the best. When we arrive at Heartland, Clara will provide a permanent anti-potion."

Beatrice handed George a knife. Molly knew there was no other choice, so she outstretched her left hand and turned her palm upwards. Teeth clenched and body tensed, Molly looked away as George cut her soft skin open. Beatrice conjured a small vial. As she waved her hand over the vial and chanted an incantation it magically filled with a silver fluid, which she then handed to George. He opened it slowly then poured the contents of the bottle over the wound. The wound instantly sealed itself as if it had never been there. A tiny light began to travel up her left arm, and straight into her heart.

"The potion worked," Beatrice sighed, "I can't sense his presence any longer," she added with a bit of a hesitation. What she didn't let on to the others, was that she sensed someone else's presence with Corcoran. It was Regina.

# CHAPTER 8

## *The dark chest.*

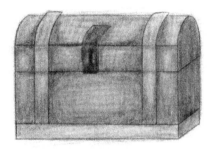

Through the magical window, Corcoran and Regina were witnessing Beatrice's interference. That image slowly morphed into the image of Molly. They muttered a counter spell, hoping to stop her. They were both slowly coming to the realization that despite their attempts, they had failed. This made Corcoran visibly angry. Suddenly, the magical window disappeared and so did the image of Molly with it.

"That's my little girl," she said, "my little Maggie."

This was the first time she got to see her daughter all grown up. Or, so she thought. She had no idea that the girl she saw through the magical portal was not her little girl. It was Molly. Regina began to hate everything about her own existence - her father for taking her precious little girl away from her, and Clara for betraying her.

"Come up with another plan!" Corcoran snarled as he headed towards the door. "But this time, do not...fail...me!"

"Aaaaah! That vile witch!" she mustered up enough strength to scream with such anger it shook the castle walls all the way down to their ancient roots anchored in the floating island. "Alright, if this is how you want it, I'm all in!" said Regina furiously as she crossed to her balcony overlooking Skyland.

The setting sun was casting an ominous shadow on the floating islands all around. Birds native to this part of Heartland, the beautiful long-tailed, green, yellow and orange feathered birds with pointy beaks were no longer flying across the sky, singing their ethereal songs. Neither were butterflies gently floating about in the warm breeze of the sunlight. Skyland, the magnificent floating islands, were slowly changing with every moment of Corcoran's reign, as though the life were slowly draining out of each living being, each moss-covered rock, grass stem and age-old sycamore tree. The rivers and lakes that once flowed through each island and cascaded over the edge far, far below, were slowly drying out leaving behind cavernous, parched troves. Sadness and hopelessness penetrated the air. It was hard to believe that centuries of peace and harmony that prevailed were so easily repossessed by Corcoran's presence. An eternal darkness was slowly but surely casting itself over the noble Skyland.

"We found it!" said Olds, the one-handed, cloaked creature clearly out of breath as he hobbled into the room, followed by two others dragging something across the stone floor with great difficulty.

"Here it is! It was hidden deep in the Dark Forest. The ancient protectors received the message prior to our arrival that their Dark Queen is ready to rise again. She will be rising through you, your Majesty."

"You bet she is! And I'm as ready as I'll ever be!" said Regina over her shoulder. "I can feel her presence inside me. Every minute she grows stronger and stronger," said Regina, trying to hide the truth that her body was growing weaker as time went on. She knew there was something she had to do to bring the Dark Queen to life, she just didn't know how to do it.

"There is one more thing, your Majesty," said Olds. "According to the ancient protectors, the Dark Queen's transformation cannot begin until the rising ceremony takes place. Which is when the two moons rise as one." He added with a stutter, "It comes at a price though..."

"What is it?" demanded Regina as she turned to face the hunched creature, taking slow and menacing steps towards him as the other two slowly backed away. "Speak, you idiot!"

"That is all I know, your Majesty," he said, as he knelt in front of Regina, fearing for his life. "The ancient protectors did not reveal that to us. All they said was that a price must be paid. I'm certain that the chest will have all the answers."

"Give it to me," snarled Regina.

He ordered the other two to bring the heavy chest closer.

"You can't open it with brute force, you idiots!" said Regina, noticing the scratched and warped metal straps.

"Da mihi hanc fenestram, aperueritis pectore ductor..." chanted Regina as she closed her eyes and ran her fingers across the top of the chest.

"You've done well. Leave me now!" said Regina as she opened her eyes and slowly lifted her gaze towards her servants. "Tell Corcoran to prepare the army for another battle. This time around, it will be a wet one!" said Regina with a menacing smile.

# CHAPTER 9

*All roads lead to Junction Manor*

Not everything is as it first appears in Heartland. Molly knew this to be true from her dreams. From this vantage point, Junction Manor appeared to be a rickety old stone cottage covered in vines. To a passerby stumbling upon it for the first time, it may seem haunted and abandoned. Uninviting, really. A short stone fence surrounded the entire house. The fence had seven stone archway openings through which Junction Manor received or bade farewell to visitors from each of the seven segments in Heartland. They all walked up to one of these openings and suddenly, as if out of nowhere, Molly heard a peculiar voice.

"Was your journey a pleasant one? Come in, come in and rest

a bit, before it takes you further on!" Molly looked around but did not see anyone.

"Beatrice, Asgoth and Thana, it is great to see you once again. You bring guests, I see!" said the voice again.

Molly looked confused. She could not figure out where the voice was coming from. She then noticed Beatrice looking at a troll sitting on top of the archway, holding a chalkboard and a piece of chalk. 'Ah, that's where the voice was coming from', she thought, 'so I wasn't losing my mind after all. Everything is alright, Molly. Just don't panic. Stay focused!'

"My name is Grindrod. What's yours?" asked the troll looking peculiarly at Molly and George.

"I am George. And this is Molly," he said as he stepped forward.

Grindrod looked perplexed at first. He kept staring at them without saying a word. One moment he tilted his head to the left and murmured something. Then he tilted his head to the right and thoroughly examined Molly from head to toe, before looking at his chalkboard.

"Are you Skypeople? I know everyone in Heartland but never have I met anyone by those names," said Grindrod with a puzzled look on his face as he continued to consult his magical chalkboard for more information about these two strangers.

"You may know me as Lord Enderby," George said as he

stepped even closer.

Grindrod was so surprised by the news that he almost fell from his perch, his chalkboard nearly flying out of his hand. This troll, that appeared to be so collected and matter of fact just a few moments ago, instantly lost his cool and turned into a blabbering fool.

"Sir. We have... been... uhm... long expecting you... uhm... hm... here, welcome!" he seemed to be star-struck and for a brief moment his brain experienced a mild power surge and as a result his mind and mouth got disconnected. He could barely utter a word, poor fellow. He cleared his throat, forced himself to take a deep breath and regained his senses before continuing.

"If you wish to stay a bit, you must have a word to give," continued Grindrod with his riddle, "Beatrice, what is the password? I'm sure you understand that due to the new developments, we have implemented stricter security measures."

Beatrice nodded, then raised her left hand and said "Altora Siractra". A shimmer of wavy light appeared in the archway opening. A place that moments ago seemed uninviting and a bit scary, if Molly had to be honest, magically turned into an elegant garden full of topiaries, exotic flowers and stone pathways. In the middle of the serene garden stood the same Junction Manor. The only difference was that it no longer looked old and decrepit. It was beautiful, like something out of an old European fairytale. Molly looked through the archway in amazement, then slowly moved her head to peek around the outside of it where she could again see that rickety old house they saw earlier.

"Well, of course this place is magical, too," she whispered, as they walked under the archway into the garden. The smell of fresh grass, flowers and clear air was dizzying at first. The sound of magical birds and bees buzzing about greatly enhanced the peaceful and calming nature of the magical garden. It all seemed so surreal that Molly kept reminding herself of the fact that in Heartland, anything was possible, and one should always expect the unexpected. And speaking of unexpected - the archway behind them suddenly sealed itself.

"Oh, my!" said Grindrod, "that was certainly not supposed to happen!"

"Looks like someone closed the Skyland entrance," said Beatrice as she looked over to George with a concerned look on her face, "I'll advise the proprietor. In the meantime, Grindrod, seal the entrance from this end as well. Just to be safe."

Junction Manor was a busy hub of magical creatures and travelers coming and going. Molly felt confused at first. Hundreds of elves, goblins, trolls, fairies, and other magical creatures were coming in and out of this tiny little cottage. How could they all fit in there? It reminded her of a television program she watched long ago, of a clown car at the circus, with an endless stream of creatures flowing in and out.

"Come along, Molly," said George. "Don't fall behind."

Molly walked up to the front entrance and found herself filing in with the rest of the magical creatures arriving at the same time. Never in a million years would she have guessed what was inside this tiny cottage. A rush of excitement came over her and as she walked through the door, she found herself entering the massive, circular shaped lobby of Junction Manor.

"I've never seen anything like this," said Molly in total amazement. She pretty quickly realized that this was a magical hotel, of sorts, a place of refuge and rest.

The place they just entered into resembled a foyer of a beautiful ancient castle nestled in the heart of Europe that Molly had seen countless images of in her uncle's books. With sandstone walls, pillars and gorgeous fabric accents in light shades of green – every vantage point provided a breathtaking view. A massive candle lit chandelier hung from the intricately carved ceiling. Large banners symbolizing each of Heartland's segments hung from above, gently flowing side to side from the small breeze blowing through. Molly looked up and saw balconies lining five stories above overlooking the lobby. There were all sorts of magical creatures moving and flying around, some appeared to be staff of the Manor, dressed in dark green uniforms, but most were temporary residents of Junction Manor. 'Lucky them!' Molly thought. She would have loved to stay here for a few nights, exploring all the rooms and trying out all the amazing food they probably served here.

A grand staircase led up to the first level. From there, Molly saw numerous staircases and doors leading to what she suspected were the various halls, rooms and dormitories. Then she remembered that moments earlier she was looking at a tiny house, and now she was standing in the middle of a massive castle.

"But how is it all possible?" asked Molly confusedly. "Wait, don't tell me. It's some sort of a spell, right?"

"Yes, you're correct. An ancient spell protects Junction Manor," explained Beatrice, "for centuries this has always been a safe place connecting our segments. I trust you are familiar with them all," added Beatrice, throwing a smile over to Molly.

"Yes, the six primary segments of Heartland are – in alphabetical order because that is the only way I remember them all," she said with a smile, "Barrenland, Shadowland, Skyland, Waterland, Winterland and Woodland."

"You missed one!" said George with a raised eyebrow and a smile.

"YES! I nearly forgot, the Capital," she added quickly, "it is, indeed, the seventh segment of Heartland. How could I have forgotten the Capital?"

They continued their way through the lobby walking towards a group of witches and wizards, led by a bald, bespectacled, olive-skinned man with a neatly kept beard. He was dressed in a beautiful cloak that lightly dusted the stone floor as he walked.

Molly couldn't help but giggle a bit. It seemed that the hair that should have been on his head was on his chin instead. She was quite amused by it, even though she knew she should be ashamed of herself for having such rude thoughts.

"Welcome, we have been expecting you. Allow me to introduce myself. My name is Trail. I am the owner and proprietor of Junction Manor. It is a pleasure to have you stay with us here tonight.

'Surprise, surprise? He's still here. I can't stand him,' thought Thana to herself.

Asgoth looked over at her sister, 'You had to know there was a good chance he would be, so just stay calm and act professional. We are here for work, not pleasure.'

"Thank you," said George, "may we have a quick word with you?" Beatrice and Trail followed him off to the side away from the others.

"This place is so beautiful," said Molly in amazement.

"It is indeed," said Asgoth, "I have fond memories of this place from my youth."

'Ha!' thought Thana. 'You mean to say from your *wild* youth? Should I tell her about the time you nearly burned down the Café?'

'Don't you dare frighten the child, sister,' thought Asgoth as she shot a look at Thana. 'We don't talk about that one unfortunate incident, remember?'

'But it was funny,' added Thana.

'There was absolutely nothing funny about that,' Asgoth retorted. She did not want to show that Thana was getting under her skin, but she was.

The ever-observant Molly picked up on this silent interlude and quickly jumped in.

"Is she trash-thinking you?" Molly asked Asgoth. Thana looked shocked at Molly's intuitiveness. "You know, it's like trash-talking, but different. You know what I mean…"

"But how do you know?" asked Thana.

"The way Asgoth looked at you," said Molly. "The expression on her face kept changing, the way normal people's expression changes when they are having a heated argument. Not to say you're not normal," added Molly, suddenly realizing she may have offended the two of them.

"No worries, Molly," said Asgoth with a smile. "The two of us are certainly far from normal."

'Speak for yourself,' thought Thana.

"I've known about your special powers for a long time. You certainly are two of the coolest people I've ever known," Molly added with a smile.

'I like this kid more and more. She's not a regular teenager, that's for sure,' thought Thana.

"Now back to our regularly scheduled programming," joked Asgoth. "On every floor there are beautiful bedrooms where all the magical creatures from this land can find a peaceful place to rest their head on a softly fluffed pillow before another day's journey."

'After all these years, look who still remembers the verbiage from the promotional materials,' through Thana, smirking at her sister. Before Asgoth had a chance to respond, Thana quickly jumped in. "The food is exquisite here, too."

"Oh yes, indeed," said Asgoth, proudly smiling right back at her sister.

"The best flavors from all the seven segments," continued Thana, "here is where one could delight in eastern fire-roasted cuttlefish, alongside a cup of the sweetest honeydew nectar with a slice of blue water chocolate delight on the side. This place is very well known for offering a delicate cuisine prepared by the best chefs from all around our world."

As Asgoth and Thana continued to share their exciting

memories of this place, Molly found herself fighting her focus as it started to drift away. She knew she needed to be a good and attentive girl, and not offend the ladies by tuning them out. At the same time, she was desperately trying to hear what George, Beatrice and Trail were talking about, only a few feet away from where they were standing. If only she had some apparatus that would allow her to hear over such a distance. Like the one the Weasley brothers invented. She knew that would be wrong, though. One should never eavesdrop onto conversations they have not been invited to participate in. Madame de la Fleur reminded her of this on numerous occasions. Molly did get caught spying on her dad and Uncle Az's meetings a few times – once while holding a cup against the wall and pressing her ear against it. Sadly, she discovered that it didn't really work as well as it was described in a few of the books she had read. Perhaps it was the thickness of the wall separating Uncle Az's office and the room next to it. Who knows...

Trail called over one of the witches that accompanied him earlier. Molly knew something was going on. Something serious. The witch rushed off as Trail lead George and Beatrice back towards Molly.

"Please, follow me. I will show you to your rooms." And with these words, Trail turned around and led the way towards the grand staircase.

One by one, everyone in the entire grand hall, whether they were standing on the stairs or the balconies overlooking the lobby, slowly turned towards them. They all whispered to each other that by the time Molly noticed, the entire lobby buzzed with an excited murmur. Magical creatures, witches and wizards stepped in from all angles to shake Molly and George's hands and welcomed them to Heartland. Some were even thanking Molly for coming, which was surprisingly odd to her, because it was not like she had any choice in the matter.

"Dad, why are they all staring at me?" Molly whispered.

"I suspect that it's because not every day someone from Earth shows up in Heartland." replied George quickly. Truth be told, he too was wondering the same thing.

How do they know who she is, she wondered? Why would they care about someone not from this land? They bowed to her and kissed her hand as if she were royalty. Molly, unsure what the etiquette was in such situations, attempted an awkward half-curtsy that left her stumbling for balance.

Trail led them straight up the stairs towards the elevators that took them to the highest floor of Junction Manor. As the elevator door opened, Molly saw a long hallway stretching ahead of them, which was lined on both sides, from one end to the other, with enchanted knight's suits of armor holding long steel swords in front of them. As Molly passed by each of them, she noticed them bowing their heads. She began to feel as if she had a much bigger role to play in all of this than she initially anticipated. But she had to admit, she rather enjoyed the attention at this very moment. Who wouldn't have?

"This is the Royal Suite," said Trail, as he opened the door for them.

"Trail, I was wondering if we could continue our conversation with you in a little while," Beatrice asked quietly.

"Most certainly!" replied Trail, "please visit me in my office after you've had your supper. Everyone, rest well. I shall see you in the morning," he said with a smile. But before he and his entourage turned around and walked down the hallway, he managed to throw a half wink towards Thana.

'I could punch him in the face. Right here, right now!' thought Thana as she watched Trail walk away. 'Did you notice he winked at me?'

'Yeah, I noticed,' thought Asgoth. 'Just forget about him, ok?'

"He doesn't seem like he's worth the trouble," Molly whispered to Thana. Somehow, Molly picked up on Thana's tension whenever Trail was nearby, leading her to think there was more to that story.

"You are correct, my friend." Thana whispered.

The five of them found themselves in a tall, oval-shaped room with ornate walls and a big window on the opposite side of the door they just stepped through. A round table was placed in the middle with five chairs tucked into it and a beautiful chandelier hanging above it. Four doors lined the walls on either side of the window. Molly walked up to the table which had a small plate with a folded card placed on it. She picked up the card and read out loud, "May you find everything your appetite desires!" And just like that, a magical spread appeared in front of them. The food plates filled every inch of the massive table. There was everything from Yorkshire pudding, a giant turkey, ham, roast beef, vegetables, and all sorts of desserts. Even if for a moment, Molly once again felt as if she were back at the mansion, having a festive dinner prepared by Madame de la Fleur.

'Let's see if the food is as good as back home,' she thought to herself.

"Let us enjoy a delicious meal inspired by the many flavors from Molly and Lord Enderby's land - Terra Nova. Take a seat, everyone," said Beatrice with a smile.

The feast was absolutely magnificent. Molly's taste buds were exploding with delight from every bite she took. As always, despite her father's displeasure, she started with dessert. 'Who decides on the order of the meal anyways', she had thought to herself many times.

After a cup of delicious fruit salad, a butter cup torte, a scoop of dark chocolate ice cream and a helping of vanilla pudding,

George looked at her and said with a smile, "perhaps some protein and vegetables are now in order?" Molly concurred and reached for a turkey leg and some steamed veggies.

Once everyone finished their meals and put their cutlery down, the food and dishes magically disappeared, leaving behind a clean table with only a couple of candelabras and tall ivory white candles burning brightly. It was the best meal Molly had had in a very long time. Not as good as Madame de la Fleur's cuisine, but a pretty close second. Then a sobering thought came to her. Molly hoped that the crazy little lady with the nuts in her pockets was safe somewhere. She missed her very much.

"Your rooms are prepared. Rest up. Our journey to the Capital will be a long one," said Beatrice as she stood up from the table. "We will leave at sunrise."

"Zonks, how are you doing?" asked George as he walked her to one of the bedrooms. "What a crazy adventure this is, isn't it?"

"I'm fine, I think," she replied. "Not a typical Friday night, is it?" she added jokingly before her mood shifting. "I miss Madame de la Fleur."

"I miss her, too." George replied. "Beatrice said she's safe. As soon as we get to the Capital, I'll see about tracking her down."

"Okay. Thank you, daddy." Molly walked into her room and sat down on the bed before continuing. "And were you ever going to tell me you are a wizard?" she added with a smile.

The honest truth was that he did plan on telling her. He was going to tell her about it, about Heartland and about everything else the day she turned fifteen. And here they were, on the eve of that day, with a lot of the secrets already having been revealed.

"Maybe," he said with a smile as he plopped himself down next to her, conjuring a little paper butterfly seemingly out of thin air.

"Can I ask you a question?" said Molly, as she reached for her dad's hands causing the magical paper butterfly to disappear. "Before we moved into the chateau, we weren't traveling from city to city because of your work, right?"

"No," George replied simply.

"We were running away from Corcoran."

"I have feeling, there will be less and less I'll be able to keep from you going forward, my smart little Zonks," he said with a smile.

"Are we going to be safe here in Heartland?" she asked.

"Yes," George replied without hesitation. "My only purpose in life is to keep you safe. Whether it is here in Heartland or back home on Earth," he added as he wrapped his arms around her.

"Why does he want me so bad?" she asked.

Before George could muster up an answer, Beatrice appeared in the doorway. "I'm ready whenever you are, George," she said.

"Don't you worry about any of it, ok? You rest up. We have an

73

even longer journey ahead of us tomorrow. I'm going to see Trail with Beatrice and then I'll be back. I love you, my little Zonks."

"Okay, daddy. I love you, too."

"Goodnight, Molly," said Beatrice with a smile.

"Goodnight," she replied.

Once Molly was safely tucked into her bed, Beatrice and George headed down to Trail's office.

# CHAPTER 10

*The dark soul.*

Whn the two moons rise as one, dark magic is at its strongest. Regina figured this out when she started to dabble in this forbidden kind of magic with Corcoran, back when they were in their late teens.

"It's almost time, Mama," said Bevan, a shy boy that stepped into the room.

He was nearly fifteen years old, with pale skin and medium length dark hair that seemed to have a mind of its own. Fully dressed in black, his mysteriously striking face, well defined eyebrows, strong jaw line, pointy nose and dark grey eyes made him seem unapproachable, even threatening. Contrary to his strong visage and the common first impression his appearance afforded others, Bevan was actually a meek and timid young man. A lost soul, with hardly any life experience who, due to his circumstances, grew up far too fast.

"Do you really have to go through with this? You don't need to, I'm...I'm...sure there is another way."

"I don't have a choice. I have to...for my little girl," said Regina. "It's the only way we'll be able to get her back, Bevan."

"Mama, I can't watch you do this to yourself," pleaded Bevan.

"You pathetic little vermin! I always knew you had a weak stomach for dark magic. You are such a disappointment to me!"

"Mama, what happened to you? I don't recognize you anymore. You raised me with kindness and selflessness. Now you hit and curse at me! You are in such a dark place...let me help you. Please! Now that we're here with Corcoran, it's as if your sole focus is to hurt and kill thousands of innocent people. That is not you! What have you become?" Bevan was so upset seeing his mother like this. "Now I know why my father left us!"

"Don't you dare talk to your mother in such way," Regina snapped back with a curse that sent Bevan flying into the wall, then bouncing onto ground. "You ungrateful child! After all I've done for you. Keeping you alive for all this time, you little ingrate! Your father left us because he could not handle the truth!"

"What truth, Mama?" pleaded Bevan.

"Aaaaw!" screamed Regina as she flew across the room,

landing hunched over Bevan on the floor, like an eagle ready to attack its prey.

"Come on...do it. If it'll make you feel better!" he said, tears streaming down his face. "Kill me now! If I've let you down so unforgivably, why don't you just end this once and for all!"

"Get out!" growled Regina through gritted teeth, holding back her tears. "Get out before I do the unthinkable! And get me Aiken. Now!"

Bevan picked himself off the ground and ran for the door. "I forgive you, Mama. I'm just not sure the rest of the world will be able to once Corcoran is done with it." Bevan ran through the door into the spiral stairwell, disappearing into the darkness of the night.

"Oh, George!" Regina started. "You see what you are making me do! THIS IS ALL YOUR FAULT! Do you and your stupid Clara really think you can get away with this?"

The pain she felt was so unbearable that she did not even know how in the world she managed to find the strength to get through each day. For not a single day went by without Regina thinking of her little girl. There was not a single being in this world that understood the hell she was going through. Not a single one of them pitied this poor woman. She felt so utterly alone. A broken shell of a woman lost in the darkness of her own mind, desperately trying to find a way out.

"I did not want it to be this way, but you left me no choice, George!" she said as she lowered herself onto the ground, pulling her knees close to her. "I never stopped loving you, my baby girl. I promised you we'd be together, once again. And we will..." Rocking back and forth, she looked like someone who had gone mad.

With the remaining strength she had, Regina crawled over to the battered old chest. She placed her hands over top of the locks, while desperately trying to focus her energy. It worked! A couple of hollow clicks echoed through the room, as if the long-rusted locks finally breathed again. A satisfied smile spread across her battered face. Regina slowly and carefully opened the chest, for she had no idea what was about to happen. In that moment, a dark haze started to seep out, and began to form a cloud hovering directly in front of her.

"Yes, the moons!" said Regina as she looked up and out the window. The time had come when the two moons of Heartland became one.

"I forever release myself from the consequences of my actions! Ascio Nox Spiritus. Ascio Nox Spiritus. Ascio Nox Spiritus!" Regina started chanting the one and only spell that had the power to do the unthinkable - take away the good in one's heart and soul and replace it with an unspeakable evil. The dark cloud started to spin faster and faster around her forming into an intense cyclone filling the entire room.

"As you wish!" said an ethereal female voice. A white light shot right out of Regina's chest. It got instantly swept up in the mad whirl of the cyclone. The two lights chased each other in an intricate magical dance, intertwining as they moved around the room. Moments later, the white light reached the speed of the dark one. For a brief moment they were fused as one. It was a beautiful interchange of colors. Then the white light slowly started to surpass its partner, leaving it behind. This exchange allowed the dark light to slow down and position itself directly in front of Regina, before shooting right into her chest. She inhaled deeply and the sheer force threw her head back as she fell into a trance-like state. The gusts of wind ceased, and the white light began to wind its way into the battered chest before its lid shut tight. Funny, how this simple act of an irreversible exchange seemed so frivolous. How easy it was - like pulling a trigger on a gun – within seconds it was over. Regina rose off the ground and opened her eyes. That love in the eyes of a grieving mother, who would do anything to get her daughter back, was fast replaced by the look of thirst for revenge. Her eyes were white, white and cold as ice.

"Gorgon! Gundula!!!!" she shouted. "Take this chest back into the forest and bury it. I don't want to see it again!!! And bring me Aiken!!!!!" she demanded furiously.

# CHAPTER 11

*Still angry?*

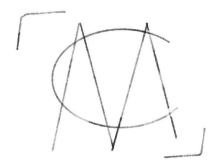

"This is absolutely ridiculous," said Maeve as she jumped out of her chair. "What is your 'educated' expectation on the outcome here? Am I supposed to feel sad, angry, hurt? Am I supposed to be moved by this story? Which part of it should I latch onto?"

"Well, only you have the answers to those questions," replied Dr. Claremore very calmly. "I can't tell you which part of the story you should feel a strong connection to, or if any for that matter. Which character do you associate with the most?"

"Are you serious?" asked Maeve crossing her arms.

"Step back everyone," said Fon shaking his head. "The lid is going to blow off the pot any minute now."

"Yes, I am absolutely serious. I want to know which character speaks to you the most. Is it Molly? Are you worried about her lack of formal educational setting in which she would, under normal circumstances, have had the chance to develop proper, real-life peer relations? Because, let's be honest, having relationships with people from your dreams isn't really the same as experiencing those relationships in real-life. It's sort of like having invisible friends. And do you think the lack of such real-life relations may possibly have negative impacts on her social and emotional development in later years? Or what about the void Molly must be feeling, as a result of not being raised by her own mother. A void that, could easily be argued, simply cannot be filled by the tender and caring Madame de la Fleur."

"What are you blabbering about?" replied Maeve.

"Or is it George?" she continued. "You know some psychologists agree that being a single dad can take a significant emotional toll on a man and if not properly dealt with, can lead to chronic medical conditions, mood or anxiety disorders."

"What would make you think these would be my first thoughts about your stupid story?" Maeve shot back. She was angry. "Who cares? Big whoop! It's just a stupid story. Besides, does having imaginary friends not lead to heightened creativity and a 'crazy wild imagination?' Your billable hour is up! I'm leaving!" Maeve said angrily, noticing the hover car waiting outside. She walked towards the door, before realizing she was missing something. She swiftly turned around and rushed back to grab her jacket and her bag.

"Maeve, if memory serves me right, your file says you have an IQ of over 130," said Fon as he circled around her. He knew very well she couldn't hear or see him, but stating this fact made him feel like a real psychologist. "I can very easily imagine how your brain works. And even though, these concerns may not be at the forefront, you've thought about them. Come on, you're not fooling anyone!"

Dr. Claremore just sat there, observing her every move. She was not surprised at all by Meave's reaction. On the contrary, she expected somewhat of an outburst from her, just as it happened with all the girls who came before her. She swiped her finger across her tablet. A moment later a quiet beep was heard coming from Maeve's bag as the mechanical door slid behind her. Meave stepped off the platform and into the hover car, which swiftly filed into the zooming air-traffic above.

"She'll be back. Just as they all have," said Dr. Claremore.

"We are running out of time," said Fon. "Did you transfer the story to her? Please tell me you transferred the file to her!"

"What do you take me for, an amateur?" asked Dr. Claremore with a smile. Then, suddenly a notification appeared on her tablet.

"Don't tell me she deleted it!" said Dorn. "They always delete the file when we get to this point, and it saddens me."

"Actually, no..." said Dr. Claremore surprised. "She opened it. And it seems she's starting to read the next chapter."

"She's hooked," said Dorn joyously. "I knew it! I knew she was going to be the one! I told you so, brother," he said as he smacked Fon's arm.

"Stop it!" Fon yelled at his brother. "Well...what's the saying about the chicken and the egg, Dr. Claremore?" said Fon as he flew back over to the windowsill, looking out towards the way Meave's hover car just flew off.

"Oh, I know..." Dorn raised his hand excitedly. "Which one came first? The chicken or the egg. Age old question. I don't think anyone on Earth, I mean Terra Nova, has figured out the answer to it, yet. I don't think anyone ever will..."

"No, Dorn," said Dr. Claremore with a smile. "Don't count them before they hatch! Let's just hope she'll continue reading it. If all goes well, we'll see her again soon."

# CHAPTER 12

*Just for a few minutes.*

**M**olly's room at Junction Manor was very cozy. For whatever reason, though, she could not get comfortable. After that wild adventure, one would think she would be out the moment her head hit the pillow. But no. She just sat at the edge of her bed, staring at the little music box in her lap, one of the two items she was able to bring with her from Chateau Azeri. It played such a lovely tune. She could not quite remember where it came from, though. One morning she simply found it in the drawer of her nightstand. At times like this, when her feelings started to get the best of her, she would play its soothing lullaby for hours and hours on end.

Molly could feel the warm summer breeze flowing in through

the partially open balcony door. She thought perhaps some fresh air would do her good, so she got up and walked out onto the balcony. The air was hot and sweet, in a very odd way. Funny things happen when we find ourselves in foreign places. To feel comforted, we desperately try to associate our current surroundings to something that's familiar to us, however accurately or inaccurately the association ends up being. The smell in the air reminded her of blossoming cherry trees out in the chateau garden, mixed with the aroma that flowed from the kitchen windows when Madame de la Fleur baked her delicious loganberry pies. Molly gazed at the night sky admiring the two Heartland moons side by side. They were truly beautiful. Like two sisters, so much alike, yet so different at the same time.

'Wow, Junction Manor sure looks different from up here,' thought Molly as she looked down below. It did not look like a small stone cottage at all. From this vantage point Molly saw a majestic castle. She felt like a real princess looking out and admiring the view from her tower room. She squinted her eyes trying to see the cobblestone paths leading away from the front door towards the archways. It looked like the trolls stayed at their posts even at night. One of them turned around and waved to her. Molly recognized him. It was Grindrod. Not wanting to be rude, she quickly waved back with a smile.

For a girl of almost fifteen years of age, who took advantage of every opportunity to sleep, Molly found herself wide awake in the middle of this peaceful night. She looked far out and saw a storm cloud approaching from a distance. A gentle smile spread across her face. She loved summer rainstorms. This one, however, was bringing with it some rather pungent scents, similar to the one back at mansion the night before.

The trolls seated on the other arches turned around and waved to her as well. She politely waved back. Then, Molly had an idea. She thought there would be no harm in exploring the castle a bit. With everyone asleep, nobody would notice if she were gone for a couple of minutes. Surely some of the staff downstairs would be working. On the plus side, she could learn a bit more about the place. Back at the mansion, she would sometimes wander down into the kitchen in the middle of the night for a cup of hot chocolate. 'Oh, a nice cup with whipped cream and chocolate syrup on top would hit the spot right about now,' she thought to herself as her mouth started watering.

'No, I can't. That wouldn't be right. I can't simply wander around all by myself. What if I get lost?' Molly went back into her room and sat on the edge of her bed, still contemplating whether sneaking out in the middle of the night was a good idea or whether it was wiser to just stay here and try to get some sleep. She laid down on her bed, wide-eyed and staring at the ceiling.

'Maybe...just maybe...I'll only go as far as the door to our suite, peek outside to see if there is anyone wandering the hallways,' she tried to wrestle with her conscience. 'Don't be silly, Molly. Remember the elevator ride up here? I don't recall seeing any other passages after we stepped off of it and into the hallway that led straight to our suite. There is no reason for anyone to come all the way up here at this late hour of the night. Hm... Maybe... just maybe... I'll go *only* as far as the balcony overlooking the lobby, and then I'll come straight back. Yes. That seems reasonable...' Molly hurriedly settled on that compromise, quickly dressed, put her little music box back in her messenger bag and headed for the door.

She opened it slowly and quietly, hoping it would not creak and wake everyone up. Luckily, it did not, so she peered out into the round room where they had that delicious supper just an hour or so ago. The room was dark with the only light coming from a couple of candles atop the dining room table. Molly slowly closed the door to her room and walked toward the main door of the suite. It appeared that everyone else was asleep in their rooms.

As soon as she opened the door to the hallway, all the enchanted armors turned towards her. It was an eerie feeling - being stared at by a row of hollow knights holding giant swords. Molly stepped out of the suite and closed the door behind her. She did not dare move. She didn't know what these knights might do to her if she moved even an inch closer to them.

"Courage, Zonks," she whispered. "You can do it. There is nothing scary about these...things..." Molly was trying to find an ounce of bravery, the kind she felt so strongly during her many visits to this land through her dreams. Those times she felt invincible, powerful and strong. Right now, not so much. "Maybe, I'll just take one step and if things get scary, I'll just run right back in." She took a deep breath and stepped forward. Shaking, she was ready to turn back in an instant. Nothing happened. "All right, now or never," whispered Molly to herself. She felt it would be safe to go so she took a few steps past the first set of hollow knights. They instantly turned facing each other. As she passed the second set, the very same thing happened. They instantly moved to face one another. She took a few fast-paced steps, and like a camera shutter closing fast, one by one the hollow knights turned once again. She put her index finger to her lips and whispered, enunciating every word. "Shhh, you are going to wake everyone up!" As she took a few steps past the next set of armors she noticed something funny. The magical knights surely took direction, Molly chuckled at the thought of it. They did move to face one another, however they moved without making the tiniest of sounds. "Good boys," she said smiling, "I see we will get along just fine."

As Molly went down the stairwell towards the second floor,

she was greeted by witches and wizards in beautiful cloaks. Everyone bowed to her and wished her a good night. She realized that the castle wasn't as quiet as she thought it would be at night. She stood on the balcony that overlooked the darkened main lobby below. Beautiful singing filled the space, but Molly could not tell where the music came from. Busy peering over the railing, Molly did not notice a crowd gathering behind her. She turned around and suddenly, there they were.

"Welcome, it is so good to have you here," said one of the elves.

"It's a pleasure to meet you," said the other.

Molly started to walk through the crowd, mustering up a shy smile. Everyone wanted to touch her, shake her hand, and wish her a pleasant stay in Heartland. She could not help but feel slightly embarrassed, for she felt so uncomfortable being the center of attention. At last, she made her way over to the grand staircase where she stopped to admire the absolutely breathtaking view of the main lobby. 'Maybe I should head back, now,' Molly thought to herself. 'Or maybe I'll just see where the music is coming from and then go right back. Yes, that's it.' Molly was trying to reason with herself once again.

A massive crowd filled the center of the lobby surrounding a circular stage, watching an elf girl with long braided red hair, a round face and big blue eyes, singing the most beautiful song

Molly had ever heard.

"Who is she?" Molly asked a witch standing nearby.

"Oh – that's Princess Eyya from Woodland. She visits here often and puts on the most beautiful concerts. She is most known for including songs from each of the seven segments in her repertoire."

"But she looks so young. Do you know how old she is?" asked Molly. "She is fifteen years young. A rare talent, indeed," said the witch with a smile.

"Eyya." Molly whispered as she slowly made her way down, completely enchanted by the sound of the elf girl's voice. 'Can it be?' thought Molly to herself. 'Can this truly be my Eyya. My best friend Eyya!"

When she got to the bottom of the stairs she just stood there, mesmerized by the beauty of the elf girl. She wore an emerald-green dress and dark brown leather boots that came up to her knees. She looked stunningly beautiful. Suddenly, as though triggered by the sight of Eyya, Molly experienced her very first dream-flashback, recalling one of her memories.

# CHAPTER 13

*First flashback.*

**M**olly remembered spending countless hours in the maze with Eyya and Aiken. It was located in a clearing just past the Forest of Inkhans in the Woodland segment. It was a stone maze, about nine feet high, covered in age-old vines, which served mostly as a training ground for all the gate keepers of Heartland.

One day they spent an entire afternoon in the maze practicing spells, including the fast-move spell, which allows the caster to move at high speed from one place to another. But the effects of the fast-move spell only last a few seconds, so the caster does not really get a chance to travel far. It turned out to be a fun version of hide and seek, more than anything.

As Molly cast one fast-move spell after another, skillfully zooming through the maze without hitting a dead end, she found herself getting further and further away from Eyya and Aiken. She paused for a bit, listening intently for the sounds of their movements, but could not hear anything.

Suddenly, out of nowhere, Molly heard laughter echoing through the maze. It sounded very eerie. Looking down one of the corridors, she saw a figure of someone emerging from one side then disappearing into the other. 'There must be a path that intersects this corridor,' thought Molly. 'Either that, or someone figured out a way to move through the maze walls.' She had a weird feeling that something was not quite right. She ran down the maze corridor and tried to follow the laugh.

"Eyya!" she said loudly. "Eyya, is that you? Where are you? This isn't funny anymore, do you hear?" Molly stopped at the end of the corridor and found herself coming to a dead end. She could hear the laughter echoing. She quickly turned around and saw the figure of a person in the distance once again. Molly ran. Yet again, the figure disappeared into another corridor. After running down corridors for what felt like an eternity, Molly turned a corner and found herself entering a small clearing. 'That's odd...' she thought to herself. She did not remember this clearing being here before. Freshly cut grass covered the ground instead of the usual cobblestone. In the middle of the clearing stood a tall apple tree, covered with ripe ruby-red apples. A girl was picking them with the help of an odd gizmo - a round piece of metal with teeth and a cloth pouch attached to the bottom of it. The girl was using some sort of a spell that basically made the chomping pouch pick the apples for her.

"Hi there," said Molly politely. "May I ask how you got here?" she paused for a brief moment, taking a few steps closer. "Are you lost, perhaps?"

The girl turned around to face Molly. It was Eyya. Molly was confused at first. Why would Eyya stop practice to pick apples?

"Oh, hello there!" said Eyya. "Would you like some freshly picked apples?"

"Eyya?" said Molly as she took a couple more steps towards her. "How did you get all the way here? We are not supposed to use the teleportation spell. That's against all sorts of rules and you know it! We are only supposed to use the fast-move spell. Are you even listening to me?! Where is Aiken, anyway?" As she walked closer, she noticed Eyya's eye was twitching.

"Have an apple, Maggie!" said Eyya with an eerie smile.

"My name is Molly..." she said confused.

"They are very delicious," continued Eyya without acknowledging that she had just called Molly by the wrong name. With a move of her hand, she made the chomping pouch come down towards them. Molly felt a little intimidated by this gizmo.

All this was so confusing to her. Not only was Eyya acting strangely, but she was playing with this weird chomping thing. Why would anyone even think of reaching inside? Arguably, one could certainly risk losing a finger or two.

"What's wrong with your eye, Eyya?" asked Molly.

"Ah, those pesky little fruit bugs, one of them must have gone straight into my eye," said Eyya quickly. "These apples are so deliciously sweet." Eyya continued in a very bizarre, trance-like way. "See the one over there, at the top of the tree? The one that is so dark red it's almost black? It looks even more delicious than the rest. But every time I try to grab it, it moves away. I wonder why? Can you try catching it?"

"I'm not good at climbing trees, you know that..." replied Molly, confused.

"Then try one. They are very delicious apples," said Eyya softly. Molly reached hesitantly into the chomping pouch to grab an apple from the top of the pile, and just as she was about to bite into it, she heard someone yelling from behind her.

"Molly don't!" As if out of nowhere, a big gust of wind blew straight through the maze. Clara appeared, followed by Asgoth, Thana and Aiken. "Igeaglor!" screamed Clara. Then, as if her spirit was leaving her body, Eyya let out an excruciating cry. Like a piece of wood chopped in half, Eyya instantly fell one way and the apparated body of Regina fell the other.

94

"How dare you cast a spell on me! You miserable piece of... Aaagh..." Eyya screamed at the top of her lungs, as she jumped Regina with her hands around her throat. "You will regret this!!!" Molly had never seen Eyya so furious.

"Eyya, let me handle this," Clara stepped in. "Seize her!" ordered Clara. Aiken helped Eyya up on her feet and held her back. Asgoth and Thana dragged Regina up off the ground, holding her tight by her arms.

"Aiken, take the girls," said Clara. "I'll meet you at the entrance to the maze. Go now!"

"Nooooooo!" cried Regina. "No, you can't do this. Don't take her! Don't take her from me!" she pleaded as she mustered up a few tears. Molly stopped and turned around to face her.

"Corcoran, sent you, didn't he?' said Clara. "Tell him to give up! He will never succeed! Do you understand?" Clara paused, contemplating everything that went wrong between them. They used to be such good friends - Clara, George and Regina. They were practically inseparable.

"You don't understand, you fool," she said plainly, her mood changing drastically from being overcome with emotion a moment ago, to becoming extremely cold and uncaring. "I am simply here to take back what is rightfully mine," replied Regina as she looked over at Molly.

"Regina, it pains me to say this, but you leave me no choice.

You are from here on banished from all of Heartland. Do not return, the benevolence we are showing now will not be shown again. Let this be a warning to you and Corcoran!" Clara paused, for the next few words would cause her deeper pain than she wished to outwardly permit anyone to witness. "Take her to the forest."

Regina dropped to her knees pleading, "…you can't…you can't send me there. Please!!! Just let the girl come with me and I promise you will never see me or Corcoran ever again."

"May the spirits of the Dark Forest have mercy on your soul," said Clara as she turned away.

"He will come find me, and you know it," bellowed Regina. "He will, and then I will find you!" she said looking over at Molly.

"I have only one message for him. If he ever tries to harm any citizen of Heartland, he and his accomplices will be sentenced to the Chambers. For eternity!"

Asgoth and Thana took Regina away. With a swift move of her arm, Clara cast a spell that made the tree and the grass clearing disappear and the vine-covered stone walls rose from the ground returning the maze back to its original state.

Molly was shaking, she was scared. Scared for herself, for her friends but mostly for the people of Heartland. Eyya and Aiken were trying to comfort her. "Could somebody please tell me what's going on here? Who is she? Why would she do this?"

Clara placed her hand on Molly's shoulder and hesitantly started, not wanting to fully divulge Regina's true motive, "Regina and Corcoran have been trying to cause havoc in Heartland for years now. Trying to get to me through whatever means necessary. This time they chose you as their target. I'm so sorry that it has come to this."

"Are you alright?" asked Aiken turning to Eyya.

"I'm fine. Regina found me in the maze, cast a spell on me then brought me to that tree. I saw Molly with my own eyes. It was as if I was trapped inside my own body but being controlled by someone else. My actions and words were not those of my own free will. I fought hard to break out but there was nothing I could do to get her out of me.

"The twitching eye..." said Molly quickly. "That was you trying to tell me something was wrong."

"Is that so? I must've looked like a freak, then, with a twitchy eye, and all," laughed Eyya.

"The imposter curse..." said Clara as she walked closer, trying to focus on the next few things. "Aiken, thank you for your quick thinking and calling for help. Eyya, did she manage to access your memories in any way?"

"Not that I can tell." replied Eyya.

"Head straight to the City of Arbor. We'll have to make sure no trace of her remains in you." said Clara.

"I'll go with you," said Aiken.

"We'll see you soon, okay?" said Eyya.

"You bet," Molly replied, wrapping her arms around both of them, tighter than ever.

"Now, don't you go all soft on me, you hear?" said Eyya sensing a slight shakiness in Molly's voice. "Everything will...."

"...will be okay, I know," said Molly. "No go! Get back to Woodland fast, so you can make sure everything is okay with you."

"Catch you later," said Eyya and Aiken at the same time before turning around. They ran as fast as they could out of the maze.

"Who knows what would have happened had you taken a bite of that apple," said Clara once Aiken and Eyya were gone.

"I don't even want to think about it," said Molly.

"It is best you return now," said Clara after a moment. "Are you ready?" she asked with a gentle smile.

"Yes, I am," replied Molly, wrapping her arms around Clara.

"You know the rules?" asked Clara.

"Yes, I do. Never talk to anyone about my dreams. Not even my dad."

"And?" asked Clara.

"Always keep my diary safe," said Molly, her eyes welling up. She looked up at Clara, trying to muster a smile to reassure her that she'd be all right but couldn't. The events of this particular visit were too much to take in for this not-so-brave little girl. At last, she closed her eyes tightly and prepared herself for the return journey, taking what seemed to be the longest path through *the passage of no man's land*. When she opened her eyes, she was back in her bed at the mansion. Awake.

# CHAPTER 14

*Re-united. For real this time.*

**M**olly drifted out of her daze, realizing she was standing at the bottom of the staircase at Junction Manor. 'Why did she call me Maggie?' she thought to herself. 'And why did she want me to go with her?'

Eyya finished her song and with grace and elegance bowed to her adoring crowd. Everyone in the room applauded vigorously.

"Thank you! Thank you, everyone. It is a true honor to be here on such a special night," said Eyya as she stepped off the stage shaking hands with her adoring audience. She made her way to the stairs through the crowded lobby, confidently working the room like a true professional. She was so talented, Molly thought.

Who would have thought she would have turned out to be such a star?

As soon as Eyya emerged from the crowd, she was about to head up the stairs but had to stop herself for she nearly ran into Molly.

"I'm so sorry," said Eyya and as she lifted her gaze she realized who was standing directly in front of her. "Molly?" said Eyya in amazement.

"Eyya!" said Molly in equal amazement.

"You're here already. How was your journey?" said Eyya.

"Yep. I'm here," Molly replied. "You won't believe what happened to me."

"Is it really you, Molly? I can't believe you're here," squealed Eyya in utter excitement as she spun her around then wrapped her in the biggest hug. What she was really thinking was 'I can't believe you look just like Maggie.'

Maggie was right. Eyya was overcome with feelings she was certainly not prepared for. From happiness to guilt, the range of emotions was all encompassing, and in some way borderline crippling. She recalled that very final moment with Maggie. 'Remember, just pretend it's me, and you'll get through it, ok? I could never have done any of this without you. I can't thank you enough, Eyya. You are the best friend I could have wished for. At times we are all forced to do things we don't fully comprehend, but please know that there was no other way. You are strong. You can do this. Keep everyone together and stick to the plan. Stick to the plan...Stick to the plan...' Eyya's mind was drifting but she needed to force herself to come back to reality.

"We all knew you had arrived in Heartland. News travels fast around here," she continued, desperately trying to get focused on the mission. On Maggie's mission. "But I had no idea you were already here!"

"Yes, we arrived a few hours ago," said Molly. "It was quite a journey, let me tell you. Beatrice initiated a free-form portal that dropped us at the Skyland Gate."

"Ah, yes, I have heard of them," said Eyya. "But only those with the highest clearance are allowed to perform that spell. I guess Beatrice is pretty high up there, so I'm not surprised."

"But, you! Look at you!" said Molly. "You look absolutely gorgeous. And where did that voice come from? You never told me you sang so beautifully. Honestly, I was so mesmerized by your voice. You have a true gift, my friend."

"Ah, come on..." replied Eyya sheepishly. "It's not as good as it could be. It's still a work in progress. I've only really been singing for a short little while. It's just a hobby, more than anything. I'm just happy that it brings so much joy to everyone. But don't change the subject on me. Tell me all about your journey over a cup of hot cocoa. I know just the place!" said Eyya as she led Molly up the stairs to the café on the second floor.

"I'm so happy I ran into you, Eyya, but I really should get back to my room. We are leaving early in the morning," said Molly, as she realized how long she had been gone from her room. Knowing her father, he would be freaking out by now had he known she was out at this hour. Eyya looked at Molly pleadingly. "Alright!" said Molly, giving in. "But only for a few minutes, since we're here already!"

Molly and Eyya entered yet another enchanting space. Small tents covered the tables and chairs, providing an extra level of privacy for the type of conversations Molly and Eyya were about to share. They walked up to one of them, where they were greeted by a little elf waiter.

"Table for two?" he asked as he parted the curtain to allow Molly and Eyya to step in.

"Why am I not surprised," Molly grinned as she stepped in and found herself inside a tent that was several times larger than it looked from the outside. In the middle of it was a low table with a few neatly arranged pillows all around. A colorful stained-glass lamp hung from the ceiling that provided just the right amount of light. Molly was trying to take in every little detail, especially the beautiful tapestries and banners draped on the walls of the tent. She had never seen anything like it before.

"Ta-da! Welcome to Café Tenta. The true inspiration for this place is our Barrenland segment." said Eyya. As they sat down on the pillows, two cups of hot chocolate appeared on the table. "I know how much you love the rain, so here's a little gift for you," Eyya conjured a small cloud above them. There were even tiny droplets of rain falling gently that instantly evaporated into a pink mist.

"I guess I should not be surprised. I am in Heartland after all," Molly stated. "A land where nothing is as it appears," they both said in unison.

"What is that word you say on Earth, when two people say the same thing at the same time?" asked Eyya.

"Jinx," said Molly. They both laughed.

"But wait!" said Eyya. "I know how much you like a good storm so here is a tiny one for you." With a wave of her hand, a few dark clouds appeared above, soon to unleash a heavy rain on both of them. "Oops, maybe not. Let's stick with the gentle rain." With another quick wave of her hand the ominous clouds turned fluffy and the tiny droplets instantly evaporated into mist. "I'm still learning the 'arts and crafts' charms..." said Eyya apologetically.

Oh, how great it was to see Eyya once again, thought Molly. In her dreams, they spent many, many hours together, they were inseparable. Molly could not remember a time when she did not know Eyya. They truly were best of friends, through thick and thin. And here they were, together once again. Molly had so many questions, so many unanswered questions that she didn't even know where to start. She came to a quick realization that for as long as she was in Heartland, their encounters were never going to be cut short by her sudden awakening.

"Molly, I'm so glad you are here! How long are you in Heartland?" asked Eyya.

Molly, her eyes welling up as she felt the reality of it all finally sink in, sighed. "I have a feeling I will be here for a while. I'm just not sure why."

These were happy tears, she assured Eyya, for she did not think the day would ever come when they'd both be in the same place at the same time, breathing the same air.

"How is everyone back in the City of Arbor?" started Molly, as she reached across the table and grabbed Eyya's hand. "Have you seen Aecus lately? I miss him very much."

"They are fine, everything is just as it always was," said Eyya quickly. "The Summerset Festival at the Capital starts tomorrow night. Everyone is very excited about it."

They both sipped a bit of their hot chocolate then lowered their cups and for a moment, just stared at each other without saying a word.

"Eyya..." started Molly hesitantly, "remember that time we were in the maze, practicing our fast-moving spells?" Eyya smiled recalling that memory.

"Yes, certainly. We had so much fun that day, didn't we? Aiken was always trying to cheat his way through the maze, and at the end we shared a delicious picnic of home-made apple-berry tarts and fresh pear shakes," said Eyya. Molly looked confused.

"Actually, yes that is how I remembered it as well, but earlier...I had sort of a flashback to that moment, and the whole day ended completely different.

"What do you mean?" asked Eyya with a worried look on her face.

"Well, for starters, you were under the imposter curse..." Molly began, "...and Regina tried to get me to climb up an apple tree inside the maze."

"Oh...well, I can assure you, that is not how it all happened," said Eyya with a reassuring smile. "Aiken won't stop talking about that day. Every chance he gets, he likes to remind me that he was the true winner that splendid afternoon."

In actuality, she began to worry something was going wrong. She needed to let someone know. Molly's memories were being altered, and that was a sure sign that things were not going according to plan. The wheels in her mind were spinning, trying to quickly change the subject. The pitch of her voice changed slightly, as it always did when she was hiding something or trying to avoid talking about something. "I'm positive it is just the crazy events of the past few hours that are causing your memories to be all...jumbled up. I know for sure we had the most splendid day in the maze. But, do you remember the time the three of us went to the Waterland and just as we returned to the docks, we got busted by Aecus?" reminisced Eyya. "Aiken took us there, remember?"

"Wait a minute, Eyya. Who is Aiken?" asked Molly, clearly confused. The name seemed awfully familiar, but she could not remember where she had heard it before.

"You have got to be kidding me, Molly," said Eyya in complete and utter amazement. "Aiken? The third musketeer, as you'd always refer to him. I think he has a crush on you, if you ask me, but that's beside the point. Aiken, our buddy Aiken. Do you really not remember him?"

Eyya was extremely worried, although she was desperately trying to appear as if she were not. One moment Molly remembered Aiken, and the next, it was as if he was gone and wiped out of her memory. There was definitely something wrong.

"No, I...I don't think I do," replied Molly sounding very confused. "Should I?"

"Where is your journal?" asked Eyya. Molly pulled out her journal from her messenger bag and pushed it across the table.

Eyya took that as permission, started flipping through the pages. She stopped when she came across a picture of an angry, winged lion, and the three of them standing on the dock at the shores of Waterland, facing it.

"You see, here he is. I knew you had written about him. This is Aiken," she pointed to a hand-drawn picture of the Skyland boy as she started to read aloud.

*"Aiken, the Skyland boy. My Skyland boy, with the dreamy blue eyes. Tall and toned dude, with his gorgeous messy locks of brown hair that he always parted on the side. And dimples, let's not forget those cute dimples. Oh, and his freckles. This guy makes my heart stop beating every time he looks at me..."*

Looking up at Molly from the book, "wow, Molly...this is like a passage from a steamy romance novel, here!!?!!" she said with a smile, "And look at this drawing of him... you made him out to be quite a handsome little devil, didn't you? He always loved his high-collar jackets. What a crazy ride that was...did you know he turned sixteen last week? He may have to take on additional duties in his segment, which sadly will mean we won't see much of him for the next little while..." Eyya nervously rambled as she always did when she was trying to keep something from someone, in this case, not letting on that Molly's memory loss was extremely concerning to her. "Anyways...that sure was a splendid morning, wasn't it? I was so excited when I got up that I nearly forgot to brush my hair. And that is unlike me, as you know. I wouldn't be caught dead without looking my best…"

Molly was so confused. She looked at Eyya, who was smiling away, animatedly telling her story. She slowly tuned out the rest of Eyya's story, distracted by what was happening at this very moment. Why could she not remember Aiken. She should remember someone that she drew and wrote pages about in her book. Eyya said they were the three musketeers. Then, just like earlier, the thought of Aiken triggered Molly into another flashback.

# CHAPTER 15

*Second flashback.*

A long, rusty wooden boardwalk with a rickety roof led out into the oceans of Waterland. It was foggy that early morning, so from the shore it was nearly impossible to see all the way to the very end.

"It's spooky, isn't it?" said Eyya as she followed Aiken and Molly down the boardwalk.

Even Molly felt a bit uneasy. As they walked further and further, the shoreline slowly disappeared into the eerie mist.

"How far do we have to go?" asked Molly hesitantly.

"Not far. We're actually almost there," said Aiken.

It was very quiet, with only the occasional thud of the water hitting the boardwalk and the wooden planks creaking under the weight of their feet. This seemed like a classic scene from a horror movie with the bad guy about to jump out at any moment to murder or kidnap somebody. Molly was trying to wipe that thought out of her mind, for she did not want to appear scared. Especially in front of Aiken.

"Here we are!" said Aiken once they arrived at a large open deck that had half a dozen distinct places where a boat or small ship could dock, each designated by a narrow post with a bell hanging from it.

"Pick a post and ring the bell!" said Aiken excitedly. "Come on, ring it!"

Molly was hesitant at once. She wasn't sure what was about to happen. Perhaps a big ship would arrive to take them all for a ride. Eyya rang her bell first, followed by Aiken. Molly did not want to be left out so she, too, rang her bell quickly.

Molly had to take a step back for the fear of being drenched by a big wave that was heading straight towards them. Out of the water emerged three water dragons, nearly twice the size of a horse. Because of their size and speed, they did seem menacing. But to be honest, Molly didn't feel threatened by them, in fact just the opposite.

"Everyone, meet your water dragon," Aiken started. "They used to live far deep in the oceans of Heartland. Over the centuries they migrated to the coast lines and adapted quite well to their new lives alongside the mermen and mermaids of Waterland."

"Aren't they vicious and deadly creatures?" asked Eyya hesitantly, taking a step back.

"Any animal, if not treated with dignity and respect can turn on you," said Aiken as he gently touched the long nose of the beast. "It's all about forming a trusting relationship. If you trust them, they will trust you back. If you disrespect them or hurt them, they may do just the same. Now, put your goggles on. They are attached to the saddle. Once we are under water, they will cover your whole face."

"How do you know all about this?" asked Eyya excitedly.

"Just as I get to spend time with you, I get to spend time with the royals from the other segments as well," explained Aiken. "In fact, Caspian the crown prince of Waterland is one of my good friends and we hang out a lot during the warm seasons."

"Is he handsome?" asked Eyya as she was putting on her goggles not knowing that they left her looking somewhat less glamorous than she thought they would.

"Do you ever think of anything other than finding yourself a boyfriend?" said Molly as she reached over and slapped Eyya's shoulder with her goggles, "and a rich one, none the less?"

"Not a boyfriend," replied Eyya. "A husband."

Much to Aiken's displeasure, they went on describing what

would constitute the perfect husband, until the conversation ended with both of them giggling.

"Okay, ladies," Aiken finally spoke up as he could not take any more of this nonsense. Molly noticed that he was starting to blush a bit, too. "He is good looking, for a merman, one might say..." Truth be told, Aiken was always a bit jealous of Caspian's natural good looks. His chiseled chest, carved abs and long blond hair were a sure hit with all the mermaids. Caspian had a light blue shimmery tail, big round blue eyes and a beautiful smile. On shore, unlike underwater, he was a true fish-out-of-water for he had no clue how best to use these characteristics to his full advantage. "But enough of that...now, it's time you introduce yourselves to your water dragon."

"Hi, I'm Eyya. What beautiful fins and horns you have? It's a pleasure to make your acquaintance," said Eyya loudly as she bowed to her water dragon.

"Oh, ok... so that's how we're supposed to do it," said Molly. "Ahem," she cleared her throat. "Hi, I'm Molly. What beautiful smooth, shimmery scales you have. Not to mention those large gentle eyes. I am so honored to be here and meeting you for the first time, majestic water dragon," said Molly as she curtsied, nearly falling over.

Well, the beasts were having none of those introductions. With high-pitched roars and a swing of their tails, they doused

Eyya and Molly from head to toe.

"No, no..." Aiken could barely speak for he was laughing so hard, "not like that."

"Dagnabbit, now I'm soaked!" said Eyya as she was wiping the water off her clothes.

"I think I got more soaked than you did, though," added Molly.

"Now what do we do? I didn't bring a change of clothes, did you?" asked Eyya looking over to Molly.

Aiken laughed once again, "Did you think this was going to be a gentle boat ride? We are going under water riding these beasts. Naturally, we will get wet!"

Both Molly and Eyya instantly felt embarrassed. 'Duh, he's right.' Molly thought to herself. 'Why didn't I think of that? He'll think I'm a total fool.'

"Now, watch me!" Aiken gently stroked the water dragon's long nose until it pushed its head forward as if to say, 'Why did you stop? Keep petting me.' "You see? If your water dragon nudges back, that's a good indication that he or she trusts you. Also, check their names," he continued, "they have a little tag on the side of their saddles."

"Hi, Meerian," said Eyya shyly as she reached out towards her water dragon. "Look Molly, I'm doing it!" yelped Eyya excitedly. Her water dragon instinctively nudged back, wanting more affection.

Molly's beast, on the other hand, had a bit of a temper and it very much appeared that it was not going to give in so easily. It let out another high squeal, spun around then dove into the water. "Clarion...girl...at least I hope you're a girl...behave!" she said insistently. A split second later, the water dragon's head re-emerged a couple feet away from the dock spitting water towards Molly, as if to taunt her.

"What now? You would like me to swim to you, is that what you want, you blueish...greenish beast?" said Molly putting both her hands on her hips.

"She likes you," said Aiken with a smile, "she's playing with you. I have a feeling she won't let you off the hook that easily. Try again, ring the bell and she'll come back to you. Now, wait until she settles in the dock. Good. The trick is, to create the bond between the two of you, she must feel your heart through your touch. She must instinctively know you mean no harm to her. Imagine she is your best friend. Project that energy and care into the touch. Now try it."

Molly could feel her heart beating a mile-a-minute. With her shaky hand she reached out towards the beast's gnarly face. Noticing her hesitation, Aiken stepped in closer, grabbed her hand and slowly, together, they moved towards the beast. Clarion's skin felt warm and soft. But also, having Aiken so close to her was very distracting. 'Focus, Molly. Focus! He's just a handsome guy, that happens to be touching your hand at this very moment...that's all. Oh, he smells so good...Focus!' Molly caressed her water dragon's long nose, until Clarion nudged for more.

"You're doing it, Molly," whispered Eyya. "Despite the...never mind," she was going to say 'distraction', for she did notice that Molly was preoccupied with Aiken so close to her.

"That's it, you're doing great," said Aiken softly as he let go of her hand.

Molly was on such a high. Not only she had just tamed this water dragon, but Aiken touched her hand. "I'm never washing this hand again," Molly whispered to Eyya. Eyya gave her a strange look then gestured towards the water they would soon be entering. "Ah, shrapnel," Molly muttered under her breath.

"Hi, girl..." whispered Molly. She could not believe that this creature could be so gentle and majestic. She could feel the affection she was giving reciprocated tenfold.

"Do you feel it? Do you feel her energy? They truly are gentle giants," said Aiken softly as he walked back to his water dragon. "Are we ready, then?" he asked as he hopped into the saddle.

Once the girls were settled on their water dragon, Aiken said, "Follow me, and try to keep up. The landing deck is just a few miles south. That is the closest point in the ocean to the City of Aecor below."

They headed for open water, Eyya and Molly following closely behind Aiken, quickly gaining speed. These water dragons sure knew how to ride the waves.

"Press the button on the side of your goggles," shouted Aiken from the front pointing to the button on his googles before pressing it. With a swift motion a shield appeared, covering his entire face. Eyya and Molly followed suit and within a split second, Molly's water dragon dove under the water.

'Wow!' Molly thought to herself. 'I can breathe under water with this thing.' Everything went suddenly silent as they went under the surface. They swam past a school of tiny turquoise fish that were barely visible because the ocean was just a shade or two darker. Molly noticed a variety of magical underwater creatures and water plants. As they swam through the ocean, stone paths, archways and what appeared to be stone buildings were starting to appear at the bottom of the ocean, far, far below. Some were small, some were large and tall, connected with glass-top bridges. Lights reflected off all the glass surfaces making the magical underwater village glitter on the bottom of the ocean.

'Was there anyone living down there?' Molly wondered. It was a breathtaking view of underwater life, and Molly found herself tightening her grip on her harness - more-so from excitement than fear from the exhilarating ride. Her water dragon found a perfect rhythm riding the underwater currents and Molly soon realized that she could ease her grip a bit. They moved fast, but it was a gentle, smooth ride that could have easily lulled her to sleep.

There was something Molly noticed about the water. It felt warm. Warmer than she had anticipated. Molly's water dragon took a sharp turn. She opened her eyes and saw something or someone in the far distance. She thought it might be Eyya since Molly seemed to have fallen quite a bit behind. She needed to catch up to her or she'd get lost in the vast ocean. She leaned forward which made her water beast swim even faster. The surface of the water above her appeared to move closer and closer with each stride. Molly did not know what was happening. Suddenly Clarion broke the surface and swam up to a floating platform. To Molly's amazement, on the other end of the platform sat a mermaid with her back to her.

Molly opened the goggles and was contemplating whether or not to disturb her. After a few moments, trying not to startle her, she quietly said, "Hi there." As she spoke Clarion rose to the level of the platform to allow her to dismount. "Are you alright?" asked Molly. The little girl turned around, tears running down her cheeks. "What happened? Why are you crying? Are you lost?"

"I ran away," said the little girl. "I ran away to find my mom."

How odd, thought Molly. There sat this little mermaid, probably no older than five or six, with her fin dangling in the ocean water all alone. Where was her father, or siblings, aunts or uncles?

"Why would you run away?" Molly asked.

"Because I want to find her. I want her to tell me why she left. I want her to tell me why she...abandoned me," cried the little mermaid.

"When did she leave?" asked Molly.

"A few days ago. I have been waiting for someone to tell me where she is, but no one is telling me anything. No one seems to want to talk about her. No one seems to want to tell me where she is and why she had to go. My father told me we will have to move away to another pod far away, in another part of these waters. I don't understand why." The little mermaid girl covered her face with her hands and sobbed.

"I'm sure it will be alright," said Molly as she knelt next to her. "Where do you live?"

"Not far from here," replied the little girl, wiping her tears.

"What's your name?" asked Molly after a moment.

"My name is Lena?" asked the mermaid.

"Very nice to meet you, Lena," she said reaching out with her right hand. The little mermaid looked at her with a confused look. Molly quickly lowered her hand since she realized a handshake was probably not a form of greeting here.

"Where do you come from?" asked Lena.

"I'm from the Capital, but I'm actually from Earth, a place you call The Land of Dreamers. Or more formally Terra Nova." The little mermaid nodded.

"A good mother would never leave her child willingly; no matter how tough things were," started the mermaid in an almost trance-like state. "The bond that is created between a mother and her child is eternal and so is the love between them. A mother would fight to get her child back. And no matter how far away she is, she will always love her little girl." With those last words, the little mermaid started to cry again. "It's not fair that they took her away from me."

Molly thought the way Lena spoke was very mature for her age, and it struck her as odd. Molly wasn't sure what else to say. After a few moments, Lena seemed as if she were starting to calm down a bit. Perhaps Molly's presence was all she needed. It always feels good to talk to someone about one's troubles.

"Do you have a mother?" asked Lena.

"Well..." started Molly, not really knowing what to say in response, "I do and I don't. It's hard to explain. You see, my mother left us when I was born and so I was raised by my father, Uncle Az and Madame de la Fleur on The Land of Dreamers. It's a long story, though."

"Do you know why your mom left you?" Lena asked, now much calmer than before. Molly shook her head in silence. "Did they tell you why she had to leave?" Molly shook her head once again.

"I have often wondered, though," Molly admitted. She had thousands of unanswered questions she wanted to ask her. In her head, countless times Molly imagined how the conversation would go. She wanted her mother to tell her why she left. What was more important than being there for her. Did she love her? Did she think of her, miss her or look for her? Or did she just selfishly walk away. She wanted to look her in the eye and ask her why she chose to leave. She desperately wanted to hear it from her.

As Molly came out of her thought, Lena was looking at her intensely and held out her hand. "Come with me – we will find her." Lena's sweet childlike voice suddenly turned dark and demonic.

Then from behind her, Molly could hear Eyya calling out, "Molly! Molly!" Molly stood up and looked behind her to see where the voice was coming from but didn't see anyone. She turned back only to find Eyya sitting by the table at Café Tenta staring right at her.

# CHAPTER 16

## *The three musketeers.*

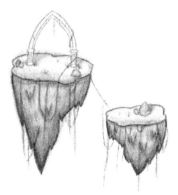

Her second flashback was instantly over, and she found herself once again back in the tent. Molly felt uneasy all of a sudden.

"And that mermaid, Lena?" asked Molly suddenly, interrupting Eyya's long tale describing how Aecus found them at the dock in the saddles of their water dragons after they returned from their visit to the underwater city. He was upset with all of them, especially Aiken for bringing the girls to Waterland in the first place.

"What mermaid?" asked Eyya confused. "There was no mermaid. If there had been I'm sure you would have written about it in your diary in great detail...have a look," Eyya started flipping through pages of Molly's diary until she came to a picture of the Waterland. "You see, your journal entry ends with exactly what I just said,

*'Aecus was very upset with us for venturing to the Waterland without proper training and guidance. Someone could have been hurt on this journey. It takes a considerable amount of practice to breathe under water with the help of the shield. He said that as one dives further and further into the waters, the body pressure needs to be regulated properly. At the speed the water dragons swim, this can be tricky. And for some even dangerous. Not to mention all the wild creatures that live in the waters and the proper training required to master protecting oneself against a possible attack. We returned to The City of Arbor without saying a single word. I betrayed my friendship with Aecus. He will never trust me again.'*

Great writing, by the way," added Eyya. Then with a look of both confusion and concern Eyya finished, "there you have it, no mermaid." Eyya thought that none of this should be happening, and that Clara needed to be told as soon as possible. Yes, the part about Aecus was all true, but she was never supposed to dream about Lena. "I still haven't found out who ratted us out to him, but I have a sneaking suspicion it was Fon!"

"But I do remember her, Eyya. I wouldn't make this up! She was there, I swear!" pleaded Molly. "Her mother was taken away from her, so she decided to run away in search of her. She asked about my mother," added Molly. Eyya did not know what to say.

Saved by the bell, at that very moment Molly and Eyya heard a distinct male voice coming from outside their tent.

"Aah! Just in time! I have a surprise for you," Eyya said as she stood up from the table, making her way to the entrance of their tent. "Close your eyes. Close your eyes, and don't peek, do you hear?" said Eyya. "Ok, you can come in, now," she said as she parted the tent opening.

A young blue-eyed boy entered the tent. It was Aiken.

"Happy birthday, to you..." he sang as he was pulling out a small candy bag and a jar of grapefruit fuzz out of his messenger bag. Eyya joined in. Molly opened her eyes and stared at Aiken in amazement. She was so happy to finally see him. Molly stood up and gave Aiken the biggest hug.

"Do you remember him now?" asked Eyya eagerly. Molly laughed joyfully. She finally remembered and it made her incredibly happy. The sound of the magical rain above turned into a beautiful symphony. String, brass and wind instruments played harmoniously together. All of her memories of Aiken came rushing back. One moment she felt excited to see him and hugged him tighter than she ever had, the next her feelings started to change and as if the world around them slowed down drastically, she felt herself giving into her emotions. She remembered how much in love she was with this Skyland elf. He made her so happy. His gorgeous smile and blue eyes made her shiver every time, without fail. Right now she was the happiest she had been in a long time. Finally, being with her one true love, for real. Their hearts started to sync up to the rhythm of the music, which played faster and faster with each of their heartbeats. She pulled away and slowly moved in to kiss him. Before their lips met, the music in her mind ended abruptly. Like a record being scratched in a comedic movie - her euphoric moment suddenly stopped and Molly felt herself freeze. With glazed eyes, she started experiencing another flashback. Random images appeared in her mind, one of which was of herself in her bed at Chateau Azeri. It was nighttime and she was asleep. Then, an image of her music box appeared, followed by an image of a tall, hooded figure lurking around.

As fast as these images started, they disappeared and Molly felt a sense of embarrassment that instantly morphed into shock as she regained consciousness, with her nose only a few inches away from his. She pulled away from Aiken instantly. With a sudden jerk of his head, Aiken quickly turned away slightly embarrassed at the near kiss incident.

"And...how does it feel being almost fifteen?" asked Eyya, trying to divert attention back to Molly.

"No different than being almost fourteen," replied Molly.

"And how about our first adventure to Waterland?" asked Eyya once again. They all laughed as they sat down around the table. Molly's face turned somber for a moment. She felt happy because she was finally together with her best friends. But she felt incredibly confused at the same time. Her mind was working overtime trying to make sense of everything she had experienced so far. All of this emotional turmoil felt very unfair to her. She found herself preoccupied with all these crazy thoughts when she should have been fully enjoying these moments.

"And these are for you...Maggie...I mean Molly!" said Aiken breaking the awkward silence. He only now realized he was looking at Molly, and not Maggie. 'But she looks just like her' he thought to himself.

"Your favorites! Toffee covered pretzels and pink grapefruit fuzz," said Aiken. "At least, I hope they are still your favorites," he added with a smile.

"Thank you so much. But I can't believe you're here!" said Molly in amazement. "In fact, how are you here? I saw the Skyland crossing at Junction Manor close right after we came through."

"Actually, I was on my way to go visit Caspian in Waterland when I heard you were coming," added Aiken quickly, "so, I sent a quick message to Eyya to let her know I was on my way."

"What are we going to do?" asked Molly. The not-so-brave

Molly was contemplating ways to help the people of Skyland. "How are we going to save your family?"

Aiken shook his head, not really knowing what to say. In that moment, the ground started to tremble. Molly, Eyya and Aiken looked at each other in horror as they grabbed onto the table. The lamp above was swaying from side to side and Molly feared the cord it was hanging from would snap at any moment.

The elf waiter peeked into the tent, "I'm so sorry to interrupt, but Trail is waiting for you in the lobby. You must get to safety, now!"

Molly hurriedly grabbed her diary along with the gifts Aiken brought her off the table and stuffed them into her messenger bag.

"Wait," said Eyya. "I can't go like this! I'll never keep up to you in this outfit!" And with a swift motion of her hand, the beautiful dress she was wearing transformed into form fitting pants and a jacket. "I learnt this little trick from Asgoth and Thana," said Eyya with a smile.

The three of them ran out of the café as fast as they could, rushing past panicked witches, wizards, elves and other magical creatures. The ground was still shaking, as if they were in the middle of an earthquake. They were desperately trying to grab onto anything they could to stay on their feet as they made their way straight towards the main staircase where George, Beatrice,

Thana and Asgoth were already waiting for them.

"Beatrice, I don't know how, but Corcoran managed to get in. Hurry and lead everyone to the underground passageways and take the train from there," shouted Trail from the bottom of the stairs. "Travelling on the surface is too dangerous. We will hold them back, but you must leave now! Thana will show you the way!" he added looking over at her with such intensity, as if he were saying his final goodbye. All Thana could do was simply nod.

The army of hollow knights started to flood the lobby from all corners of Junction Manor. It seemed they were not there to just decorate every hallway and room. They were finally able to honor their motto – to protect and defend.

Trail, ready for battle, fighting through the panicked masses led a small group of witches and wizards along with his steel army towards the front door.

"Follow me," said Thana as she led everyone down a corridor that seemed to lead to nowhere. There was a window overlooking the front garden at the end of it. Through it, Molly could clearly see the battle heating up. Outside, it looked like the Battle of Helm's Deep from Lord of the Rings. Hundreds of Corcoran's warriors were coming towards Junction Manor. But even more were spilling out of it ready to fight against the incoming enemy. Will Trail be able to hold off the evil Corcoran?

Will they be able to escape in time? Molly's mind was once again reeling, so much so that she completely forgot about how upset her father must have been with her for sneaking out of her room.

"Is this it?" asked Beatrice. "Is this the entrance to the catacombs?"

"Don't let the window deceive you, it is not real," Thana explained as she raised her left arm. "Recludo!" she said. The entire wall with the window moved back to reveal a secret spiral stone stairwell leading downwards. "After you, Beatrice."

"Follow me!" ordered Beatrice. "And stay alert! We don't know if they managed to find their way into the underground passages."

~~~

Outside, Gorgon and Gundula were having a grand old time torturing poor, helpless Grindrod, who seemed to be running out of hiding places.

"I got you!" gleamed Gorgon as she cast a spell that grabbed poor Grindrod from his hiding place and lifted him into the air. He did is very best, casting spells that managed to create small clouds of dust, causing Gorgon to lose her momentum and dropping him. This gave him the needed time to find a new hiding place.

"Aaaa-hahahahaha," laughed Gorgon maliciously. "Where are

you my little pumpkin spice?"

"Come out, come out, wherever you are?" added Gundula as she tried to quietly tiptoe towards a large fallen tree. "I think I found you," she added with a big laugh as she leaped across the crown of the tree. "Boo!" she shrieked.

"He's not here," said Gorgon as she leaped over to Gundula's side. "Where can he be?"

"Over there!" shouted Gundula pointing towards a large hole in the ground.

Luckily, Grindrod managed to find the place where all the other Trolls were waiting for him. As soon as he joined them, the hole in the ground disappeared instantly, leaving behind a small dirt pile.

"Aaah, how could you let him get away!" screamed Gorgon. "I was going to make a key chain out of his tiny head."

"Never mind that little vermin. Look!" shrieked Gundula. "The housekeeping staff is out in full force."

"Let's show them who's the boss, here," said Gorgon with a smirk followed with the biggest laugh.

As the door to Junction Manor swung open and Trail made his way out into the courtyard, he realized the full intensity of the attack. Dozens and dozens of magical creatures, wizards and witches lay across the garden injured in battle, screaming in agony. Flowers and shrubs were crushed to the ground in burning heaps, and the majestic ancient trees were uprooted. The once beautiful garden had been left in ruin as though a violent tornado gnarled its path across the landscape.

"Charge!" he ordered, as thousands upon thousands of hollow knights rushed out the door towards another group of Corcoran's incoming warriors heading straight for them.

In the distance, Trail locked his eyes on Corcoran. He was just standing there, observing the devastation of his attack. He noticed Trail, too, and apparated closer.

"We meet again," snarled Corcoran.

"I sure hoped I was never going to see you again," said Trail, remembering the last time the two of them saw each other.

"I don't want to hurt you," shouted Corcoran. "My beef is with my brother, not you."

"Then why are you here?" asked Trail calmly as he circled around Corcoran.

"You know why I'm here. Release her to me!" Corcoran ordered.

"No. I can't do that," replied Trail. And a fight between the two wizards erupted. "I see you've gained some new skills," said Trail as he disarmed one of Corcoran's attacks.

"And I see you're still just as predictable as before with yours," scowled Corcoran.

The fight continued. Spells were flying. There were moments

when Trail looked like he could use reinforcements, but that was just his way of assessing Corcoran's new abilities all the while tiring him out. Trail could tell that Corcoran was having a hard time, he seemed out of breath more so than out of strength. With one swift move, Trail flew over top of Corcoran and positioned himself between his enemy and the entrance to Junction Manor. A group of witches and wizard gathered behind him.

"What, am I too much for you?" snarled Corcoran as he continued throwing one spell after another. "Little Trail needed backup?"

"You're no match for me. Impedemus!" screamed Trail as loud as he could. The others close behind him followed suit. This spell cast a massive thrust against the damaging spells coming from Corcoran and his army. It simultaneously created a sphere-like protective shield that pushed the enemy inch by inch to the outer perimeter of the stone wall. The final thrust from Trail threw them hundreds of feet further back, landing on the ground with an incredible force. Corcoran and his small army were defeated - for now.

"I will be back, mark my words, Trail!" screamed Corcoran just before he disappeared into the night.

"Take everyone inside, now!" ordered Trail. He then turned to the wounded enemies, who were begging for their lives to be spared.

Over the broken stone garden wall, he caught a glimpse of Gorgon and Gundula trying to slither away. He was furious and with one leap, he flew up over the fence and landed in their path.

"How dare you show your faces here and attack us?" said Trail towering over them as they lay helplessly in the grass. "This action of yours bears heavy consequences! You know what the punishment is for traitors, do you not?" asked Trail, trying to regain his composure.

"Please, Trail, spare us!" begged Gorgon.

"We were under his spell, I swear, we would never..." pleaded Gundula.

"Do not send us to the Chambers. Anything but the Chambers..." Gundula and Gorgon were practically frozen in terror.

"You two leave me no choice. You sealed your fate when you joined forces with Corcoran." Trail raised his hand and cast a bright red beam of light straight into the air. It was to serve as forewarning to all the lands that war was indeed upon us all. Simultaneously, a gust of wind swept through the garden sending dust swirling in the air, making it hard to see. The dust settled and a half a dozen white cloaked figures appeared. The Attendees had been summoned.

"Take these miserable creatures to the Chambers," ordered Trail. "Category six will do. I wish you both a pleasant life in The

Land of Dreamers."

The Attendees pulled Gorgon and Gundula off the ground. They cried and pleaded but in an instant, they all simply vanished into a cloud of dust.

# CHAPTER 17

### *The great escape.*

B eatrice led the way down the stairs. As they stepped off the staircase, the glass lanterns that were hanging on the wall lit up one after another, revealing what appeared to be an underground maze of tunnels. A beautifully ornate and intricate design of tiles covered the walls that continued up towards the rounded ceiling. After a few steps, they all stopped for a moment, listening intently for the slightest possible sound of the enemy coming from the tunnels.

"Stay here! I'll scope the place out to make sure it is safe to pass," said Beatrice after a moment.

"Molly, where were you?" whispered George, who seemed very upset with her. "After our meeting with Trail, we went back to the room and I went to check in on you only to find out you weren't there. Do you realize how worried you had me? I was scared something happened to you, Zonks..."

"I'm so sorry, Dad. I just wanted some hot chocolate and on the way I ran into my two best friends. By the way, this is Eyya and Aiken," said Molly sheepishly, her head bowed low. She wasn't too embarrassed about being scolded by her father in front of her friends, but she did feel truly ashamed for sneaking out in the middle of the night. All these years she never once left his side. She just stood there, quietly hoping he wouldn't say anything else. She could not bear the thought of disappointing her dad for the very first time in her life.

"Ah, nice to meet you," said George. "I'm Molly's father," he continued. "If we were back home, you could call me George. Here, however, etiquette insists you address me by my proper name. I am Lord Enderby."

Eyya and Aiken could not believe their ears.

"Lord Enderby?" they said at the same time.

"Yep, in the flesh. I was just kidding about you having to call me Lord Enderby! I only wanted to see your reaction," said George with a smile. "I'm a pretty 'hip' dad, if you ask Molly. I'm not much for customs or traditions. You can call me George."

"I am so honored to finally meet you...sir...George," said Eyya in amazement.

Zonks and The Gate Keepers

At that moment, Beatrice came running back towards them. "The tunnels are clear. Follow me!"

After a few turns left and a couple more turns right they finally emerged at a train platform. Molly had never seen anything like it before.

"Wow, this is beautiful," she said.

"Look at those stained-glass inlays in the roof and the mosaic of tiles on the walls," said Eyya in amazement. "I've only ever seen anything like this in old books. This is a true testament to the creativity and ingenuity of the elves from all of the segments and it's a shame that no one really comes to these old train stations anymore."

A steam engine attached to a dozen individual carriage-like compartments was waiting for them. The engine had many chimneys poking out the front-end of it. Some were small, some were larger, some had round bulb-like tops, others had cone shaped metal caps. The carriages were another marvel. Each were oval in shape with a steel frame and eight gear-like wheels supporting each carriage. The sides were burgundy red with stained wood inserts along the bottom and full glass on the top capped with a curved stone slab roof.

"That is very interesting," said Molly. The tracks did not resemble those on Earth. Instead of a flat track, the steam engine and the carriages rode on a gear track. "Those tracks are pretty

137

cool. What a clever idea!"

"It has been decades indeed since these gear trains were in service," said Beatrice as they headed towards one of the carriages. "They truly were an invention ahead of their time but were quickly abandoned in favor of travel by dragon."

Thinking back to her wild ride aboard Ceara, Molly thought to herself, 'I'd prefer the Hogwarts Express here over a return trip on Dragon Airlines any day.'

They walked closer to the train, where they were greeted by a stoutly little man, dressed in the same uniform as all the other staff upstairs at Junction Manor.

"Welcome, everyone," he started, "I am so glad you made it safely. I trust Trail briefed you? Good. The train is pre-programmed to follow a specific course, so there is no need to worry. It should be safe, but stay alert at all times. We don't know how far the enemy has spread across our land." With that, the little man opened the door to the first train car for them all to climb aboard.

For a gear train that hadn't been used for years, the interior of the carriage was meticulously preserved. Dark green leather covered seats lined the whole perimeter. Brass tacks decorated each cushion and polished wood covered the entire floor. Once they were all seated, the little man closed the door and wished them a safe journey.

"It will be a long ride. Buckle up and try to rest if you can," said Beatrice as they started to move.

The train started to pick up speed as it entered the tunnel leading out of the platform. The clear glass windows that wrapped around the entire upper portion of the carriage transformed to display an advertising montage of unique elven-made wares.

"Are those gims...or gizmos?" asked Molly.

"Yes, Zonks," said George. "Although they seem quite old. These look like the old advertisements from the time this train was still operational. The finest creations in all of Heartland, all hand-made by the elves. They are very resourceful creatures and I don't know where we would be without them. Notice their differences. The elves, I mean. These are the Woodland Elves from the City of Arbor. You can tell by their appearance and type of clothing they wear. See that elf holding the gozer? We can see if we can find one at the Capital. You would be amazed at how useful they can be. They are like a Swiss Army knife of battle weapons."

"What kind of a knife?" asked Aiken, confused.

"It's a....sort of a specialty knife from our land," replied George. After the chaotic crossing and a brief stay at Junction Manor, George was slowly starting to think like a true Heartlandian again. It was all coming back to him.

"I'm sorry, I guess I'd forgotten myself for a moment, there. Two worlds colliding in my head. It will be a bit of an adjustment on my part, so please bear with me," he added with a smile. "But enough of me blabbering, for I see you are all tired. Why don't you rest a bit? We'll wake you when we get there."

Molly closed her eyes and within seconds she fell asleep. After a few minutes passed, Eyya noticed that everyone, including George, was dozing off, gently rocking from side to side to the motion of the train. Everyone, except for Beatrice. She thought this would be a perfect moment to bring up how worried she was about Molly.

"Beatrice?" said Eyya, "may I share something with you? I don't know if this is the right time, but I really need to tell someone." Eyya knew she could confide in her. Beatrice was one of her teachers in school. She taught the defense class among other subjects, but since she left to serve a higher cause, Eyya wasn't certain if that changed their relationship at all.

"But of course, Eyya," Beatrice nodded. "And just because I serve the royal family now, doesn't mean you ever have to feel like you can't come and talk to me. I'm still the same Miss Bea - and I'll always find time for you."

Eyya nodded with a smile, relieved that one stress had been alleviated – she knew she could speak freely with Beatrice. Now she just needed to figure out how to articulate her fears about what was happening.

"I don't want you to think I'm crazy but I'm afraid something strange is happening to Molly. Earlier, when we were talking and reminiscing about our adventures, a couple of things were going on. In one moment, we were talking about Aiken, then seconds later, she didn't know who he was. I even pointed out a picture of him in her diary along with some of her notes, but it didn't seem to trigger her memory. It wasn't until Aiken arrived that she remembered who he was," Eyya paused for a moment before continuing.

"And then there were a couple of instances when she appeared to relive a moment in a flashback. She remembered things differently than how they actually happened in her dream and were captured in her diary," continued Eyya. "One was our fateful trip to Waterland, you know the one…" added Eyya, shyly bowing her head in embarrassment. "Through her flashback, she seemed to have experienced the…the 'actual ending' of that adventure, and not the alternate ending, if you know what I mean. But even when I flipped to the pages in her diary that described the alternate ending, she insisted that it happened as it did in the flashback. I know this sounds very confusing."

"Interesting. Very interesting," said Beatrice as she pondered this over. "The memory of Aiken was reset when he became physically present. Until she had that flashback, the key element, in this case Aiken, did not exist in her mind. But that still doesn't explain it all. The memories, with the alternate endings, should remain intact, by design. That is how the protocol is written. There is no way she should remember anything other than what was presented in her dreams. How did you react?"

"I stuck to the plan," she said bravely, fighting back tears. Eyya was an intelligent elf, wise beyond her years with a sharp mind. She was struggling to put together the pieces of what Beatrice was telling her in a way that made any sense.

"So, I get the memory part with Aiken, which actually better explains her reaction when she did see him," said Eyya as she recalled the near miss of a kiss. "But I'm struggling to understand why she is remembering the actual versions of the events…"

Beatrice paused for a moment not saying anything, just waiting to see if Eyya could piece the puzzle together on her own.

"Something caused an override in the protocol," Eyya paused with a confused look on her face. "But what? I'm positive I accounted for every variable when I programmed it." Beatrice was proud to see Eyya using the tools she had taught her in analytical thinking.

"You are correct, something did interfere with the protocol," said Beatrice. "Can you think of anyone that might have a reason to do this?"

"You mean Corcoran and Regina?" asked Eyya in disbelief.

"Yes. I can't help but think that they are involved in this, somehow. This memory rated at the top of the list, that is why we included it in the protocol. But you know what you have to do. Stick to the plan, at all costs!"

"Yes, Beatrice," said Eyya finally giving in to the tears that so desperately wanted to flow. Sticking to the plan and not being able to reveal the secret was becoming harder and harder, with each passing hour. She never thought it would weigh on her so much, despite all her training. "Molly's just a little girl. She never signed up for this," said Eyya.

"I know, Eyya," said Beatrice with a heavy heart. "Maggie told us to trust her plan, and trust each other, right? We will make sure to get Molly to the Capital safely. I am sure with the help of Clara we can reverse all of this. And then, we can focus our combined efforts to protect her. Just like Maggie wanted us to."

Eyya nodded as she looked over at Molly sleeping peacefully, with her head resting on her dad's shoulder. This girl, that reminded her so much of her best friend, Maggie. This girl, so blissfully unaware of the great responsibility she was burdened with. She needed their help and Eyya needed to find her strength to carry on with the mission. There was no turning back, no matter how hard things get. Maggie was counting on them. But more importantly, she was counting on Eyya.

# CHAPTER 18

*We don't have much time.*

The moonlight was shining through Molly's window at Count Azeri's mansion, while the curtains danced in the warm summer breeze. It seemed like a storm was approaching. A smile came across Molly's face, as if she knew that the long-awaited rain was at last on its way. A dark, tall, hooded figure creaked the door open, and slowly stepped into her room. One foot in front of the other, he quietly moved across the wooden floor, carefully navigating the room towards the nightstand. It was like walking through a minefield. With each step, the old floors creaked but he managed to cross without waking her up. Very slowly, he opened the drawer. At that moment, Molly stirred in her bed, causing the hooded man to jump back, and stumble into the nearby dresser. Gentle music started to play. The hooded figure realized that it was coming from inside of his bag. The music box must have opened when he bumped into the dresser. He pulled it out of the bag, examined it briefly to make sure nothing happened to it, then placed it gently inside the nightstand and closed the drawer. He then hurriedly turned around and left the room, hoping he did not wake her.

"Zonks. Zonks. Zonks! Can you hear me! Zonks?" said a familiar voice. George was trying to wake her up. The train started to slow down and it seemed they finally arrived at their destination.

"Happy birthday, Zonks," he said. "I'm sorry I don't have your birthday present with me. I left it on the kitchen table at the Chateau. It's probably gone by now," he added remembering the fire they left behind just before they stepped through the portal.

"That's alright, Daddy," said Molly still half-asleep. "Where are we?" asked Molly. "Why are we here?"

"We took a train from Junction Manor, remember?" said George, gently caressing her face as he always did when she first woke up from a bad dream.

"The what Manor?" asked Molly confused.

"Did you have another bad dream?" asked George.

"No, I didn't," Molly replied simply. Beatrice and Eyya exchanged a glance. The memory loss seemed to be progressing faster than either of them expected.

"One must be alert at all times," said Beatrice. "Now, when the train stops, everyone wait in here. We will see if it is safe to proceed." Within a few moments, the train pulled to stop in an underground station.

"Lord Enderby, may I have a word with you?" asked Beatrice as she stood up to open the carriage door.

Beatrice, Asgoth and Thana stepped out of the train compartment and disappeared into the steam filled platform. George followed right behind them. Molly, Eyya and Aiken jumped up and pressed their faces against the windows, trying to look towards the direction they headed.

Sensing everyone's anxiety rising, before he got too far, George turned back and said, "All right everyone, don't panic. Everything is going to be fine. The next leg of our journey may be a bit of a bumpy one, if I recall. We will be flying to the Capital from here. We will fly around Mount Kiragar, which should take us a couple of hours," George paused for a moment before he continued. "Relax. We'll all be safe. I'll be back in a few seconds. You wait here, okay?"

"Dragons?" asked Molly, quivering.

"Yes, dragons," said Eyya with similar sentiment.

"Lord Enderby..." started Beatrice slowly, "the imposter curse. The side effects are worsening. Even though we administered a counter curse, they are much worse than I anticipated."

George fell silent, because deep down he knew that there was the likelihood that they would run out of time before they reached the Capital. He knew that bringing his precious little Zonks to Heartland would put her in grave danger. He had no choice, but he was prepared to protect her at all costs. He knew that her chances were better here in Heartland than back home on Earth. The rumors were proving to be true. Corcoran's men managed to get through the gates to wreak havoc on Earth despite the gatekeepers and their families' efforts. Corcoran's men captured a lot of them and tortured them to gain intel on the location of Chateau Azeri. It really was only a matter of time before they found Molly and George. Running away and hiding on Earth with the risk of being discovered was not an option. Coming to Heartland was George and Molly's only chance of survival, at least that is what he thought.

"Is there anything else we can do right now?" asked George.

"I'm sorry, but I'm not certain if there is. If everything went according to plan though, Fon and Dorn are waiting for us outside. I'll send them ahead to alert Clara. She'll have the treatment ready. I trust that she will know what to do. Our only option is to get Molly to the Capital safely and quickly," she paused briefly.

147

Before she could continue, George interjected, "How much time do we have before all her memories are either altered or lost altogether?"

"We don't have much..." she replied, "but you already knew that, didn't you?"

"I understand," he said simply. For George, a man who lived on Earth for so many years, over time he allowed himself to show vulnerability and emotion. Especially since Molly was born. In Heartland, as Lord Enderby, he had to remain calm and composed at all times, showing little or no emotion. He never thought he could feel such hatred as he did right now. Corcoran and Regina were going to pay for this. "Then what are we waiting for? I know of a quicker route," he said as he turned to head back to the train compartment. Beatrice took Asgoth and Thana to explore the platform.

"Change of plans, kids," said George when he got back to the train car. We will be flying up to about two thirds of Mount Kiragar's height, instead of going around it. The mountain is about 25,000 feet high. The Capital is located on the other side and it is faster to go through than around. There are tunnels that we can use to cut through." Molly immediately tensed up.

"Given the options, I'd much rather fly around, Dad..." said Molly sitting right back down. Instantly, Eyya sat next to her and grabbed her hand to comfort her. George crouched down, trying to find words to console Molly.

"I know, Zonks," said George gently. "That would take hours, though. And we don't have that much time. Flying up to the tunnels should take us no longer than half an hour. It'll be a breeze, you'll see."

"What was that lady's name, again? The one with the beautiful white hair?" Molly asked. George paused for a moment before answering. He gently placed his hand on her cheek.

"That's Beatrice, my little Zonks. Her name is Beatrice," said George with tears welling up in his eyes. He had to stay strong, though.

"Daddy, are you ok?" asked Molly.

"Yes, my Zonks." he replied. "Everything will be fine."

"Lord Enderby...I mean, George," said Eyya, trying to divert his attention. "What's that flickering light outside?"

A beam of circular light traveled across the platform as if it were scanning every square inch of each wall.

"That is a sensor spell that Beatrice cast," said George, regaining control of his emotions. "It is a form of echo locator that scans the perimeter of the platform for traces of any danger."

The light beam traced the walls and penetrated the thick steam. It was obvious they were in a large open space with a very high ceiling.

As the steam dissipated, Molly noticed they were still

underground. This station was even more grand and beautiful than the one at Junction Manor. The structure of the building seemed to have been carved out of ebony wood with the windows and doorways skillfully inlayed with etched-glass inserts depicting vignettes of magical creatures from all the seven segments. The beautiful floor was covered in stones of different shapes and sizes with a purposefully laid out design that resembled a unity symbol of some sort. The steam fog had all but vanished and Molly could now see a row of doors, through one of which walked in Beatrice, Asgoth and Thana.

"Come this way!" said Beatrice. "It's safe to proceed."

After they exited the train platform, they found their way to a rickety old steel elevator. Molly wondered whether it would have the strength to carry them all the way up to the surface. Luckily, they made it. Light filled the elevator cabin as the rusty steel doors opened. Molly noticed they were entering a small, horseshoe shaped building, with a rusty green steel frame and weathered windows. The glass panels let in just enough sunlight. There was some sparse foliage that, despite all odds, seemed to have taken up residence and survived in the old planters. This place was long abandoned, no longer used by anyone and already forgotten by many.

As soon as they stepped outside they were greeted by Fon and Dorn.

"Fon, Dorn. Fly ahead and alert Clara of our arrival," said Beatrice, "we will be right behind you. Everyone else, your dragons are here. Let's head to the Capital! The Councilors are anxiously awaiting our arrival."

# CHAPTER 19

*Bad news bear.*

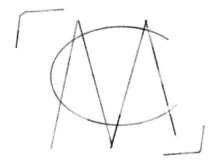

The door to the office opened slowly revealing a mysterious hooded figure striking a peculiar pose. The office hours were over, so this was definitely an unexpected visit at the office of Dr. Claremore.

"I'm sorry, the office is now closed," said Dr. Claremore, not even lifting her gaze from the book she was reading at her desk.

"Dr. Claremore, huh? Nice name. Sounds like you're from Oklahoma or somewhere around there! Dr. Margaret Claremore. I must admit it does have a ring to it. Maggie, are you certain you can't make an exception for an urgent appointment?" asked the mysterious figure.

"I would recognize that voice anywhere!" said Maggie with a

big smile as she jumped up from her chair and rushed towards the door. "What are you doing here, Eyya?"

"Just popped in for a visit," she said with a smirk as she embraced Maggie. "You look great! That 'age refining therapy' is truly doing wonders, isn't it? You don't look a day over 30."

"Yes. Anything is possible with a bit of magic, regardless of which side of the gates you find yourself on," said Maggie pointing at a little music box on her bookshelf across the room. "And you? You don't look a day over 25."

"Well, you know. Benefits of being introduced to magic at a young age. Aging myself a bit comes in handy occasionally, let me tell you. A sixteen-year-old me running around the streets of New York would sure have raised some suspicions. The last thing I needed was to get detained," she added with a laugh. "But where are Fon and Dorn?" asked Eyya.

"They should be back shortly," replied Maggie. "Please don't take this the wrong way, but why are you here?"

"That little turd!" said Eyya as she plopped herself onto the love seat. "He didn't tell you, did he?"

"Tell me what?"

"I knew it! I just knew it!" said Eyya. "I hate being right, you know. I knew this was going to happen, and that is why I told Clara to send me here just to make sure you got the message. I don't know where Fon's head is these days. This was critical *information that was supposed to be passed on to you urgently. Plus, he was supposed to deliver a confirmation that the message was delivered. That part was my idea, by the way. Because I knew Fon would either forget, or deliberately delay telling you. This is why I have to do everything myself. I guess that is the only way to ensure the job gets done."*

*"Don't blame him," said Maggie. "He's really having a hard time with this assignment. What was he supposed to tell me?" Just as she finished asking the question, Fon and Dorn flew into the room. Fon noticed Eyya sitting on the love seat and was about maneuver his way right back out.*

*"Where do you think you're going?" asked Eyya as she moved towards the door using a fast-moving spell to block his way.*

*"I…I…I forgot something," stuttered Fon.*

*"You are in trouble, brother," said Dorn with a giggle.*

*"Don't you move an inch, mister," said Eyya. She was really angry with him. "Now, since you decided to finally grace us with your presence, I'll let you have the honor to DO THE JOB YOU WERE ASSIGNED TO DO IN THE FIRST PLACE! Come on, tell her!"*

*"Would someone care to fill me in? What is going on?" Maggie was really confused.*

*"Fon has a message for you from the Capital, that he is deliberately neglecting to share." said Dorn from the other side of the room. "I heard him finishing his call with Clara earlier. He*

*wouldn't even tell me what it was about."*

*Fon let out an audible grunt suggesting he was not at all pleased with his brother for throwing him under the bus. "It's because you're such a blabber-mouth!" shouted Fon.*

*"Were you even going to tell her, or were you planning on keeping it a secret all along?" asked Eyya angrily.*

*"I was going to deliver the message. I swear I was," said Fon as he flew across to the other side of the room, away from Eyya, mainly for fear of being smacked by her.*

*"And why didn't you?" asked Eyya.*

*"Because...because I think we're getting somewhere with Maeve," he said.*

*"Aha, then you admit that this is working!" said Dorn victoriously.*

*"Shut up, you!" said Fon throwing Dorn a stern look.*

*"Well, if you won't tell her, then I will," said Eyya crossing her arms. "Not let this visit go to waste."*

*"I'm growing tired of these arguments between the two of you," said Maggie. "There's obviously something there that needs to be unpacked and dealt with. Why don't you just talk it out?"*

*"Don't psychoanalyze the situation, Maggie," said Eyya. "Now is not the time!"*

*"I know you're still mad at him for calling Aecus on you all! Remember that time when you decided to take a little swim in*

the ocean and visit Caspian?" said Dorn as he snacked on something, observing the battle erupting between Eyya and Fon.

"Stay out of this, brother," said Fon.

"Alright, enough! Both of you," Maggie couldn't take this any longer. "Fon, would you be so kind and tell me what the message is?"

"Uhm...I was supposed to deliver a message from Clara," said Fon not really knowing how to say it. "The message said that this was...to be...our final try...and..."

"Oh, shrapnel! I'll age tenfold just standing here listening to you blabber," said Eyya impatiently. "Clara said that this is your last and final attempt. If you fail, you are to report back to Heartland and Protocol 24601 will be terminated. No more life cycles."

"But...that can't be," said Maggie. "They can't just terminate her! There is a way to counteract the effects of the dark magic, I just need a little bit more time."

"I know, Maggie," Eyya started. "I know how hard this is for you and I know how bad you want this to work. Clara said that you have had dozens of failed opportunities already. Maybe this is just not meant to be. Some souls are just not meant to be saved."

"I know," said Maggie with a sigh. "How much time do we have?"

"You have as much time as Maeve gives you. If she decides to take her life, like all of the other girls before her, then we'll have no choice but to follow through with Clara's orders. She does not trust Regina, and who could blame her. Clara is determined to fight this battle without Regina's help. But don't blame yourself if it doesn't work. We all know you have done everything you could to save her."

"I'm so sorry, Maggie," said Fon as he flew closer to her. "I knew how hard it would be for you to hear this. I just couldn't bear to tell you."

"That's ok, Fon," said Maggie. "I get it."

"And how is it going with Maeve?" asked Eyya.

"Well..." started Maggie, "...I think it's actually going quite well. She's still reading the book, which is a good sign. This is the furthest we have gotten with any of them before."

"That's good to hear," said Eyya. "I'll let Clara know that you are making some significant progress. I have to get back now. Come here, give us a hug," she added with a smile as she reached out to pull Maggie in.

"You better get going," said Maggie. "We wouldn't want Clara waiting."

"Catch you later?" said Eyya.

"Catch you later," replied Maggie with a smile.

# CHAPTER 20

## *Heartland*

**M**olly walked up to her dragon with hesitation, as she certainly did not want to do this again. The thought of riding a dragon scared her less than the thought of flying thousands of feet high up in the air. No seatbelt, nothing. Just her in Ceara's saddle holding on for dear life.

"Zonks, it'll be fine," said George as he helped her mount the dragon. "I'll put your bag in the side pouch, ok? Just hang on tight. Your dragon knows the course, so if you really want, you can just close your eyes and breathe slowly. The higher we get, the less oxygen there is going to be, so we all have to pace ourselves." Molly silently nodded. "But if you really want to see something spectacular from up there, just open one eye, briefly," smiled

George, trying to lighten her mood. "You will be amazed how beautiful Heartland looks from above."

'Heartland...Heartland...Heartland...' Molly kept repeating the word in her mind, over and over again. Why did that word seem so familiar to her? She knew she heard it before, somewhere, but she could not recall when or where, no matter how hard she tried.

"Hi girl. Here we go again. No shenanigans this time around, alright?" said Molly. Ceara brought her giant head around and nudged her a bit. "Alright, alright. I trust you'll get us up there safely." Ceara gently closed her eyes as if to say 'but of course.'

Molly closed her eyes tightly. With a couple of wing-flaps, Ceara rose off the ground and was headed straight for the mountain. Then Molly started to recall that day she spent sitting in the library with her Uncle Az listening to him tell a story about a mysterious place for the very first time. Often, the stories he would tell were about his amazing travels all over Earth. But at times like this one, when George was away, he would tell some very special ones. Stories of a world that was altogether different. George would frequently leave for a day or two, though he would never tell Molly exactly why. The truth was, he would do so to send messages through the nearest gate to Heartland. He never gave up hope that one day he there would be a message waiting for him. A message from Clara.

'Heartland...' Molly thought to herself.

"Presently, Heartland consists of six self-functioning land segments - Woodland, Skyland, Waterland, Barrenland, Winterland, Shadowland; and a city segment called the Capital," started Uncle Az. "These are, coincidently, the seven remaining founding segments of the Heartland Commonwealth. The Commonwealth was much larger in its heyday with many more segments. Years of battles and confrontations with the Overlanders dwindled it down to the seven that exist today. The Commonwealth was governed by the noble Heartland family who lived in the Capital. Unlike the other six segments that were lands, the Capital is a giant city located at the top of the tallest mountain called Mount Kiragar.

"The Capital was also often referred to as 'The City of Magic'. Out of all the inhabited places in Heartland, the Capital was situated at the highest altitude. Therefore, it seemed natural to make it the place where the Councilors of each segment would meet with the rulers of Heartland to discuss matters of utmost importance and urgency. Beyond the Commonwealth and the lost segments there are other pockets of land inhabited by magical creatures that have not yet evolved, or simply did not see the benefit of joining the Commonwealth.

"Visiting the Capital was like going to an elegant medieval market. The heart of the city had a number of streets and squares with meticulously designed houses, and the best pub this side of Mount Kiragar called The Tipsy Shrew. It was nestled right on the banks of a massive infinity lake with its water falling over a cliff hundreds of miles down where it then funneled into a calm river running through the ancient forests below all the way to the oceans of Waterland.

"The area around Mount Kiragar is home to the most diverse population of magical creatures from all around this world. The trees around the base soared so high that from up above you'd look like a small ant next to them. These trees were the homes of the Woodland elves, who lived harmoniously with the Inkhans, the ancient inhabitants of the region who had occupied the land ever since the dawn of civilization.

"Mysterious tall trees..." he continued spinning this magical tale, "...hollow from the inside but beautifully green from the outside, with vines resembling a tangled net falling down from their tall branches. These vines were their source of water, among other things. They also served as both a plumbing and a communication system. There were many incredibly unbelievable things in this world, but somehow, they all seemed to make sense. Everything had its purpose; however obscure it may have seemed. When you thought you had it all figured out, when you thought the deepest secrets of Heartland had all been revealed, another one or two surfaced. A new fascinating fact to add to what you already knew.

"Fairies lived up in the tall branches of the majestic trees of the Forest of Inkhans. They lived in tiny houses connected by rope bridges. It almost looked like a miniature treehouse community amongst the green leaves. Although they were small in size, fairies played an important role in the balance of Heartland. Some fairies worked alongside wizards and witches and some alongside the Gate Keepers, serving their employers proudly.

"The elves from this region were most known for making gims. Gims were, among other things, extra futuristic yet medieval gadgets, that everyone in Heartland loved. Gims truly made lives easier. Each season, one of the Elves, specially appointed by the Ministry of Gims, Gizmos and Gadgets, would come up with a new invention. If the gim was successfully received, it would become instantly marketable. My favorite gim was the gozer - the enhanced version of it, not the original design. The gozer was a bow-like instrument combined with a hooked zipline, arrows and a net. It was especially useful for hunting and in battles.

"The area at the very edge of the Forest of Inkhans, that sprawled up the side of the mountain was inhabited by a unique group of magical creatures. Centaurs, unicorns, griffins and shrews made this region their home. It is said, that the ancient spells of the ancestors guided these creatures here to serve and protect the great leaders of Heartland.

"Goblins lived deep inside the mountain, which was often referred to as the place of eternal darkness. They managed to carve out a wonderful world of underground burrows, tunnels and hideaways. It was fascinating how the mountain regions were so in tune with the needs of the goblins. The entrances into their underground world were hidden, for the most part. However, when accidently uncovered by someone unwanted, the mountain would make these entrances instantly disappear forever, as if magically swallowed by the luscious ground-cover greens, never to be seen again."

A strange sound interrupted Molly's memory of Uncle Az's story, which made her slowly drift back into reality. As they flew higher and higher, the sound of the dragon wings flapping was slowly swallowed by a deafening humming sound.

"Zonks! Zonks!" yelled George, trying to get her attention. "Zonks, whatever you do, do not open your eyes. Just listen to me and do as I say, okay."

Confused, Molly did as she was told and kept her eyes shut tight. "What's going on Daddy? What is that humming?" asked Molly with a panicked sound in her voice.

"We are approaching a waterfall...I need you to keep your eyes closed, okay? The dragons will have to speed up to fight the power of the falling water. You just grab onto your saddle as tight as you can, Zonks! Can you do that for me?" asked George.

Molly nodded, panicked, not fully understanding what was about to happen.

"In a couple of seconds, we will have to fly through the waterfall to enter the tunnels."

Hearing this, with eyes wide open, Molly yelled "WE HAVE TO DO WHAT?" Panic stricken, she looked at her father, then looked ahead to see the waterfall coming closer and closer, then looked below to see how far down the water fell, and then clutched the saddle so tight her fingers practically turned white.

"Hang on, it will only take a second!" George yelled louder, hoping she would hear him through the thundering sound of the falling water.

"I'm gonna diiiieeeee," shouted Molly as Ceara picked up speed in preparation to dart through the massive waterfall.

# CHAPTER 21

## *The forgotten tunnels of*

## *Mount Kiragar*

Despite the speed at which Molly's dragon flew through the waterfall, its landing was surprisingly controlled. Molly was drenched, though. She reached inside her messenger bag to check the damage her diary sustained due to the unexpected shower and was relieved to find it to be minimal. She jumped a little in her saddle as she looked up, because in that moment she found herself staring into the eyes of a short little creature standing on a wooden platform.

"I'm sorry," said Molly a bit startled. "I didn't mean to react that way. I've just never met a..." For a second she was at a loss for words. Here she thought she knew all the types of magical creatures in Heartland, but as it turned out she had yet to meet this one.

"I'm a goblin, and my name is Corinuss Tomuss," he said with a smile. He was a short fellow, with pointy long ears, who as he spoke, gestured with hands a bit too much. When he wasn't gesturing with his hands, he kept placing one hand over the other, gently caressing his knuckles with his thumb. He was such a chatty fellow, too, as Molly would soon discover. His voice reminded her of that old man on the radio show she listened to most Sunday afternoons. "Welcome. We are thrilled to have you among us," the goblin said as he motioned for everyone to gather around him. Molly just now noticed dozens of goblins poking their heads out of round holes that covered most of the cavern walls.

"Alright, everyone. Please join me here. There..." he continued. "I hope your flight was enjoyable. We really do have the most amazing views from up here. I know flying through the waterfall can be a daunting experience. It should have, though, prepared you for what you can expect next."

'Oh no', Molly thought. 'Could this just be over, already?'

"We are presently in what we call the old dragon slipway. Visitors on spccial assignments by the royal family would travel to the Capital through here to save time. They were the only ones permitted to travel through the tunnels during the uprising that took place three centuries ago. Since the formation of the

Commonwealth, we no longer receive visitors through the waterfall, therefore this is predominantly an area where our dragon companions spend most of the warm season. Now follow me. Don't lag behind, these tunnels can be dangerous. You may notice the very interesting ridges on the upper half of the tunnel walls, these are due to..." he continued as everyone else followed right behind him.

"I'm not trying to sound rude..." whispered Eyya to Molly and Aiken "...but it feels a bit creepy being stared at by all those goblins up there. Also, is this going to be a tour of the forgotten tunnels of Mount Kiragar, or what? If so, can I opt out of this excursion?" All three of them giggled.

"Here we are at the upper deck," said Corinuss as he led everyone into another open cavern with a train platform and gear-like tracks, reminiscent of the ones the train from Junction Manor travelled on. "From here, we will take the train. Ah, and here it is, right on time." He added as four small carts rolled in. "Hop on in, there is room for up to four in each cart. Pick the one you fancy the most and don't forget to buckle up!"

Corinuss climbed in the front car, which presumably was the one that controlled this train that somewhat resembled the big thunder mountain railroad ride, but with more gears and levers than the contraption behind the curtain in Emerald City. Molly, Eyya and Aiken took the second car, George and Beatrice climbed into the third and Asgoth and Thana claimed the last cart.

"Is everyone ready?" asked Corinuss with a smile. They all nodded, anxious to get this over with.

This train was more like a roller coaster and made the one at Disneyland seem like a kiddie ride. Corinuss navigated the winding tracks with precision while the train jerked left and right depending on the direction he selected. His hands moving skillfully across the intricate control panels as though playing a complicated musical instrument. He obviously knew this maze like the back of his hand. The tunnels were dark, for the most part, with only the spill from the sporadically recessed lanterns providing some visibility.

"Molly, are you alright?" yelled George from the car behind, seeing she looked a little pale.

"I think I'm going to barf," replied Molly holding her mouth desperately trying not to, for the fear of yet again embarrassing herself in front of Aiken, more than anything. The train started to slow down as they exited a long tunnel into an open cave. Molly looked over the edge of the train cart and could see they were travelling across a tall metal bridge, the cavern below so far down that even the lights from the lanterns could not reach it. The train slowed such that it felt as though they were practically gliding across the bridge.

"This is the Pevibis Caverns," whispered Corinuss. "Please

refrain from speaking. We don't want to disturb the sleeping Katydid Luminous. Do you see the glow all over the ceiling of the cavern? That's them. Presently, they are asleep and although they are certainly not dangerous, they can spook easily. There are over 4,000 of them in this cavern alone, and waking them would make our passage through here very, very difficult, to say the least." He added with a nervous giggle. Moments later, they passed through a short tunnel and then arrived at the end of the track.

"Here we are," said Corinuss, as he brought the train to a full stop. "This is as far as my journey with you goes. Beatrice will lead the way from here."

"Thank you so much, Corinuss," said George. "Being able to cross through the mountain saved us some very valuable time."

They all piled out of their carts, anxious to move on. Molly stumbled a bit as she got out. All she wanted to do was crawl into a bed and sleep for three days straight. She was so exhausted from this journey already, but she had no choice but to find the last ounce of strength left in her to carry on.

Once they were all off the train, Corinuss wished them safe travels and waved goodbye as the train pulled away and then disappeared back into the tunnel.

"Daddy?" Molly leaned over to George, whispering. "Why are we here? Where are we going? Is Madame de la Fleur going to be waiting for us with some hot cocoa?" George looked at her, only able to muster up a nod.

Beatrice led the way up a set of stone stairs, that curved and twisted, until they finally reached a wooden door with a picture of a rodent on it.

"We made it," said Beatrice. "I'm so glad this door is still here."

Beatrice stretched out her hand, cast a spell and the rustic old door that had not moved for centuries, creaked open. A light breeze flowed through the open door, a sigh of relief to once again be able to move freely.

"We are now in the back storeroom of a pub called The Tipsy Shrew," said Beatrice. "We will exit through that door over there, which leads into the pub itself. Stay here, I will make sure it's safe to proceed. We don't want to raise any suspicion."

Beatrice left the storeroom while everyone else found a somewhat comfortable place to sit down and rest a bit.

"Hello, who are you?" asked Molly as she sat between Aiken and Eyya. "My name is Molly," she said stretching out her right arm to shake Aiken's hand. He looked confused, first down at Molly's hand, then at Eyya, who was fighting back tears. All she could do was mouth the words 'Shake her hand...'

"I'm Aiken, nice to meet you," he said. As he gently grabbed Molly's hand and shook it.

"When you meet someone for the first time you shake hands. It is customary in the world Molly comes from..." said Eyya, wiping away the tears. "I never should have agreed to this," she said quietly, shaking her head. Eyya was aware of the dangers. They all were. But no one could have prepared her for any of this and she knew it was way too late to back out now. Eyya needed to stay the course...for Molly and for Maggie. Beatrice returned before Aiken could ask more questions.

"Follow me! Keep your heads low and don't make eye contact with anyone in the pub."

In a straight line, they all headed for the door opposite the one they entered through moments earlier. As they walked out from behind the bar, Molly noticed that the pub was packed with magical creatures, drinking, smiling, dancing and some were even fast asleep on top of the tables – most likely passed out from all the drinking. One thing seemed odd. Everyone was motionless. As if frozen in time. One could hear a mouse squeak it was so quiet.

"Is this a wax museum of some sorts?" whispered Molly as she diverted from the line and moved about the pub freely.

"Zonks, come on. We don't have much time," said George as he rushed towards her and quickly pushed her towards the main entrance.

Once everyone was through, Beatrice turned around and cast

a spell and the frozen picture came back to life, as if someone wound up the record player. The noise came back and the pub was buzzing with life once again.

# CHAPTER 22

## *The Capital*

**M**olly walked right next to her dad, holding his hand tight. She didn't say a word, just kept on walking with her head bowed low, desperately fighting to stay awake. She never thought it was possible to feel such complete physical and mental exhaustion. It felt as if every energy store in her body was running on fumes, barely staying operational. Thankfully, there was just enough to keep her moving, one foot in front of the other. Beatrice was a few steps ahead leading the way with Asgoth and Thana, ready to take a turn if it seemed they were heading into a busy and congested area. They had to cross the city as fast as they could. They could not spare a single minute fighting through any potential crowds that were already starting to gather in the streets. Eyya and Aiken walked right behind, trying to keep up the pace. They were walking past excited elves carrying baskets full of flowers, ribbons, fruits and other assortment of items used for decorating. Always observant, Molly noticed something odd as she moved her long hair out of her face. The rushed, panicked urgency in which they were hurrying down the cobblestone roads towards the Grand Hall was in contrast to the excited energy of the elves. It was as if they had no idea what was about to happen. Focused on their individual tasks, they were singing their carefree happy little tunes.

The Grand Hall was often referred to by the locals as Heartland's mission control center. From the outside, it looked exactly like a larger version of Count Azeri's mansion. Even if for a moment, Molly felt as if she were back on Earth, walking up to the house that was her home for longer than she could remember. She let out a small smile before bowing her head once again and grabbing onto George's arm a bit tighter.

"We made it, Zonks," he said gently.

"Finally," she replied with half a chuckle.

Regular meetings of the Councilors were held here at the Grand Hall. Although the building was many centuries old, it looked well cared for. Not everything was as it appeared in

Heartland and the same was true for this beautiful historic landmark which had a rather deceiving façade. From the front one would think it to be a simple, ordinary two-story mansion with a tall, light blue rooftop with dozens of chimneys of various sizes poking out from it. Small rectangular windows were symmetrically aligned along the upper floor, with wrought iron balconies sporadically sticking out overlooking the front promenade. At street level, a covered arched walkway lined the whole length of the building. Right in the middle were steps that led to a set of big double doors carved out of dark mahogany wood. Detailed with black metal trim and a lion head knocker perfectly centered on each one, they looked no different than any of the other doors on the buildings that lined this street. What an ordinary city visitor didn't know, was that the Grand Hall was built at the edge of a cliff. It in fact had twelve additional floors beneath the visible two-story façade that were built into the cliff face of the mountain. What appeared simple from one angle, was intricately complex from another. When at the bottom of the cliff looking at the Grand Hall from the back, one could see a massive fourteen story building nestled into the side of the mountain.

They made their way up to the double doors and upon their arrival, they were greeted by Theseus, a minotaur towering eight feet tall. Molly jumped and instantly pulled behind her father.

Theseus seemed very stern and unapproachable. With his

175

imposing horns, a large snout, hooded eyes and big muscular arms, he looked very threatening. Contrary to that, he was a gentle creature with a very soft tone to his voice.

"You must be Lord Enderby," said Theseus, stepping towards George, bowing to him. "My name is Theseus, the High Chancellor of Heartland. It is an honor to finally meet you, your Highness."

"Likewise," replied George.

"Beatrice, I am relieved to see you all," said Theseus looking over to her.

"Well, Chancellor, given the circumstances, our journey could have been much worse," replied Beatrice. "I see the Summerset Festival preparations are in full swing. Based on the current situation, how certain are you that we will be able to proceed with the festivities?"

Theseus took a few seconds to respond. He was not known to hesitate when given a chance to respond to a question, which obviously made Beatrice feel uneasy.

"We have made all the necessary preparations and safety precautions..." started Theseus very thoughtfully. "We have doubled our surveillance in the mountain regions, as well as along the seashore and in the open waters. So far everything appears to be calm. The Councilors have decided that we in fact will go ahead with the celebrations tonight.

Beatrice led out a sigh of relief. "That's comforting, thank you,

Chancellor. We must not panic the citizens and guests of the Capital. Let's head in, the Councilors are waiting for us."

Theseus put out his hand to help everyone up the steep stairs. When Molly grabbed onto his outstretched hand, she noticed how soft the light brown fur was on his palm. It took her a moment to realize that his hand was just like hers. Very much a human hand. She could feel his gentleness and his warmth from just a single touch. It was a familiar and comforting feeling. Molly lifted her head as she walked up the stairs, catching a glimpse of his big gentle brown eyes. He smiled as he bowed his head to her. She remembered those eyes but couldn't quite figure out why.

They walked through the entrance door directly into a tall circular space that resembled a greeting room of sorts. Except, there were no benches or chairs to sit on and wait, which seemed very bizarre to Molly. She really needed to sit down, for she felt her knees could give out on her any moment. 'Just a bit longer,' she kept telling herself.

This ordinary room had walls covered in beautifully crafted royal green and gold fabric. Massive gold framed pictures lined the upper half of the walls. Molly turned around, taking in every detail of each painting. As she scanned across the paintings, she realized that the pictures appeared to illustrate a battle scene that continued around the entire perimeter of the room. She felt as if she were standing in the middle of the battleground.

Suddenly blinding light burst through one of the paintings. An explosion. Molly's eye caught a knight in silver and gold armor with a torn red velvet cape being knocked to the ground. With the last of its remaining strength, the wounded knight lifted his head, and outstretched his hand. He seemed to be calling out someone's name, Molly thought...but she could not hear him. The sound of battle all around her started to intensify.

"Zonks...Zonks...Zonks! What are you looking at?" asked George. Molly quickly came out of that daze. She stared at George with a blank look in her eyes, before glancing over at one of the portraits. There was no battle scene depicted in any of those portraits. The portraits that lined this room were of old men with beards or twirled moustaches and women with meticulous hairdos holding leather-bound books, all dressed in some interestingly embroidered cloaks. "It's just some old portraits, that's all," George said.

Molly shook her head, closed her eyes tightly then opened them right away to see that the paintings really were as her dad described them. "Yes, how interesting," she said.

A set of windows on each side of the main entrance door provided just the right amount of light to reflect off the two gold bald eagle statues towering over them in the center of the room. The eagles were positioned opposite one another with wings outstretched which created an ominous, gold feathered corridor.

Molly stood there, taking in every detail as if she were seeing it for the first time. She had been here many times before in her dreams, but sadly could no longer recall those memories. Eyya stepped closer to Molly, grabbed onto her arm and mustered up a gentle smile. She knew that Molly was not well.

"Walk with me, girl," she said as she placed her head on Molly's shoulder.

Theseus walked up to the elf sitting at a very tall desk directly opposite the front door. It was so tall, in fact, that even he had to look up to get the elf's attention. The carved façade of the desk depicted a scene with a warrior holding his arm high, in his hand a golden staff with a half-moon symbol which extended over the top of the desk. What Molly didn't remember was that this image was of the final moment of one epic battle out of which the new Commonwealth emerged. That knight was her great, great, great grandfather.

"Greetings," said the elf. "What brings you here today?"

Theseus placed his hand directly through the half-moon that also served as an access scanner. Its sole purpose was to confirm or deny if they could continue past this point.

"Ah, I see. No need to say a word. I understand," said the elf.

Strange clicking sounds were coming from somewhere in the back of the room, as if a set of locks were simultaneously being opened. Suddenly the desk lowered itself revealing the elf sitting on a tall hydraulic chair with levers, gears and gadgets sticking out of its sides. Once the floor completely swallowed the desk, the chair lowered itself allowing the elf to hop off. He started to make some odd little grunting sounds, as he shuffled around to the back of the chair. With a pull of a lever and a push of a few buttons, he made the chair disappear into the floor as well, leaving behind an empty space as if nothing had ever been there in the first place. He then proceeded to continue making those odd little noises as he made his way over to the floor-to-ceiling portrait of a winged lion hanging on the wall directly behind him. He took a deep breath and with his outstretched hand murmured a spell of some sort. The canvas inside the large gold frame simply vanished. Molly and Eyya looked at each other in amazement.

"Welcome to the Grand Hall," said the elf, as he stepped aside revealing another circular room ten-times as big as the one they were presently standing in.

Gold-plated carved banisters lined the staircase that seemed to elegantly descend down several stories, ending at a pair of tall, winged lion statues.

Opposite the staircase were dozens of glass elevator shafts connecting the five stories that overlooked the lobby. The shafts had gear tracks attached to them on the inside to assist the oval shaped elevator capsules to move up, down and sideways. Molly could see dozens and dozens of magical creatures exiting and entering the elevators, going about their daily lives. The oval shaped capsules appeared to be coming out of the ceiling, stopping then moving again, until they disappeared into the floor below. Each of these exposed floors would reveal offices, meeting rooms and hallways where more creatures were seen coming and going. Everyone appeared to be very busy. This place was buzzing with excited energy.

Theseus led them to one of the elevator capsules. Once they were all in, the retractable metal door closed behind them. No one said a word, but somehow the attendant seemed to know exactly where to take them. He pressed a bunch of buttons in a particular pattern giving the elevator the coordinates of the place to which they were heading. And with the push of the last button, the elevator started to move, and they were on their way.

They were travelling at high speed through the maze of an intricate net of shafts. Given the appearance of these elevators, Molly was instantly bracing herself for a bumpy ride but was surprised when it was exactly the opposite. The elevator moved smoothly down, then took a sharp right turn heading through a dimly lit tunnel. Molly noticed the light of another capsule moving closer to them. There seemed to be a second track alongside the one they were travelling on. In it rode two young female elves, probably around the same age as Molly. The two girls looked at each other in excitement, then started to wave at Molly. Eyya noticed them, too, and quickly nudged Aiken.

"Aiken, look! That's Maya and Ritana," started Eyya but before she could finish, the elevator capsule with the two elf girls swiftly passed them by and turned into one of the tunnels.

After a few turns the elevator capsule once again headed downwards, and within moments, the bell sounded signaling the arrival at their destination.

"We are here," announced the elevator attendant. "Third floor, the private rooms of the royal family and the Heartland Library." One by one, they all started to pile out of the elevator.

"Are you not coming with us?" asked Molly noticing that Beatrice, Asgoth and Thana remained in the elevator.

"We have some important business to tend to, but we shall see you shortly," said Beatrice. "Alright? Now go. Knowing Clara, she's probably already worn out the hardwood floor of the library, pacing back and forth anxiously waiting to finally see you," she said with a smile before the elevator doors closed.

George and the kids followed Theseus through a long hallway decorated with oversized paintings. They seemed to depict illustrations of past events, among other things. Events such as the coronation of the queens and kings, pictures of the Councilors in The Oval Room, some of mermaids and mermen of the south seashore and creatures living in the mountain regions.

While everyone continued going down the hallway, George slowly walked back to one of those paintings they just passed. Molly noticed, and asked Theseus to wait for a moment.

There she was. That beautiful girl...well now a woman. George was staring at a life-size portrait of Clara. The only image of her that George had was a picture from their school years. She looked beautiful in this painting. Dressed in an elegant, fully embroidered and beaded royal gown with a long cloak that draped over her shoulders, flowing down to the ground and partially covering the steps she was standing on. She was almost unrecognizable. Something didn't seem right to George. The way she stood there, the way she carried herself with poise and elegance, she looked like someone who could command a room with the snap of a finger. Someone who was most certainly ready to be at the helm of this massive Commonwealth, leading the nations to a better tomorrow. But, at least to George, in Clara's eyes the artist who captured this moment seemed to have also captured a different story being told altogether. A story of so much internal conflict and resentment.

"Who is this, Daddy?" Molly asked as she rushed back to her father's side.

"I think that's Clara," he replied.

"Yes, that certainly is her," said Theseus as he walked closer. "After the passing of King Zahar, she was crowned the Queen of

Heartland." Thinking this might be a good time to explain a few things, Theseus continued.

"There are certain expectations around how everyone must address the Queen. And I cannot stress this enough. Although it is altogether Her Majesty's privilege, the Imperial Council have very strict expectations and reservations around any public display of affection." George was confused but nodded to show agreement. He had so many questions floating through his mind...but promised himself he would be patient.

"Fon! Dorn!" Theseus noticed the two fairy brothers flying over to them. "Welcome back! Please, escort Eyya and Aiken to their suites." The fairy brothers nodded at the same time, ready for their next assignment.

"But, we'd much rather stay with Molly," protested Eyya.

"Yes!" added Aiken.

"Don't worry," said Theseus. "Molly will meet you shortly. The Imperial Council asked to see Molly as soon as she arrived. You two rest and don't worry about anything. You will find a change of clothes in your rooms. They are a generous gift from Queen Clara herself, so make sure to thank her the first chance you get. Go. Get ready for the opening fireworks of the Summerset Festival, I hear the Woodland elves have something quite unique planned this year," he added with a smile as he winked at Eyya.

"Yes, I know all about it. I also can't wait to see what this season's gim is going to be," Eyya said excitedly. "It is supposedly being unveiled tonight."

"I can take your bag, Molly, so it doesn't get in the way," offered Aiken.

"Thank you, but that's alright. It's no bother at all," said Molly.

"Alright," said Eyya, "we'll catch you later, okay?"

Theseus waited until both Eyya and Aiken were escorted by Fon and Dorn, "Queen Clara wishes to see you before we enter The Oval Room. She is waiting for you and your father in the library."

They continued down the long hallway, when suddenly Molly began to feel dizzy and stumbled a bit into George.

"Are you ok, Zonks?' he asked.

"No," she said just as her knees buckled under her and she lost consciousness. George quickly grabbed her before she fell to the ground.

"Zonks! Zonks, what's going on?" cried George, his heart racing.

"Hurry, we have to get her to Clara," said Theseus.

George scooped Molly up into his arms and ran down the hallway towards a set of massive doors. Theseus hurriedly threw them open and ran in.

"Your Majesty, we need you," he said.

185

"You're here!" said Clara as she rushed towards them. "George, what happened?" she said noticing Molly in his arms.

"She was fine one second, and then she collapsed," George replied still not being able to comprehend it all. Everything was happening so fast.

"Bring her here!" said Clara as she ran across to a seating area by the window, throwing the decorative cushions off the settee.

"It's the curse, isn't it?" he said as he lowered her down.

"Yes," Clara said plainly as she checked Molly's pulse. "She's still with us. Theseus, please run and get Astoria. Tell her we must see her urgently."

Without hesitation, Theseus turned around and ran for the door, his heavy footsteps echoing through the long hallway.

"We don't have much time, George," said Clara as she reached for a vial containing some dark green liquid. "Lift her head. She needs to take this potion, but I need Astoria's powers to activate it. My powers would have only worked, had she been awake."

George lifted Molly's head. "I'm so sorry...I..." said George, "...I failed as a father. My only task was to keep her safe and I couldn't even do that." No amount of training could have prepared George for this. He felt so much anger inside, fused with disappointment... mostly in himself. He was also utterly disappointed in Regina and his brother Corcoran for stooping so low as to harm a child, his baby girl, to get what they wanted.

"They will pay for this," he said, tears streaming down his cheeks.

"George, none of this is your fault. We will fix this, I promise. And then we will figure out how to make sure this never happens again," said Clara with such fire in her eyes, George had forgotten how fierce and determined she could be. She's not a vengeful woman, but no one messes with her family. Ever! George composed himself.

Footsteps were heard coming from outside of the library. Heavy footsteps, followed by the sound of galloping. Within a split second, Theseus and Astoria appeared in the doorway.

"Have you administered the potion, yet?" asked Astoria as she swiftly walked over. Her accent sounded distinctly familiar to George.

"Yes, just now," replied Clara.

"Good. Good," said Astoria.

"Wait a minute, but you are..." George couldn't spit out the words. There was a...lioness... standing in front of him. A talking one, none-the-less.

"Yes. I am a lioness," Astoria replied as if absolutely nothing was out of the ordinary. "George, now will you please step aside so I can get closer to Molly?" she said a bit impatiently. She had absolutely no time and zero patience to go into the details around how and why she was able to speak. She had a job to do, and he

187

was in her way. She needed to save Molly.

George hesitated. He was at first a bit taken back by being addressed so informally by this lioness. He looked over at Clara, confused. She reached out to him and pulled him closer to her so Astoria could get to work.

"It's alright, George," said Clara.

"Are we ready?" Astoria started. "Clara, please place your hand on Molly's shoulder. George, you do the same." Astoria placed her paw on top of Molly's chest and closed her eyes. A small pulse of energy entered Molly's body. It was winding through her veins, as if looking for a way out. The spell seemed to be doing what it was supposed to do. It activated the potion that was already flowing through Molly's veins pretty much instantaneously.

The room was filled with brightness, creating a floating circle of light all around them. Molly's head tilted back, and as she took a deep breath through her open mouth a beam of light shot out. As Molly exhaled, the light in the room vanished. It was over.

"Did it work?" asked George.

"She will be fine," said Astoria. "It will take some time, though. Just be patient. Little by little, the counter spell will start to decompose all the imprints of the curse of the invader. Her time imprint is affected, but I don't see no real long-term concern there. We have to leave the next part of the healing process up to our ancestors." After a moment, Astoria looked gently at Molly, "Rest now my little squirrel."

George looked at Clara slightly confused. There were only two people in the entire world that called Molly little squirrel. Before he could ask her the question, Astoria spoke up again.

"Right then! My job here is done. I have to return to the Oval Room. Someone has to keep that old boys club in order," she added with a hint of sarcasm. "It's a chore, let me tell you. I will see you shortly."

"I will give you some privacy, now," said Theseus as he bowed.

He followed Astoria out the door and closed it gently behind them.

The room suddenly fell silent. Clara and George just stood there, looking at each other, neither of them saying a word. He waited so long to see Clara and now all he could do was to slowly close his arms around her.

"Clara…" started George, "you have no idea how trying these past fourteen years have been. Why didn't you come see us?"

"My father forbade me to. He said it would not be safe for you or Molly. In your world, I could have been easily traced by Corcoran's men, who, unbeknownst to us, were slowly crossing the gates and combing every part of Terra Nova in search of you. My presence would have been an instant giveaway and they would have found us in no time. I would have been risking not only my life, but yours and Molly's, too. I couldn't do it, George. I wanted to be with you both so much. There was not a single day I did not regret it all. I don't think you know what it's like to give birth to a child and have her literally taken away moments after!" Clara broke down. She could no longer keep her strong façade up. "The only option left for me was to watch Molly grow up through a hologram. You don't realize how precious time can be, until you see your very own daughter, all grown up, only a couple weeks after she was born. Because that's how little time has passed for me here in Heartland. I feel like I was robbed years of our lives together. I can't….my brain can't comprehend that," Clara paused for moment, just looking into his eyes, then realizing he looked very different. "You've aged. But… how is that possible?"

"I look like someone in their mid-thirties…and I feel like it, too."

"Ah…now I see the wrinkles when you frown like that," said Clara with a half-smile, wiping the tears off her cheek. "It's not becoming at all."

"Don't be cruel…just don't!" said George as he stepped away from her.

"I'm sorry, but how is this even possible?" said Clara shaking her head. "I thought our time imprints were synchronized."

"I don't know," he said. "It started to happen after Molly was born. As the years went by, I started to notice the grey hair, the extra pounds..."

"We can reverse the aging, you know?" said Clara gently caressing his face.

"Yes, but it won't take away the years of being alone," he said bluntly.

Clara continued, "the one thing somebody should have prepared us for was to understand how excruciating all this would be. I guess, if anything, this entire awful experience has made me understand the suffering Regina went through when Maggie was taken away from her."

"Don't compare yourself to her," he said sharply. "She doesn't deserve an ounce of our sympathy after what she has done to us."

Clara looked into George's eyes before continuing. "George, I need to tell you something. Your family has been part of our world for many, many centuries protecting all that is sacred between our worlds. The Enderby's are paramount to our success, leading and guiding the Gate Keepers on Terra Nova. Molly is the only living Gate Keeper of our joined lineage and so when we first started hearing about Corcoran sending spies over to Terra Nova to find you, my father acted fast. He made the decision to arrange for you to move to Chateau Azeri and sent Aecus' wife to help you raise her. We used a transfiguration charm. Having a lioness with the ability to speak on Terra Nova would have caused quite a stir," said Clara.

"Astoria is..." said George as he made the shocking realization.

"Yes. Madame de la Fleur was in fact fully in charge of monitoring Molly's dreams, to ensure that the initial stages of training were covered as per the Gate Keeper Educational Plan. I am very much in debt to her for all that she has done for us."

"But the training of a Gate Keeper doesn't start until they turn fifteen years of age! I should know, my father wrote the latest curriculum with so much consideration and thought put into it. No one, before the age of fifteen, is ready for the immense training that is required mentally, let alone physically. I thought, once Molly turned fifteen, I could finally tell her all about this and start the training with her." George was so upset with Clara. The Gate Keeper training is his family's responsibility, and he felt that a line was certainly crossed here.

"I know, George. I know. But believe me, we didn't have much time. We had no choice but to start the training earlier?"

"Ten whole years earlier?!?" shouted George, suddenly remembering that dreadful first night at Chateau Azeri. After Molly had that nightmare and Madame de la Fleur rushed out of the room crying. "Oh - this all makes sense now. This is why her diary is filled with images from Heartland. How could I be so stupid not to see it sooner." His blame now turning from himself back to Clara. "Do you realize how much danger you've put her in?!"

George's eyes revealed a tremendous amount of pain. Pain that Clara could simply not reconcile in herself, for she was single-handedly the cause of it. She would never forgive herself for that.

Clara remained silent. George was overcome with emotion as he pressed his forehead against hers and continued, "I remember that first day very well. I remember it so clearly that I dreamt about it every night and no matter how hard I wanted the ending to be different, it was always the same. I was standing there, holding Molly not knowing whether to run or stay. I was there for her first words, her first steps – alone and without you, Clara. I tried to pass through the Gates numerous times only to be told to turn back and take my post immediately. Fon and Dorn took dozens of my messages for you. Why have you not responded to them? Why?"

"I don't think I have a good enough reason as to why," Clara started, "besides that a lot has happened in the past fifteen days here in our world. Which, I realize that for you and Molly was nearly fifteen long years. Corcoran was gaining power rapidly and shortly after I came back, my father joined the battle between Skyland and the Overlanders. We learnt a few days later that he had been killed by Corcoran himself."

"I'm so sorry. I didn't know," he said. His own brother was the cause of her father's death. George looked away, partly because of the shame that came over him.

"That same evening, I was crowned the Queen of Heartland. All this happened so fast, and with the Council's inability to make quick decisions, the days blurred one into the other, with me trying to gain control of one bad situation after another." Clara paused for a moment, trying to force her brain to think clearly once again.

"Our first priority needs to be to get Molly and the kids to safety. Their job is far from being over, if Corcoran gets his way. If things turn worse, they will be our only hope. I'll be there, by your side. We will protect her. No matter what. Do you hear what I'm saying?"

"Clara, where is Maggie?" he asked.

"She's safe," Clara replied quickly. "She's in The City of Arbour. And that is the safest place for her, Molly and the rest of the kids."

"Daddy, where are we?" asked Molly as she slowly started to wake up. Clara and George both rushed to her side.

"Zonks! You're okay?" said George as he helped her up. "I'm so sorry," he said as he embraced her. "It is all my fault, but I promise I'll fix this."

"Hi, Molly," said Clara as she knelt next to the settee. "You are in the Capital."

"Are you Clara, the Queen of Heartland?" asked Molly looking at Clara with hesitation.

Clara nodded. She was desperately trying to fight back tears. Molly didn't remember her at all. Had Molly remembered her, this surely would have been a different moment altogether. Clara imagined how it would be, re-running every second in her mind a thousand times. Her heart was full of happiness, for she finally got to see Molly in person. But the bitterness she felt towards Regina was starting to wear on her.

"You have a pretty smile and beautiful deep green eyes," Molly continued. She was mesmerized by Clara's beauty and could not stop staring at her. "I don't know anyone else who has that color of eyes, except for me. And I love your hair. My hair is always a mess, no matter how hard Madame de la Fleur tries to tame it. Will you teach me how to pull my hair to one side, like yours, and clip golden pins all the way to the end of the braid?"

"Absolutely! I have been waiting for such moment for a very long time."

"May I ask another question?" said Molly.

"But of course," replied Clara.

"Do we know each other?"

"Yes, very well, as a matter of fact. You're just having a little trouble with your memory right now, but hopefully that will be fixed soon," Clara replied, brushing Molly's hair off to the side.

"I was right. I knew we were friends the moment I saw you!" said Molly as she threw her arms around Clara, giving her the biggest of hugs. Clara was so happy to have her little girl in her arms once again.

As Molly looked up, through the big window she saw a beautiful garden that stretched all the way over to a ledge overlooking the Forest of Inkhans thousands of feet below. Molly visited that garden on many occasions before, but those memories were still lost in the abyss with the others.

"I know this place," she said as she looked around the room in awe. "Is this the library? The Heartland Library?" asked Molly excitedly. "I've heard so much about this place from my Uncle Az."

The library was two stories tall with a balcony around the entire perimeter of the room overlooking the main area below. The walls all around were lined with floor to ceiling shelving with dozens of books practically bursting out of each shelf. Among others, there were beautifully bound books on the history of Heartland, books about every creature that ever lived here, books about spells, books about herbs and potions. Small carved stairs covered in emerald-green carpet connected the two levels. Up there is where the special section was located, where Molly's diary would soon find its place amongst the diaries of all who came before her.

"There is something great ahead of us and I want you to know that I will be there every step of the way!" said Clara. "Do you have your diary?"

"It's in here," said George as he handed Molly her bag.

"Oh, good," Clara paused for a moment. "Let's try to figure out what you do remember. Do you remember Eyya and Aiken?"

"No...I...don't really know..." said Molly confused. "I feel that I should, but I can't seem to remember anything, no matter how hard I try." Molly paused for a moment.

"It's the side effect of the invader's curse," said Clara.

"The what?" asked Molly.

George deflected, hoping her recent memories were intact. "Do you remember how we got here?"

"As much as I don't want to, yes I do," she said with a smirk.

"I'm so proud of you, Zonks," said George as he sat down next to her. "And I'm sorry you had to go through all of this."

"That's okay, Daddy," said Molly as she grabbed his hand. "What do we do next?" asked Molly, looking at her dad then over to Clara, trying to be brave. After the adventure that got her here, her scared little heart was desperately trying to be courageous. She had a feeling that sitting here, idling, so to speak, was not in the plan. She still felt tired, but her brain was so wound up, she felt the need to move. She felt she needed to do something.

197

"Your diary. Just as your ancestors did before you, it is now your time to archive yours," Clara stood up and walked over to the staircase leading up to the balcony.

"The Gate Keepers?" asked Molly as she followed.

"Yes," replied Clara. "You are a member of one of the oldest Gate Keeper families – the House of Enderby. Your diary contains information we have carefully revealed to you through your dreams. Given that we had to keep you away from Heartland for this long, dreams were our only form of communication with you. They were our only means that allowed us to pass on the knowledge, the history and training needed to prepare you to become a Gate Keeper."

"I don't really understand," said Molly. "Who are these Gate Keepers and what gates do they keep?" Molly started to panic. Not being able to remember anything about Heartland, with memories of her childhood and growing up at Chateau Azeri slowly fading, she felt utterly lost in this world. "And why was I chosen to be one of them? And what if I don't want to be one..." suddenly, Molly stopped. A wave of calmness came over her as the panicked look on her face quickly faded. "I think something is happening..." said Molly calmly.

"What do you mean?" asked George.

"Something good, I hope," said Clara.

"Well..." started Molly. "Ever since we left Junction Manor...I don't know how to explain this…I felt almost like a breeze flowing through me. Taking away all my memories one by one. I felt them slowly fading away, becoming distant and faint. But just now, the breeze stopped."

"That's great to hear, my darling," said Clara with a reassuring tone. Finally, a light at the end of the tunnel. "It's working," she said looking over at George with a smile. "We don't have much time. Onto the next task," Clara gestured up the stairs.

"But how do I know…" Molly attempted a question.

"You will know," Clara said with a smile. "Your diary will show you the way."

# CHAPTER 23

*The Gate Keepers' Library*

**M**olly slowly walked up the stairs, clutching her diary in one hand and steadying herself on the railing with the other. Despite her heart beating a mile a minute, she was convinced she would do what she must when the time came. She would know, somehow. She came to the realization that this was going to be the grand adventure she was destined for. After so many years of living practically in isolation and wondering what this world held for her, she was finally going to find out! All was about to be revealed to her, she thought. Well maybe not all, but some, which in her mind was a step towards wherever this journey was about to take her. Even if at this very moment the prospect of a grand adventure scared her, she knew she needed to be brave.

Something strange began to happen as she reached the top of the stairs. The books on the shelves directly in front of her began to move like a rubik's cube, folding and moving apart, until at last they revealed an opening. Molly just stood there, mesmerized. A long tunnel emerged out of the books in front of her, with a pool of light shining from its far side. Through this opening Molly saw that the tunnel was filled with diaries molded into its walls. Diaries just like Molly's, except their covers were embossed with different symbols. These diaries shuffled from one place to another, moving about in an intriguing pattern. It was dizzying at first. As she stepped into the tunnel, Molly found the sound of shuffling paper quite soothing, and the air filled with that distinctive smell of old books took the edge off her nerves. Strangely, she felt comforted by it as she walked down the long tunnel.

Molly stopped forcefully when she reached the end of the tunnel. She could not move further. As if a force field of some sort prevented her from moving forward into the big open room. 'This must be the place...' thought Molly to herself. 'But how can I get through this invisible shield.'

She raised her hand, hoping a circular motion would unlock this invisible gate. Nothing happened. Then she remembered the spell Beatrice cast at the Junction Manor archway. She raised her right hand again and said, "Altora Siraaaactra". Nothing happened. "Altora Siractraaaa." That one didn't work either.

A sense of panic started to come over her. The stress started to become overwhelming. She felt lost with no one to help her, no one to guide her along this journey. Not even her dad, or Clara or Madame de la Fleur. She was on her own and the thought of that made her feel angrier and more scared with each passing minute.

"What if I can't do this? What if I'm not cut out for this? This is impossible! Why do I have to go through this on my own?"

A split second before she gave into her uncertainty, she heard familiar voices in her head say 'You can do anything if you believe. Impossible is just a word. Your diary will show you the way. Your diary will show you the way.'

"Clara…yes, my diary," Molly said with excited realization. There has got to be something in it that will help. She opened it and started flipping through the pages, hoping to find a hint, an image, or a spell of some sort. And then, strings of light started to flow out of the diaries inlayed in the walls of the tunnel. It seemed as if they were looking for something. Then suddenly, they found it. With a jolt they shot straight into Molly's diary, only to bounce right off projecting images onto an invisible screen that formed all around her. A flood of memories came rushing back. Molly could see every moment, every memory coming to life all around her, in vivid pictures. This time, however, these were also memories she had not dreamt yet, as they showed Molly growing up, playing with her best friends from all corners of Heartland, walking through the forest of Inkhans with Aecus, laughing, playing. Molly could not stop crying, she was so overcome with emotion, for she started to remember again. Her memories were not lost after all. She just needed help remembering them. "I remember..." said Molly through the stream of tears flowing down her cheeks. "Daddy, I remember!"

All her memories started to merge into a single one. Clara standing right in front of her, dressed in a beautiful silver-blue gown with long draping sleeves, laced with a golden trim around the waist. "Now, place your diary against the force field," said Clara's memory. Molly was about to close her diary when she noticed something. She was looking at that exact image of Clara sketched on her pages, with those precise words written out. She remembered this very moment because she dreamt about it before. Molly looked up but Clara's image was already gone. "Thank you, Clara," she whispered.

Without hesitation, Molly closed her diary and pushed it against the force field. A wave rippled through the shield until it reached the very edges of the tunnel, then came back, making the shield shrink inch by inch until it reached the spot Molly had her book pressed against. She felt her diary falling over to the other side of the shrinking shield and grabbed it with her other hand before it had a chance to drop to the ground. The invisible shield disappeared.

~~~

"There is something you need to know, George," said Clara. "There is so much I need to tell you and I promise to explain it all. We don't have much time, though. Your brother...we had no idea how it even happened. I'm told, he looks much...different now. I just received news that he conquered Skyland. Our seven founding segments have always been unbeatable against enemy forces. Nothing like this has ever happened in Heartland. We don't know what his plan is, however the Councilors fear the unthinkable could happen if he unleashes his power on Terra Nova."

"In the past, we managed to fight our own battles and the enemies that threatened our segments. There was no need to involve our Gate Keepers. But with Corcoran having full control of the Skyland Gate, that has now changed. I fear his ultimate plan is to destroy Heartland and conquer Terra Nova.

"I am not sure how to say this," continued Clara with great hesitation for she knew that what she was about to ask him would not be easy for either of them. She had no option left, for the Councilors backed her into a corner with this one. "We need you on a mission. On Terra Nova," said Clara, her words resonated without the slightest emotion. George picked up on this instantly.

"You want me to go back to Earth? What mission?" he turned around with a military-like focus, his mood shifting drastically, yet in his eyes Clara could clearly see the pain she had caused. "And why me? Do you not have anyone else that can be sent instead?"

Clara turned away from George, for she could not bear to look at him. "I tried to reason with the Councilors, given that we've spent nearly fifteen Earthly years apart." She paused, gathering the courage to stay strong, even though her heart was breaking into a million pieces. "As the head of the Enderby house, it is your duty to secure the Gate Keepers, and if need be, lead them against the Corcoran rebellion. The Councilors will provide you all the necessary details."

George didn't know what to say. She could have fought harder for him, she could have tried to keep their family together, but in his eyes, she failed. "I guess I have no say in this...your Majesty. What do I have to do?" asked George coldly.

"Don't, George! Just don't." Clara shook her head, pleading him not to be so cruel by insisting on this social division between them and addressing her by a title given to her not by her own will, but rather by the sheer circumstance. They were both hurting but the truth of the matter was that they had to be strong. When they parted shortly after Molly was born, they promised each other they would protect her, no matter the cost. Clara stood there, motionless, as she didn't know what else to say to make things better, to make things easier to accept for both of them. There was nothing else to do, and it killed them both to be so powerless. Powerless against the wishes of the Councilors. Powerless against their duty.

"All I am is just a figurehead of the Commonwealth, nothing more, nothing less," she continued. "I know that now. The power remains in the hands of the Councilors. We both made sacrifices we would not have had to, if our lives turned out to be other than the ones we were dealt by our circumstances. We have to stay strong...not only for each other, but also for Molly and Maggie. Otherwise, all will be for naught."

"I know, my love," said George.

"It's my turn to look after Molly," said Clara, as they embraced.

~ ~ ~

The Gate Keepers' Library was even more impressive than Molly could have imagined. Dark oak shelves full of diaries, just like Molly's, lined six wide hallways stretching as far as the eye could see, with beautiful paintings on the ceiling depicting scenes of cherubs frolicking amongst the clouds. The hallways shot out of the central room like spikes on a bicycle wheel from its hub. In the middle of the room stood a wooden podium with a large, leather-bound book placed atop. Past this podium, on the opposite side of the room Molly saw a couple of steps leading up to a landing. It was draped with a velvet red curtain, framing a mural of a lion and a lioness. Molly recognized this painting as it was an exact replica of the one that hung above the fireplace at Chateau Azeri.

Molly slowly walked towards to the podium. She could hear her footsteps echoing throughout, a sound that was desperately fighting to be heard against the hypnotic rustling of the books coming from all around.

As she slowly came around the podium, Molly noticed that the big book was closed. Seven circles surrounding the words Grimoire of the Gate Keepers were etched into the front cover. Three on either side of the large book's title, and one directly below. As she ran her hand over them, each circle gave out a glow and a name of one of the six founding land segments appeared. The last circle, directly below the book's title gave out a glow, but no words appeared. The rustling of the books suddenly stopped. Only the sound of Molly's breathing echoed through the library.

She tried to open the book, but it wouldn't budge. Molly wondered what magic spell she'd have to use to open it.

"Open sesame," she said with a bit of a giggle. "Reveal your secrets!" said Molly impatiently. "How am I supposed to figure this out? I am not from this land...I...I know no magic..." Molly thought to herself. 'I'm not brave, or smart. There is nothing special about me. So why me?'

The rustling of the books started again. This time, however, the sounds were intensifying by the second. A big gust of wind blew through the library. All of this made Molly very, very scared. Then, just as unexpectedly it all started, the rustling and the wind stopped.

A sense of dread came over her as she remembered that her dad, Clara, and the Councilors were still waiting. She had to hurry and there was absolutely no time to waste. Molly needed to finish what she came here to do, so she stepped towards the bookshelves that lined the center room. There must have been hundreds, no thousands of books here all neatly placed on never-ending rows of dark wooden bookshelves. So much history, Molly thought to herself. How will she ever know where to place her book? She tried to pry open a spot between two books, but that did not work. She started to walk around the perimeter of the room, holding her breath in anticipation of something magical happening as she walked past each hallway. Nothing.

Molly was getting anxious, she needed to figure this out, and fast.

She made her way back to the podium, placed her open diary on top of the grimoire and started flipping through pages after pages, once again desperately trying to find a hint of some sort. 'There has got be something here...' Molly said to herself. After searching through her diary front to back, and back to front she found nothing of any help.

"I can't believe it...I can't believe there isn't anything in here that could help me." In desperation, she shut her diary, left it atop the grimoire and walked away.

"Someone else is going to have to file that stubborn book on my behalf, I'm done with it!"

Just as she was heading towards the way she came from, those nagging thoughts started to probe and prod. Something inside her was literally forcing her to stop and go back. Intuition? Perhaps not. Rather it was her conscience that would not let her simply walk out and pretend everything was fine. It was the dread of not completing the task and abandoning her diary in the middle of the library that made her stop and turn around.

"Fine. Fine... fine... fine!" said Molly huffing like a little steam engine. "I'll figure it out, even if I have to stay here all night."

And with that new-found determination, Molly headed straight back towards the podium. She closed her eyes and tried very hard to clear her mind.

"Ok, think of...kittens...kittens running around...kittens chasing each other...kittens drinking milk...argh...this isn't working..." Molly was getting frustrated with herself and her own inabilities to do this seemingly simple task.

"Think of...Caspian and Eyya, Maya and Ritana and Aiken." An image of each popping into her mind as Molly recalled her friends one-by-one, remembering just how much they meant to her. She really felt the incredible bond they all shared. She loved them very much. She trusted them with her life. In all honesty, they were the only friends she had. The only ones that were close to her age, at least. She briefly drifted to memories of her life on Earth. How sad and lonely she was at times during the day, but how happy she was at night, asleep, spending every minute with them. Even though she only got to know them through her dreams, her friends, her crazy friends, meant the world to her. They were there for her for all those years, and now the time had come for Molly to be there for them.

"Pull yourself together, Molly. There is no time for self-pity," she said as she wiped her tears away. "Just focus."

Molly kept her eyes closed as the rustling of the books intensified again. She focused her mind, then through the noise of the shuffling pages, she started to slowly make out a voice... a female voice that was repeating something over and over again. "Ostende mihi viam. Ostende mihi viam..."

"Ostende mihi viam," said Molly as she opened her eyes. And with those words, a bright light illuminated one of the hallways. Molly grabbed her diary and headed straight towards the direction of its source.

"This is it..." Molly thought to herself. She ran past a dozen bookshelves until she finally reached the one. She knew she was in the right spot. The light was shining through the books on the entire shelf. High up, out of Molly's reach, on one of the upper shelves the books parted, leaving a perfect opening for Molly's diary. She was filled with strange emotions, for parting with her diary was far from what she thought she would ever have to do. She knew that the diary and its contents had to be protected, what she didn't understand was why. Why would anyone care about her childish hand-drawn images and absurd stories? Perhaps one day she would find out why all of this was so instrumental in all of this.

Molly noticed a rolling ladder on the far side of the bookcase. She dragged it over and proceeded to climb up until she reached the right height. She took a deep breath and without even thinking twice, pressed her diary into the opening. Then something incredible began to happen. The spine of her diary rolled off the book and made its way onto Molly's outstretched right hand. It wrapped itself around her wrist and was instantly absorbed into her skin, leaving behind a thick tattooed band with the same round symbol of the winged lion as the one that adorned the cover of her diary.

As Molly climbed down the ladder, the diaries on every shelf started to shuffle, mix and jumble, until her diary disappeared among them.

"Farewell, my old friend. I'll miss you!" she said before she climbed down the ladder to leave. As she passed the center platform, she noticed a strange light coming from the big book on the podium. She walked up to it slowly.

'Oh, no, what now! Don't tell me there is another task I have to complete,' she thought to herself. The grimoire opened itself on its own. A few pages turned until they revealed one with a list of names on it.

"What is this." said Molly as she ran her finger down that list. "I don't think I recognize any of these names. These must be all the gate keepers that have left their diaries here." She kept skimming down the list of names until she reached one she certainly recognized. "Maggie Enderby. Wait a minute." Molly forced herself to focus even more. *"Maggie Enderby, born May 31, 1991 on Terra Nova. Parents: Regina Nubilus and George Enderby."* Molly could not believe what she just saw. "No...this must be a mistake." Then she suddenly remembered that her dad and Clara were still waiting for her. "

Molly slowly backed away from the podium. After everything

she went through these past hours, her brain simply could not fully comprehend what she was reading. She turned around, stepped off the platform and ran towards the tunnel that led out of here. At that moment, the grimoire revealed the next entry before it closed itself.

*"Molly Enderby, born August 31, 2006 on Terra Nova. Parents: Clara Heartland and George Enderby."*

The entrance into the tunnel sealed itself behind her. Molly took a deep breath, for she was a bit relieved it was all over. The feeling of triumph was overshadowed by the memory of the crawling spine of her diary that found its new home nestled around her wrist.

Clara and George were waiting at the bottom of the stairs looking at the panic-stricken Molly.

"What is this?" asked Molly as she desperately tried to rub the tattooed wrist band off. "Why won't it come off?"

"It's alright, Molly," said Clara calmly. "That is your key. The key to the Gate Keepers' Library, to your diary, to the Grand Hall and ultimately your passport, so to speak. We are all connected this way." With a quick magical incantation, George and Clara both revealed their wrist tattoos. "I'll show you how to disguise yours," she added with a smile.

Molly didn't quite comprehend it, but she trusted that in time it would all make sense.

# CHAPTER 24

## *The Oval Room*

The Oval Room wasn't too far from the Gate Keeper's Library, but getting to it meant taking a short elevator ride. It was not too long before they arrived at the big door leading into it. Molly felt extremely nervous, thinking it would be a room full of grumpy old men that were probably going to eat her alive. George and Clara kept reassuring her that she had nothing to worry about, for they saw how stressed she was. Just as Molly was about to question why she had to appear in front of the Council, the big doors opened in front of them.

"Her Majesty, Queen Clara. His Highness, Lord Enderby and Molly Enderby," announced an elderly female elf, donned in a ceremonial robe that looked nearly as old as she did. Her hair was long and white. She propped herself up with a long stake, atop of which perched a glass head of a lion. Her name was Ismene. She was the High Secretary of the Imperial Council.

'This is it!' Molly thought to herself. The Oval Room, the place where the Imperial Council Members gathered. She had heard of this place but never had the opportunity to step foot in it before.

It was a long room with walls made of pure ivory stone. Rows of tall arched pillars lined both sides of the room giving The Oval Room a certain elegance. Banners representing each segment of Heartland were hanging between them, three on each side of the room, gently swaying forward and back. A Councilor from each segment sat atop a light gray, satin cushioned ivory stone chair that was nestled into the bottom half of the stairs that emerged from below each banner. The chairs each looked slightly different from one another. They were carved to resemble the style from each particular segment. Past the other side of the banners, the stairs led up to the private offices of each Councilor, where only a select few were allowed to enter. There, just a couple steps behind each chair were large, framed mirrors that reflected the light from the glass ceiling high above.

High Chancellor Theseus stood at the bottom of the stairs leading up to a platform opposite the massive ivory wooden door leading into the big room. Two chairs, bigger and grander than all the other seats in this room were placed atop the platform.

Beautiful grey curtains with a white ornamental pattern craftily draped above them, prominently drawing focus in the room.

Behind the two chairs, a large stained-glass arch framed an opening that led out onto a balcony overlooking the Commonwealth Square below, which was buzzing with excitement as a large crowd started to gather around. The sun was setting, making the ancient forests glimmer in the distance. In the center of the room was a circular stone, standing on top were Aecus, a winged lion, and a lioness named Astoria.

With the announcement of their arrival, the framed mirrors illuminated, each displaying an image of a person. These were the Kings of each segment, dressed in beautiful regal robes of colors predominant in their world and culture. All, but one. The Skyland mirror was empty. That mirror reflected the objects in The Oval Room. The Councilors rose to their feet to greet Molly, George and Clara as they followed Ismene into the room. They paused briefly to acknowledge the Councilors before continuing.

"Aecus," whispered Molly in utter amazement as she stopped dead in her tracks. Clara motioned her to continue walking. The walk from the doors to the platform in the center of the room seem to take forever. It took a tremendous amount of restraint for Molly not to run past everyone and head straight towards Aecus. Her eyes welled up. She did not want to cry. She did not want to be seen as weak so she bit the inside of her cheek as hard as she could, careful not to cause injury or too much pain. She missed him so much. Ever since crossing to Heartland, she was most anxious to see him again. And here he was at last.

Kids her age often confide all their secrets and wishes in a stuffed toy, a doll, or a best friend. Molly had none of these, but she did not mind that one bit. Her very best friend was a lion, a winged lion none-the-less. And who could compete with that? They followed Ismene up onto the circular stone, as Aecus and Astoria parted allowing them to pass. Clara stopped and bowed, George and Molly followed suit. Molly could no longer restrain herself. She rushed up to Aecus, still amazed and astonished, and wrapped her arms around his massive mane. This embrace was for real and it felt nothing like the ones before, in her dreams. She could feel his soft mane against her cheek, she could hear each heartbeat, as clear as a bell.

"You are here!" said Molly. "I've missed you so much."

"I've missed you too," said Aecus with a gentle rumble in his deep voice.

"Your Majesties. Please follow me," said Ismene with a disapproving look on her face, as she gestured towards the stairs leading up to the platform at the end of the room. It seemed that the rest of the Councilors did not approve of this behavior either.

"Molly, stay here with us," said Aecus. Molly nodded.

"Lord Enderby, it is an honor and privilege to have you in

217

Heartland," continued Ismene, "and an even greater one to have you finally sit in your rightful place, next our beloved Queen Clara." George held out his hand to help Clara up the stairs. His heart was beating so fast, it was making his hands shake. When they reached the top, they both turned towards each other before facing the room. Clara sat down on her throne first, then gently motioned for him to sit down next to her.

"May we get started?" said one of the Councilors impatiently. Molly remembered her father's tales about the different elves from the different lands on the train ride to the Capital. This one, was dressed in deep dark green robes with brown and ruby red detailing. He was a Woodland elf. "The Councilors have conferred. Given the current circumstances, my fellow Councilors and I have decided that Molly is to be relocated to the City of Aecor located in the Forest of Inkhans. Aecus and Astoria are going to escort her and her friends there at sunrise."

'Her and her friends?' thought Molly to herself. I'm right here! There is no need to speak about me in the third person.

"I agree with that decision," said Clara looking over at George. "It is the safest place for them."

"That is all we wanted to share with her. She may go and join her friends," said the Woodland Councilor.

'There he goes again.' Molly thought to herself. 'Hello! I'm right here in front of you! Can't you see me? How rude!'

"The next order of business is..." but before he could finish his sentence, Molly stepped a closer and spoke a bit louder, as to be heard over him.

"May I say something?" asked Molly. The Councilors looked at each other disapprovingly, muttering under their breath. No child had so brazenly interrupted one of the Councilors before. For that matter, no child had ever been allowed to address the Councilors of Heartland. This certainly was an unprecedented situation. But after everything Molly had gone through thus far, she felt she had every right to get answers to some of the questions that were burning a hole in her mind.

"Of course, you may," said Theseus with an attitude that contrasted that of the Councilors.

"Firstly...and I don't mean any disrespect by saying this, but I feel a need to address this otherwise it'll just fester in my brain, so forgive me. This is just how my brain is wired." She paused for a moment, then took a deep breath before she continued. "There is really no need to speak about me as if I'm not here. I'm right in front of you. This situation seems to have a whole lot more to do with me than anyone has been willing to share. And I'm okay with that, because I trust that you will all make the right decisions in order to protect me. But please address me directly. I feel that after everything I have gone through to get here, that is the least I could ask of you." Aecus had a hard time restraining a smile on his face. She reminded him so much of her mother right now. George seemed shocked at his daughter's choice to address the Council, but Clara on the other hand felt a great deal of pride. Finally, a woman standing up to the old guard. Molly was absolutely correct! There was no need to address someone like that when they were standing directly in front of them.

"Secondly," Molly continued, "the Forest of Inkhans is known to be a sacred place. And as my limited knowledge of Heartland tells me, someone like myself has never been allowed to set foot there. It is not a place for someone like me, so...I do not wish to...in any way question the decision...but...I was just wondering...if..." Molly paused, for she noticed she was rambling once again, and quickly collected her thoughts and very calmly continued, "with all due respect, why are we being sent there? Why can't we stay here? Isn't the Capital the safest place in Heartland?"

The room fell silent. It felt as if no one wanted to speak, either for fear of saying too much, simply not knowing more, or not wanting to entertain a question from such a child at all. In the case of the Councilors, it was mostly the latter.

"The ancient Forest of Inkhans..." started Theseus as he stepped forward breaking the long and awkward silence that made everyone in the room most uncomfortable, "... is a place as old as time. It is the most sacred place in all of Heartland.

Although many creatures live in both of our worlds, the forest is protected by ancient magic that forbids the entry of anyone from outside of Heartland. That is in order to protect and safeguard all the magic and secrets of our land.

"We are at the brink of war with Corcoran," continued Theseus, "and so, just as Her Majesty said, the ancient forest is the safest place for you."

"I certainly don't want to be difficult. If that is what you believe is best, then I trust you," said Molly as she looked at each of the Councilors and Kings around the room. This made them all a tad uncomfortable. Her gaze finally landed on the empty Skyland mirror. "I have one more question. Do you know what happened to Aiken's parents? Are they alright?"

"We don't know much at this point," said Theseus. "We have sent out envoys to provide updates on the situation in Skyland."

"Why does Corcoran want me?" asked Molly calmly. It was now or never, she thought to herself. If anyone had any answers, surely the Councilors would know. Molly was never one to hesitate to ask the tough or complex questions. She had a very inquisitive mind. What she learned in her short little life is that adults like to talk, and they like to talk for hours. Most of the time about nothing. These kinds of conversations were a waste of time, in her opinion. She never understood why adults liked to beat around the bush instead of simply getting to the point of the matter, quickly and efficiently. Instead, these conversations always tended to turn into some elaborate demonstration of one's masterful ability to conquer the English language by showing off their vast and expansive vocabulary.

"Molly..." said George imploringly as he stood up from his seat. "The Councilors have a lot of work ahead of them, let's not take up any more of their time." He knew this was not the place or time to get into any of this.

"It is quite alright, Lord Enderby," replied Theseus. "but with respect to your question, I don't have the answer to that. Now I realize that is a heavy burden to place on you...but you have nothing to worry about. You will be safe. Aecus and Astoria will see to it and we shall take care of the rest."

George looked at Clara and could not help but smile. Molly seemed so calm and collected, but more so she was respectful and polite. She handled herself with such confidence and elegance. She was growing up fast, right there in front of their eyes.

"Molly, further to your question about Aiken's family," said Clara as she rose from her seat. "Corcoran rose to power at an unprecedented rate when the lurking creatures of the Overland were seeking a new leader. We have heard grave news about Skyland and we know that Corcoran has already gained full control over that segment. We have not yet been able to reconnect with the royal family of Skyland. Our only hope is that they are still alive." Clara paused before continuing. "Theseus, may I ask a favor?"

"Of course, your Majesty," replied Theseus.

"Could you please escort Molly to her room?" Theseus nodded. "Molly, go and get ready to join the festivities with your friends. And happy birthday, darling. There is a little birthday gift waiting for you in your room. Your father and I will see you later," said Clara with a gentle smile.

# CHAPTER 25

## *As-stinky-as-a-skunk Team*

The mood in The Oval Room changed once the big white doors shut behind Molly and Theseus. Now not only was it somber, but it was also filled with tension and uneasiness.

"We have never encountered a situation like this before," said the Woodland Councilor. "Can you please try to establish a connection with Skyland?"

"I'm not hopeful," added the Winterland Councilor.

Ismene moved onto the center platform and placed her shaft into the little opening along the edge that was directly opposite of the Skyland Councilor's chair. The mirror initiated but the picture was blank. Everyone in the room became even more anxious. This certainly was an unprecedented situation and none of them had a clue as to what to do about it.

~~~

"Molly," said Theseus, "it is truly great to see you."

"It is great to see you, too, Theseus!" said Molly. She then realized an apology was due. "And I am so sorry for the way I reacted when we arrived. I...I didn't remember you," said Molly, shaking her head in disbelief.

"I know. Beatrice filled me in," said Theseus.

"Magic is a powerful weapon," Molly continued as they walked down the hall, "and it almost caused me to lose all my precious memories of Heartland forever, not to mention the memories of my closest friends. I don't mean to sound like I'm complaining, but my journey to the Capital was not the most pleasant one." Molly paused, taking a deep breath which did seem to calm her nerves, "I'm certain the Councilors hate me after the way I behaved. Nevertheless, I am very happy to be here."

"I'm going to take my High Chancellor hat off for a moment. I'm very glad you spoke up, Molly. It was very brave of you, and most importantly the right thing to do. Those old buffoons need to be reminded that we are all living beings and that talking about us like we don't matter, like we are just another problem to be solved so they can move onto the next thing on their agenda, is simply not okay. Their actions and words do have consequences and they need to be held accountable. I am very glad that you have your memories back. Let me walk you to your room. Eyya and Aiken have quite a surprise for you."

"A surprise?" said Molly in excitement. "I love surprises!"

For the next few moments, they walked side by side without saying a word. Molly recalled her memories of Theseus, with whom she spent countless hours learning the art of classical sword fighting, how to handle a bow and arrow, and how to fight. She remembered how brave she was in her dreams, fighting in battles alongside Aecus and Theseus. The truth was, she didn't want to let anyone down. She didn't want anyone to know that the real Molly was not as strong and brave as the one that visited Heartland through her dreams.

"Can I ask you a question?" asked Molly, breaking the silence.

"Most certainly," said Theseus.

"What do you think is going to happen now that the Overlanders have found a new leader?"

"I honestly believe that you are safe here among us. You have nothing to worry about, as long as you follow the instructions set out by Queen Clara. She knows what is best for you. The Forest of Inkhans is a place where no evil spirits or evil powers can penetrate the ancient spells protecting it. The rest...well...we shall see. All in its own time. One step at a time," Theseus paused for a bit before continuing. "There are many evil creatures living in our land. Many, however, have not dared to even come close to our segments for centuries. Creatures from Overland are some of the most vicious, blood thirsty ones. They are bottom feeders that have no real purpose in life. We occasionally see them lurking around the far, far outskirts of Heartland. There is an unwritten law that defines the relationship of the Overlanders and the segments of Heartland. There are certain rules that are not to be violated by either side, and thus we can live in peace with one another."

"What do they look like?" asked Molly.

"They are dark creatures with large, tattered wings and a dozen tentacles, with magic too strong for some. They can go on living for centuries without eating, drinking, or sleeping. They feed on the young and weak - animals or magical creatures - to them it does not matter - they suck the blood straight out of their victims by simply pressing one of their many arms on their prey's chest, right where the heart is.

"What about Regina? How did she get wrapped up in all of this?"

"This unprecedented alliance between a magical creature from one of the Heartland segments fighting along the creatures

227

from Overland is not to be taken lightly. We don't know what Regina is capable of, especially now that she has joined Corcoran. We do know that under his rule, the Overlanders can become a great threat to our segments, not to mention to our entire world. Even yours, Molly. We have to do everything in our power to defeat them."

They walked through the hallways in silence the rest of the way to Molly's room. She was tired, both physically and mentally. She did not want to think anymore, she did not want to talk anymore. She longed for those quiet times at the mansion when the most exciting event was the weekly grocery delivery.

"We have arrived," said Theseus with a gentle smile as he opened the door.

"Thank you, Theseus," said Molly smiling back at him. "Thank you for everything. Will you be at the Summerset Festival Ball later?"

"Dances are not my cup of tea," said Theseus with laugh. "I will however join you for a cup of watermelon juice, if you wish."

"I would love that," replied Molly.

"Till we meet again," said Theseus as he turned to leave thinking that although Molly looked like Maggie, they were so different in so many ways.

Molly walked through the door leading into a room resembling the one at Junction Manor - oval in shape, with a large table in the middle, two fireplaces on opposite ends, and seven doors lining the walls. The room instantly transformed into a magical forest, with tiny multi-colored butterflies zooming about; baby squirrels chasing each other up and down the trunks of age-old trees; and baby foxes frolicking in the bushes below. Molly could not help but giggle not only at the ornately clad Eyya stepping out of one of the rooms, but also at the megaphone she was carrying through which she started speaking in a silly voice.

"Our esteemed guest of honor. Please step onto the center platform," said Eyya giggling, while gesturing to the table in the middle of the room, "and await the arrival of your humble servants." Molly was very hesitant at first - back home she would never dare to stand on top of any table. She looked around as if to check to see if there were any adults nearby, mostly out of habit, for she realized the likelihood of that would be slim. With one foot on the soft cushion of the chair she hoisted herself up onto the top of the table. This felt invigorating. For the first time in her life she felt fully in control of her decisions without worrying about the tiny little voice in her head cautioning every one of her actions. It was there, she just ignored it this time, and shockingly it felt great!

"Allow me to introduce to you, Prince Aiken, from Skyland." The table Molly was standing on instantly transformed into a floating grass covered island with magical clouds hovering above her. A great fanfare blared out of Eyya's megaphone and just like Peter Pan descending into Wendy's room, Aiken flew victoriously through the door into the dining room. He flew circles around the chandelier that had transformed into a tree branch with luscious green leaves. He landed on the floor straight into a deep bow. He did look great in his festive robe and tights with his hair greased back, Molly thought. She bowed like a princess, holding out the fabric of her pants as if she were lifting a glorious dress.

"Don't you wish you could fly, too?" asked Eyya.

"Sadly, only Skylandians can," added Aiken with a smile.

"True that," replied Eyya. "Up next, your Greatness, "giggled Eyya, trying to remain serious. "You will not believe your eyes. We bring you, from the far, far away land of the eternal cold...."

Molly gasped in amazement and instantly started clapping. Could it be, could it really be who she thought it was going to be. She was shaking - partly because the room transformed into a snowy valley with her standing on a mound of snow below a breath-taking icicle chandelier, and partly from excitement. She was jumping up and down like a child that was just told she could have any toy in the entire store.

"... none other than..." a cool breeze and a blast of the tiniest snowflakes burst out of the overhead clouds. Molly knew right away who was next. She could hardly contain her excitement.

"Princess Maya from Winterland."

Everyone cheered and applauded. Maya blasted through the doorway of her room riding the snow, that with a wave of her arm transformed into an ice path that circled all around Molly. Maya was a shy and timid elf girl of fourteen years of age, with long wavy ivory hair and light blue eyes. She wore silver rimmed round glasses that were a bit too big for her small round face. Often, they slid down her nose. Dressed in white pants and a form fitting long sleeved white jacket and a cape, she looked marvelous spinning around like a professional figure skater. Molly had fond memories of little Maya, who was the youngest of this bunch of crazy misfits. For an elf, whose wardrobe consisted of outfits in only white, she had an incredible sense of style. Molly jumped off the snow hill she was standing on and ran straight to Maya and gave her the biggest hug. They spun around together, laughing, and sliding around barely being able to stay upright, all the while talking at the same time. Neither could understand what the other was saying, but it did not matter. Molly felt so much joy. Aiken rushed to them both, split them apart but trying to speak through his excited laughter, at the same time moving Molly back onto the snow-covered hill in the center of the room. Who was it next, Molly wondered? By now they were all shaking from excitement. Despite the incredibly trying start to her journey, Molly thought things could not be any better. There was no possible way she could feel more happiness right now, being surrounded by her best friends.

"And now..." continued Eyya with a low and mystifying warble in her voice. At this point both Aiken and Maya joined Molly on the snowy hill. Light colored fog of sand filled the room, making the magical snow and ice disappear. Under her feet Molly could feel the warmth of the fine, white sand. Suddenly the lights turned dim in the dining room, the chandelier transformed into a round moon shining down on the masqueraded creature that appeared in the doorway of the fourth bedroom. "Let us celebrate as we present to you, the magnificent creature of many disguises...Princess Ritana from Barrenland!"

As the cloak spun off Ritana, it magically wrapped itself around her creating a funnel-shaped cloud of sand that darted around from one end of the room to the other until she twirled so fast, the cloud of sand disappeared. The room then returned back to its original state revealing a beautiful elf girl with tan colored skin standing in front of Molly. Her gorgeous outfit had more shades of brown than Molly could ever find names for. The gold accented pieces on her dress were a key part of every item in her wardrobe. She was tall, with mysterious deep brown eyes, and long, dark brown dreads pulled into a ponytail. She looked fierce and gorgeous at the same time.

Molly was beside herself. Not even in her wildest dreams

could she have imagined she would finally be with her best friends, together, in one place and time. Eyya, Aiken, Maya and Molly rushed to Ritana. They all embraced. The excitement in the room made them practically levitate off the ground.

Molly rushed to the next door, ready to be greeted by the last member of the crazy bunch, Prince Caspian from Waterland. She looked back at her friends, expecting another grand and silly introduction followed by another magical transformation of the room. They looked at her, not really knowing what to say.

"Caspian technically can't leave the waters. He has not yet turned sixteen," said Eyya. "You know how it is...the underage merpeople of Waterland don't develop their glamour until they turn of age. We pleaded with his parents, but...rules are rules...they said. He does wish he could be here, though, and hopes when this is all over, we will visit him soon."

"What do you mean 'glamour'?" asked Molly, not fully understanding what Eyya meant by it.

"It's a fancy word for clothes," replied Ritana.

"Oh, so if they haven't developed their glamour then..." said Molly.

"Yep, once they get out of the water, they'd be completely butt-naked," said Ritana with a smirk. They all laughed.

"Do you remember us all now?" asked Eyya.

"Yes," said Molly with a giant smile. "Yes, I do."

"Let's enjoy our last night in the Capital," said Eyya with a smile. "Who knows when we will be back here again. Besides, I've been waiting for the Summerset Festival all year! I can't wait to try some of those loganberry tarts – they are said to be the best on this side of Mount Kiragar."

"Before we go," started Aiken with a curious smile, "can we stop at the library?"

"Yes, yes, I want to see it, too," said Maya with immense excitement.

"Molly, please, let's make a quick stop on the way," Eyya instantly jumped on the bandwagon.

"I just don't know if I should," said Molly hesitantly. "With everything going on the last thing I want to do is break any rules and get us all in trouble."

"Please, please, please!" begged Eyya. "We just want to peek in through the door. Just a tiny little peek. Just a little one."

"Just a little one!" said Maya in a whiny voice.

"Just a tiny, little one!" said Ritana with an even whinier voice, but much quieter.

"Just an itty-bitty, tiny, little one!" said Aiken, in a barely audible whispered high-pitched whine. They all huddled around Molly, staring at her pleadingly with puppy-eyed looks and clasped hands.

"You are one pathetic looking bunch of weirdos," said Molly.

They all laughed. "Alright," she continued, "just this once, but you will do as I say! We will go after we check out the festival. Now go get changed. Go, go, go!"

They all left for their rooms and closed their doors behind them. Now finally with a moment to herself, Molly walked over to the window overlooking the gardens. It looked so serene from up there. The setting sun was casting a beautiful glow. The serenity of the garden contrasted her current feelings. She felt confused and somehow lost despite that she and everyone she loved so dearly were for once in the same vicinity. Well, almost everyone. She no longer had the stressful feeling that she had in some of her dreams. In order to protect her loved ones, she had to gather them all up in one place; but each time she returned with one of them, the others would trail off somewhere. In her dreams, it felt like herding kittens, in a way. One would think that having everyone near at last would provide a sense of comfort and assurance. But with the impending war with Corcoran, she instead felt a growing sense of responsibility over everyone and everything. As if it were all her doing, all her fault. She had to figure out a way to make it all right. Back home, she'd huddle up in a corner trying to find the courage, but here...here she needed to be brave, for real. She needed to be as brave as the Molly that regularly visited Heartland through her dreams. This was it, this was her real challenge. 'Don't let this overwhelm you!' Molly said to herself quietly as she felt her eyes well up. 'You have to do this! Little by little, you will figure this out.'

"I am ready!" said Eyya as she stepped out of her room. "Molly? Is everything alright?" asked Eyya as she got closer.

"Yes, quite alright!" said Molly, looking over her shoulder as she tried to wipe her eyes unnoticeably. By now, the rest of the gang came out their rooms and walked closer.

"Molly, don't you ever feel that you are alone in all of this," said Eyya as she gently reached for Molly's hand. "You have us! We will figure this out, together. After all, we are your "A" team!"

"The 'A' team!" joined everyone in a group hug.

"Yes, as-nutty-as-a-squirrel team," said Molly, breaking up the hug with a laugh.

"As-brave-as-a-lion team," said Eyya.

"As-mighty-as-an-eagle team," said Ritana.

"As-stinky-as-a-skunk team," said Aiken.

"Hey! Speak for yourself..." replied Eyya. "I bathed yesterday."

"Thanks, guys," said Molly with a smile.

With a big laugh they all headed for the door. Trying to outwit one another, they continued coming up with outrageous "A" team names.

"Oh, wait," said Molly. "I still have to change out of these clothes. You all got a new fancy outfit, I hope there is one waiting

236

for me in my room, too. Give me a couple of minutes and I'll be right back." Molly turned and rushed into her room. "And, thanks. You are truly the best bunch of weirdos a girl could ever wish for."

# CHAPTER 26

*A new leader is born...*

T he conversation was slowly heating up back in The Oval Room. Clara had a tough time keeping control of the room and quite frankly, was starting to lose her patience with the old boys' club.

"Well...I think we should. Tough times call for tough actions. We should in fact, close the Skyland Gate and cut the bleeding before it's too late," said the Shadowland Councilor.

"Well...that is easy for you to say," responded the Woodland Councilor with disdain. "You have nothing to lose, do you. You just going to sit there and watch this all unfold from the safety of your...position. Perhaps what we should be discussing are... charges of treason! Would you not agree, Councilors?"

"I second that stance," added the Winterland Councilor as he looked towards the Barrenland Councilor for support.

"What are you suggesting, Councilors?" shouted the Shadowland Councilor through gritted teeth.

"Councilor! Let me address these accusations," said King Nubilus of Shadowland very calmly. "Brothers. Duty above family is a motto we live by every day. For it is that duty and responsibly I have been entrusted with by my people to ensure their safety and prosperity! We are all in this with equal responsibility. And do not fool yourselves! The fact that our own daughter is partially responsible for these disastrous series of events, does not, in any way, absolve us from any accountability to ensure we collectively see this through. Nor does it mean we will be protected or spared if or when the situation gets past of the point of no return. These are unprecedented times! Let us not fool ourselves and be ready for the darkest of outcomes. It was with a very heavy heart we made the decision to ban our daughter from our world… and our lives." He continued as his wife appeared in the mirror by his side. "Azusa's guidance and expectation of us are very clear – love your people, honor them with your devoted work and respect the power and responsibility of your status. Her actions were not the forgiving kind. And believe me when I say, that given the chance, she would end our lives with no hesitation." He glanced over at his wife with a pained look in his eyes before continuing. "So - no!

You are in fact incorrect in suggesting that we, the people of Shadowland are going to ride this out...how did you put it...'from the safety of our position'. I can't be responsible or accountable for the actions of my daughter, but what I will do is ensure that no matter what, my people and I will walk along beside you to bring justice to Heartland and to Terra Nova. Times are changing and what we need now is a united front."

"We shall see," grumbled the Woodland Councilor.

"Thank you for your rectitude, King Nubilus," said Theseus. "Lord Enderby. I fully realize the heaviness of the following request. Do trust it is done so with the utmost thoughtfulness for the greater good of both of our worlds."

"Duty above...all!" said George, briefly glancing over at Clara. He knew very well what Theseus was about to ask of him. "Just as my father instilled in me, and as did my grandfather in him."

"We are unsure as to how Corcoran and his men gained access to cross one of the Gates in search of you and Molly, before he conquered Skyland," continued Theseus. "We are still investigating the matter. However, with Corcoran having full control over the Skyland Gate, we have received some unsettling news from our Gate Keepers. Dozens of Heartland Chancellors and their families living on Earth have been searched out and eradicated by Corcoran's army. We are certain it is only a matter of time before Corcoran discovers the whereabouts of the remaining six gates on Terra Nova. We need you to return and ensure our gates and our people are safe."

"I don't understand. What's to stop Corcoran from attacking and conquering another segment in Heartland, and therefore gaining access to yet another gate?" asked George.

"We have increased our security in all of our segments," said Theseus. "We now need to ensure our gates are safe and that Corcoran cannot use them to attack our lands through them."

After a moment of silence, Theseus continued. "Lord Enderby. The rules forbid the use of teleportation on Earth; however, you have our permission to do so to expedite your travel between the six remaining gates. So long as it is done with extreme caution. We do not wish to raise any suspicion amongst the citizens of Terra Nova as to any magical activity happening around them."

"Understood," replied George.

"Travel to each of the gates, and once they have been secured, your next task is to ensure the safety of our Chancellors, their families, and the families of all of our Gate Keepers. Our duty first and foremost is to protect our own. Unbeknownst to the citizens of Terra Nova, nestled in the Black Forest located in the country of Germany lies a city protected by an ancient spell. This city is large enough for everyone. Crossing through the Woodland Gate will take you to the Rakotz Bridge, just north of the City of the

Black Forest.

"Now that we have briefed Lord Enderby, I believe the imperative question is whether we continue with tonight's festivities or not?" asked the Winterland Councilor.

"In order to eliminate any sense of unrest that has slowly propagated through the populous of the City of Arbor, I believe we must continue as we have planned," said the Woodland Councilor.

"I agree," said the Shadowland Councilor. "Altering the course at this stage would have the potential to create wide-spread panic.

"Continuing with the celebrations will allow us the time needed to work out the details of removing Skyland from the Commonwealth," added the Woodland Councilor with such a lack of emotional attachment, as if removing or adding segments to the Commonwealth were a simple daily task, or part of some elaborate board game they were all enjoying at the moment.

Clara had had just about enough of the formality. She could not contain her thoughts anymore.

"With all due respect, "she began. "do you honestly believe that hiding behind a façade of a celebration, pretending that losing one of our own to the grips of our enemy, continues to be tolerable? I will not stand for that. How will you continue to live with yourselves? I watched both my grandfather and my father struggle to guide this Commonwealth, to help it achieve the greatness I truly believe it can. And so do many of our people. Throughout these centuries we lost sight of what really brought us together. It was my family's belief that forming this Commonwealth came out of the necessity to show our greatest enemy, the Overlanders, that we are a united front, and we will not stand by watching our villages being pillaged, women raped and killed and children taken away from us. But I don't believe that is what this Council's understanding is any longer."

"Well, the most unfortunate by-product of this unity, is that the strongest segments thrive and survive, whilst the weaker segments succumb to their fate. That is the course of nature, is it not?" said the Winterland Councilor.

"When our fellow man is fighting a war with their enemy," continued Clara, "we don't turn away, pretending it is not happening. No! We just sit here, watching it unfold like some cruel, barbaric game. We keep both eyes on the score when we could have lent a hand to save lives. And many have been lost as a result of it."

"But, your Majesty," interjected the Barrenland Councilor, "over the years, the agreement has evolved to such level where we no longer interfere with the affairs of the other segments. May I remind everyone that commerce is now at the forefront of this union. And if one segment is lost, we all figure out how to divvy up the shares to continue serve this great Commonwealth. That is the nature of the agreement we have all signed."

"Divvy up the shares? So that's what this is all about for you. The ones left standing get a bigger piece of the pie?" George interjected. Theseus couldn't help to let out a small smile. He too shared George's sentiment towards the matter.

"How dare you speak to us in such a tone?" said the Winterland Councilor.

"You are wrong!" Clara jumped in. "Let me remind you all that the people of the founding twelve segments rallied to form our Commonwealth with one singular purpose. Unity! Our individual strength is not enough to defeat the evils of this world. It is our greatest weakness as a Commonwealth. Losing Skyland continues to prove that. Our enemy poked and prodded, for centuries, from all angles in all segments. All the while, unbeknownst to us, they were seeking out our weak spots. Until one day out of twelve segments there are now only six. What do we do about it? Chalk it up to the collateral damage of war?! Thank you, King Nubilus, for urging us to be united in this battle, for the very first time. For that is what we must do now!

"The news of Corcoran's rise to power and his capture of Skyland has already percolated throughout the Capital as well as all the other segments. There is no use in pretending otherwise. The ripples of unrest have already begun," said Clara very matter-of-factly, desperately trying to compose her feelings. "The citizens of the Capital demand action. While we were busy tallying up the score, they have been silently crying out for their fellow friends from the other segments. I don't believe we have any other choice in the matter. For the first time in the history of our Commonwealth we will live up to the expectations of our people and join forces, capture Corcoran and free the citizens of Skyland. Before it is too late for all of us!"

The room exploded with shouting, fingers were pointed towards Clara, as the Councilors moved towards her. George stood up, ready to protect Clara if the situation were to get out of hand. The Councilors continued to have their heated conversations, as if Clara were not even in the room. Astoria was fuming. She was getting angrier and angrier and simply could not take it any longer.

"Are you just going to stand here and do nothing?" she asked Aecus. He didn't reply.

"Then I will!" Astoria simply could not restrain herself any longer and leapt off her center platform and positioned herself between Clara and the oncoming mob of Councilors. The noise from the square below started to make its way into the room through the balcony.

"Enough!" Astoria shouted, trying to be heard over all the noise in the room. "Can we please have order!" She roared with such power that her voice reverberated throughout the entire room. The Councilors seemed to have regained their composure and one by one sat back down in their seats.

"Can we, please, allow ourselves a dignified conversation, respect each other's opinions, but most importantly, keep an open mind and open heart to truly hear one another," said Astoria as she walked back to the central podium. "Gentlemen, is that too much to ask?"

"What do you then suggest that our next course of action be?" asked the King of Winterland. "We have never interfered with the matters of the other segments. Are we all to risk our own people's lives and saddle up for a battle with Corcoran on Skyland territory? This motion is highly unprecedented!"

The shouting began once again.

"Are you seriously not going to do anything about this?" asked Astoria as she turned to Aecus.

Clara could not take this any longer. She ran out onto the balcony. Astoria, too, had had just about enough and ran after her. To their surprise, thousands of witches, wizards, elves and other magical creatures were flooding the Commonwealth square shouting 'We are the people! We are the people! We are one! Save Skyland. Save Skyland!'

"Can't you hear it? It is what the people of Heartland are crying out for!" said Clara passionately as she rushed back into the room. "They are tired of standing by and watching their friends and neighbors perish in wars that could have been prevented, had we shown a stronger and more united front to our enemies. They would much rather fight side by side, protecting the Commonwealth, than watch it crumble, one segment at a time because of your individual pride and selfishness." George stood there, proudly watching his beloved Clara fighting these powerful men of Heartland with words that cut deeper than any weapon could.

"Look. Look!" begged Clara. "See for yourselves!" Clara grabbed George's hand and led him out onto the balcony. The Councilors made their way up the stairs and were astonished at the sight of thousands of citizens of the Capital filling every inch of the Commonwealth Square. Clara raised her hand and the crowd went silent.

"Friends. Thank you. Thank you for being here with us tonight. It is with a heavy heart that we stand before you. The people of Skyland fought a brave and strong fight, however, their enemy did so tenfold. We were shaken by the news we received this morning. It has been confirmed that Corcoran, the new leader of the Overlanders, conquered the Skyland segment." Clara paused before continuing. "How did we get here? How did we, as the leaders of a free nation let this happen? I believe an apology is long overdue. As leaders, we let our pride and selfishness stand in the way of ourselves, and as a result we failed to honor the promise that our ancestors made to every single one of us at the dawn of our Commonwealth. We have been listening to you, but it has taken us centuries to hear what you were saying. I am standing here before you, acknowledging our past mistakes and I promise you that from now on the Heartland Commonwealth will stand and fight the evil, not as individual segments, but as a single nation." The crowd erupted in cheerful celebration. The people of Heartland had long given up the hope of hearing those words again. "Please, let us celebrate the Summerset Festival tonight, for tomorrow we will witness the dawning of a new Heartland. Your Heartland!"

"Gentlemen!" said George turning to the Councilors. "You have all seen your Kings and Queens rule. Watch and learn, for this is how you lead a nation!"

The crowd erupted and the Councilors found themselves not fully understanding what had just transpired. Astoria returned into The Oval Room looking for Aecus.

"Why didn't you step in?" she asked as she walked back up to the center platform. "I don't understand why you just let them at her like that."

"I chose to not interfere, dear, because I knew Clara was going to find a way out of all of this. I know her well. It had to be on her own terms...by her own strength."

# CHAPTER 27

*It's time to reveal the truth...*

E yya was becoming very impatient because nobody else seemed as interested in getting to the festival as quickly as she did.

"Come on guys!" she said. "We'll miss the grand opening of the festival! I cannot wait to see the merry-go-round. I hear it is going to be out of this world! Wow, look at all these people arriving...come on, come on...we have to sneak ahead of them to get in line first!" Eyya was just a bit too excited, thought Molly. She was tired and didn't want to say anything for the fear of ruining Eyya's excitement. Taking this moment away from Eyya would not have been fair. Molly forced her mind to allow herself the joy of these last few precious moments of freedom with her best friends, for she knew that soon all of this would change.

"That's a pretty necklace," said Maya.

"Thank you. It was a gift from Clara," replied Molly.

"Come on, come on!" urged Eyya. "We won't be the first in line if we don't pick up the pace."

The Summerset Festival is the most splendorous event of the season that always takes place at the Capital. The Woodland Elves were responsible for organizing the festival this year. Creatures from all over the land come together to visit and to celebrate the past, the present and the future. It is a time full of festivities, wonderful company, magical midway rides, delicious food and wine. All-in-all, a day to remember. But it wouldn't be the same this year. Many magical creatures looked forward to this day, to spend some time with their friends from the other segments. Sadly, a lot of their Skyland friends wouldn't make it this year. It was quite a bittersweet day for a lot of them.

In the past, each year's Summerset Festival seemed to top the last. The Elves were in full preparation mode and were busy decorating the streets, sprucing up the shop windows and the city square. They prepared something very unique that was surely going to make this year's festival better than the last. Their 'ace' card that would help with just that was the Byzantium Merry-Go-Around. This was no ordinary merry-go-around. The structure was made from elm wood brought in from far away.

Gold plated decorative ornaments encased the crown and the bottom part of the ride, with beautiful paintings of creatures from every corner of Heartland. The midpoint of the ride was covered with tall mirrors framed in gold trim. The enchantment of the ride was the platform full of magical horses that came alive as the ride started to move. This type of ride had never been seen before, so the Elves knew they had something that everyone would be talking about for years to come. This year's Festival, however, on the eve of the battle against Corcoran and the Overlanders, would also be a celebration of a united nation, fighting together, side-by-side, stronger than ever before.

"Look at those majestic horses!" said Astoria. "They are absolutely gorgeous."

"Aecus, Astoria! You're here!" said Molly in amazement, as everyone bowed their heads slightly, greeting the lion and the lioness.

"Just you wait," said Ritana. "I have it from a reliable source that these horses also do some special tricks."

"Looks like the festivities have already started," said Aiken.

"Let's go, let's go, Molly," pleaded Eyya. "There's hardly any line up for the merry-go-round, yet. But that's about to change with the masses approaching. Come on!"

"Actually, I think I've had enough of crazy carnival rides for one day," said Molly. "All that flying did me in. If it's alright, I'll just sit on this bench, and watch you from here."

"Are you sure, Molly?" asked Ritana.

"I'm sure. Go, just go! Have an absolutely amazing time. Really, I'll be fine," she replied with a smile. Truth be told, Molly was exhausted, and just the thought of going round and round...and round...and round made her feel nauseous.

"Alright, we'll wave to you," said Eyya with excitement as she ran towards the star attraction of this year's Festival.

"Are you alright, Molly?" asked Astoria.

"I'm taking it all in slowly, considering..." replied Molly. "I can't let it overwhelm me, otherwise..." Molly paused for a moment. She was desperately trying to be brave and trusting that the adults had everything under control, that they knew what was best in these kinds of situations. The truth was, she was scared. She was scared because she did not understand how she fit into all of this and why Corcoran and Regina were so obsessively trying to hurt her.

"In times like these," started Astoria, "one must keep a sharp mind. You can do this, by simply closing your eyes and clearing your mind. It's sort of a way to reset your brain so you can focus better."

"But how can I clear my mind when my whole world is falling to pieces?" replied Molly.

"It's easy, my little squirrel. Simply close your eyes and focus on your breathing. Don't think of anything other than trying to guess your next thought. I know this sounds silly, but I bet you simply won't be able to."

"I don't think it's possible," said Molly. "How can it be? Stressing over what my next thought is going to be would simply cause me more anxiety."

"Trust me," said Astoria. "Just give it a try."

Molly reluctantly closed her eyes, took a deep breath, exhaled and tried to figure out what her next thought will be. Astoria was right, she simply could not guess. It is impossible to predict what the mind would think of next. When there are millions of thoughts floating around in our brain, it is simply not possible to guess which one will be the next one. To her surprise, this did not stress her out at all.

"By trying to guess your next thought," started Astoria, "you are in fact forcing your brain to create an open space. It also creates a sense of quiet and calm. With each passing moment, it is as though that open space of quiet and calm grows bigger and bigger, until it fully envelopes you. When you open your eyes, I promise you will feel much calmer and focused."

Molly took a deep breath, opened her eyes and said in total amazement, "you called me, little squirrel. The only two people that ever called me that were Madame de la Fleur and my Uncle Az." It finally dawned on Molly now why the tone of Astoria's voice, her intonation, the subtle way she pronounced her r's and her th's seemed so familiar to her. Molly also just remembered that she had not seen Madame de la Fleur since the night they left Chateau Azeri. "Dagnabbit, you are…"

Astoria looked over at Aecus and with a smile replied "Yes, it is I, my little squirrel."

"But how did you escape?"

"Well, Aiken. Don't ask me how, but he managed to message Clara to let her know that Corcoran found you and George, and was on his way to Chateau Azeri. Without hesitation, Clara sent Beatrice, Thana and Asgoth after him. Once they arrived, I knew that everything was going to be alright. So, I teleported to the nearest Gate in north-eastern part of Germany and crossed to Heartland. Don't even get me started on the amount of paperwork I had to file afterwards for the unauthorized teleportation. But I had to do it. I was able to alert Clara that Beatrice made it on time and that you and George were soon going to cross through the free-form portal to Heartland. She then made sure Trail at Junction Manor was notified of your arrival."

"There is something I need to tell you," Astoria said after a long pause. "When you arrived at the Chateau, you were only five years old. By that age, children of the royal families of Heartland or the children of the Gate Keepers would under normal circumstances begin completing their preparatory training. To lay the foundation, so to speak and to prepare them for their primary training when they turned of age. Since it was impossible to accomplish this with you in Terra Nova, the decision was to do the training through dreams. In addition to being the stoutly housekeeper of the Chateau Azeri, I was also assigned by King Zahar to ensure you progressed through the training curriculum without any delays. The regular dreams you had of Heartland served to teach you about the world you belong to. They also helped to teach you the spells and skills you relied on during the battles we fought alongside King Zahar and our Barrenland friends a few years back."

"But I am not that Molly. I am not as strong or brave as she is. I know no spells, no battle moves. I'm just ordinary little me," said Molly, staring down on the ground, feeling extremely overwhelmed by all of this.

"Little squirrel, little squirrel, climbed up a tree. Then he fell, then he fell, and broke his little knee…" sang Aecus with a gentle rumble in his lion voice as he raised Molly's chin with his front paw.

"Uncle Az?" Molly's eyes welled up. "You are my Uncle Az! As morbid as that song is," Molly laughed, "you were always able to cheer me up with it." She embraced both of them at the same time. There was no point in contemplating how Uncle Az and

Madame de la Fleur turned into a lion and lioness. It just felt right. 'Of course.' Molly thought to herself. 'Of course, they are part of this world, too.' As she remembered all those little pivotal moments of her life on earth that fit so well with this final realization. Like the countless moments she caught Madame de la Fleur flirting with Uncle Az. Or the moments she caught Madame de la Fleur in the kitchen conjuring her famous pies seemingly out of thin air. Molly sensed that Madame de la Fleur had some sort of magical powers, but she would always skillfully explain how she was able to create those illusions. Or those moments during the games of hide and seek, when Uncle Az managed to simply appear out of nowhere, always right behind Molly when she was about to give up because she couldn't find him. No matter how hard she tried to look for him in the secret rooms, hallways and passages, she was never able to find him. He, on the other hand, was always able to find her within a few minutes. Strangely it all fit, everything made sense now and everything felt as it should.

"Aecus," said Molly as she wiped the tears from her cheeks, "can I ask you a question and will you answer me honestly?"

"I will," said Aecus after a moment, not really believing that he would have the strength to. He knew the time had come. He feared it was here and now where secrets would have to be revealed. He knew exactly what Molly was about to ask.

"Every single time I asked my dad," Molly started, "if he would mail her a letter I wrote, if she'd be coming to visit us, or if she sent me a birthday card... he said, she was simply too busy to read my letters, too busy for any of that, too busy living her New York life. Then finally, after asking you about my mother for a hundredth time, you told me she lived far away, in America, and that she had left soon after I was born, because...because she did not know how to be responsible for herself, let alone for a child. At least one of you gave me some form of a reasonable answer. At least one that a child of my age could comprehend. That is not why my mother left me, is it."

"No," said Aecus matter-of-factly. He no longer had the strength he thought he would have to be able continue this conversation. He turned, and started to walk through the crowd, leaving Molly and Astoria behind.

Molly ran past Aecus, then stopped in front of him, not letting him take another step. "Is Regina my birth mother?" she asked. Molly and Aecus stared at each other for what felt like an eternity. "Is she or is she not my mother?" pleaded Molly, crying. "Answer me!"

Even though he promised to be honest, he could not get himself to say it. A mother bear will do anything to protect her cubs, and Regina tried as well. However, along the way she caused pain and destruction of an unimaginable scale. The last thing Aecus wanted was for Molly to know she was connected to that monster, if only through the skillfully crafted magic of the Chambers.

"Well, if you're not going to tell her then I will," said Astoria, her voice shaking as she walked to Molly, pushing Aecus out of the way with her shoulder. "Molly, this old buffoon loves you, very, very much, you know that, right? He would give his life to protect you, to make sure no harm comes to you. And so would I, proudly. But no...Regina is not your mother. Open that pendant Clara gave you."

"I had no idea it opened. How do you know she gave it to me?" asked Molly. "Never mind," she added with a smile. Molly slowly reached for the pendant and opened it. There, set inside was a picture of George and Clara holding a baby girl. "Is that me?" she asked.

"Yes," replied Astoria.

"And that is my dad and Clara. Does that mean... "

"Yes, my little squirrel. Clara is your birth mother," said Astoria.

"No, that can't be true. What do you mean?" Molly asked bewildered. "She would have told me. Can one of you please just stop... stop this nonsense and tell me what is going on here! Why is it so hard for adults to speak the truth? I hate it when you sugar-coat things. It serves no purpose. This doesn't make any sense. Tell me the honest truth!" she demanded.

"You are so much like her," said Aecus. "The way you flip your hair out of your eyes when you are upset."

"It's a bit windy, here..." said Molly "I hate having my hair down for that very reason. It gets in my eyes..."

"Clara is your mother," started Astoria.

"Then why didn't she tell me herself? Why didn't my dad tell me the truth?"

"How would one go about bringing something like that up in the midst of everything that was going on?" asked Astoria. "I don't know. I honestly don't know how he managed all those years. There are way too many intertwined secrets and I think as for your dad, he opted to pick the easy, normal route by raising you as an ordinary girl to shield you from all of this. As hard as it must have been for him. George and I didn't speak much, but I could sense there were times he truly needed and wanted to confide in someone. At those moments, the burden of it all must have been altogether unbearable for him. I truly respect and admire the man for everything he did throughout those years."

Molly closed her eyes and breathed in deeply. She was trying to calm her mind.

"You are right, Astoria," Molly started. "After everything my dad and I went through since we got here, I can see how there just was no single moment when he could've simply said 'Guess what? On this trip you'll get to meet your mom.' I wish I would've known what he was going through all these years. He kept everything to himself. He must have felt so alone, all those times. I guess Clara's way of revealing the secret was through this pendant, wasn't it?"

"I guess so," replied Astoria with a smile.

Molly paused for a moment. "Maggie" she said calmly. "Who is she and why do I remind everyone of her?"

"How do you know of her?" asked Astoria.

"Intuition, I guess. When we first crossed, despite our terrifying last night at the mansion, for the first time in my life I felt like I finally got to live in the place I'd spent most of my time dreaming about, the place I belonged in. Everyone was nice to me – the folks at Junction Manor, Eyya and Aiken. But something about all of it felt...artificial in some way. I don't feel the same closeness to my friends as I had in my dreams. It's the way they look at me...with a hint of sadness in their eyes. I don't feel the same self-assurance and confidence. Aecus, I'm desperately trying to remember every spell you've ever thought me, every minute detail about Heartland, but my memories seem to escape me, as if they were not my own...as if they were just borrowed. Does this have something to do with Maggie? How does she fit into all of this?"

Aecus turned to Astoria and pleaded, "Astoria...it's not our place to…"

"But, my dear, it is, and I think you need to be the one to tell her," said Astoria looking over to Molly with a sense of resolution in her eyes. "She needs to know. We are just as responsible for all of this as they are. She may as well hear it from us. It is time Molly learns the truth." Aecus nodded.

"Corbus Damwich," he started. "is the oldest Oracle of Heartland that foretold this day to come. When an outside force dares to break the promise of alliance, it shall bring forth a new-found sense of faith and unity brought by a child of both worlds."

"A child of both worlds…" Molly contemplated this statement for a moment. "Do you believe that the child foretold in the prophecy is me?" asked Molly plainly. "I was never much of a fan of prophecies. They give you the high-level details, leaving you to figure out the rest. I don't suppose you know how I'd go about saving our worlds, do you? If that is, after all, why I'm here."

It took every ounce of courage for her to say this. On the inside she was shaking, but on the outside Molly mustered all her strength to keep herself composed. She knew she had to ask this. She did not want to be wrapped up in any of this, but somehow, she felt she had no choice in the matter. Courage is what she needed most. Courage to understand and to accept her fate.

"To put it simply, yes, we believe the child spoken about in the prophecy is you," said Aecus.

"Ok," said Molly. After all, it was not like she had much of a choice in the matter. At least she finally had an answer to one of her questions. This was her purpose. To be the one to save Heartland and Terra Nova. How to do that remained a mystery for now. She trusted that she'd know when the time came. "Now tell me about Maggie."

"Okay," said Aecus, knowing full well it was time. "Please come and sit. Let me tell you a story of a young man and a young woman," started Aecus, "who loved each other very much."

# CHAPTER 28

## *It must be done!*

Clara was convinced there was no other choice. They were faced with an unthinkable scenario and an unprecedented decision had to be made.

"After careful deliberation, I am afraid that we are left with no other options. The Skyland Gate must be sealed," said Clara with a heavy voice.

The Councilors immediately stood up and took a step closer towards her.

"First a revolution and now this? We don't know the implications of these actions, your Majesty," said the Woodland Councilor with an accusatory tone in his voice.

"For all we know we are opening ourselves to even more

danger," said the King of Winterland.

"The gates have never been sealed," the King of Waterland added his view on the matter. "How do we know that is the right decision? As we discussed already, can we not continue with the plan of sending Lord Enderby to Terra Nova to ensure the balance is not threatened by having one of the six gates under Corcoran's ruling?"

"I hear your concerns," said Clara. "We have also never lost one of our primary land segments to our enemies before. Sealing the Skyland Gate would mean, however, that Corcoran and his army are not able to access Terra Nova and cause damage and destruction on that front. We have lost far too many lives there already. We shall send patrols to ensure that any magical creatures sent by Corcoran are captured and brought back to Heartland for immediate sentencing."

"At this rate we may as well seal the Shadowland Gate," muttered the King of Woodland.

"How dare you continue insulting me and my people!" shouted the King of Shadowland.

A massive argument erupted, with Kings in the mirrors shouting and pointing, as did the Councilors in the Chamber. Complete panic ensued.

"George, I can't do this. I will not continue watching this nonsense," said Clara turning to George.

"Enough!" Clara shouted. "I am done being patient with you gentlemen! In all honestly, I now realize just how difficult of a job my father had working alongside you. For better or for worse, we are all in this together and we will see this through, together!" Clara paused. "Our shield is at its weakest at our Gates, and rest assured Corcoran will be counting on that. While we are busy fighting the battles at the front of our segments, he'll be marching in through our back doors, like a virus killing us from the inside. We cannot count on Regina not sharing this information with him. We have got to be prepared for anything. I hope you understand that our only option is to stop the bleeding - stop Corcoran's men from crossing over to Terra Nova by sealing the Skyland Gate. Yes, the risks are unknown, but the consequences of not doing so are inconceivable. Lord Enderby, please share the procedure with us all."

George started as he rose from his seat, "sealing one of the gates requires the remaining Gate Keepers to initiate the closure protocols from their respective gates on Earth, I mean Terra Nova. Forgive me, old habits die hard. These protocols are carefully documented, however as we are all aware, there has never been a need to retrieve them. The documents allow the Gate Keepers to reset the gates and designate the remaining six as the primary gates between Terra Nova and Heartland. This procedure will lock the Skyland Gate immediately. Clara, we will need your assistance to retrieve the gate closure scrolls that are kept in a secret vault carefully hidden away deep in the Forest of Inkhans. Only the King or Queen of Heartland can release the ancient spells guarding them. I will send Fon and Dorn to advise King Silva of Woodland of your arrival. Theseus, will you escort Queen Clara and me?"

"Certainly," replied Theseus."

"Thank you," said George. "Once we have the scrolls, I'll use the Woodland Gate to cross and deliver them to each of the Gates on Terra Nova."

"Raise your hands to indicate your agreement with the presented plan," said Ismene, as she lifted her cane out of its place in the platform. One by one, although hesitantly, the Councilors and the Kings rose their hands. All, but the Woodland Councilor. "With ten votes to one, proposition is accepted." With those final words, Ismene tapped her staff on the floor. The Kings in their mirrors disappeared, and the Councilors carried on their conversations as they all exited into the Woodland Councilor's private chamber. All, except the Shadowland Councilor.

"Your Majesty?" he started.

"Yes Councilor?" Clara replied.

"I am truly sorry about all of this. Please know, I am here to help in any way I can. I know that King Nubilus shares the same sentiment." He paused for a moment before continuing, "I watched your father over the years navigate these troubled waters. Our Councilors did not always see things the way your father did. Or the way you and I do. Their reactions are often out of fear, not defiance. In light of recent events, may I suggest that you, too, seek safety in the ancient forest along with the children. We will continue to follow your leadership from there via the mirrors. Theseus will be here to ensure we carry out all the necessary tasks as per your wishes."

"Thank you, Councilor, for your concerns about my safety. I truly appreciate it. I'll seriously consider your suggestion," replied Clara.

"Have a safe journey," said the Councilor before turning around and heading to his private chamber.

"Let's not waste time, Your Majesty," said Theseus. "We should head out immediately."

"There is just one thing I need to do. Come with me George. We'll meet you in the gardens, Theseus." said Clara as she headed for the door.

# CHAPTER 29

*A long, long time ago…*

Aecus found a comfortable spot right next to the bench Molly was sitting on and laid down. After all this time, Molly was finally going to learn the truth.

"Since the dawn of our Commonwealth," started Aecus, "one of the most important families living on Earth, or Terra Nova as we call it, was the House of Enderby. Being the Head Gate Keeper family comes with a heavy responsibility. This was passed down the Enderby line for many generations with close to one hundred and twenty thousand presently in the Enderby family tree. They are also often referred to as Sentries and their primary role is to train, guide, mentor and assist all the Gate Keepers and their families. Your father is one of the Sentries. In addition to what may seem to an untrained eye like a bunch of mundane tasks, though let me assure you they are not, Sentries serve a much higher purpose. This may come as a surprise to you, but the Heartland Commonwealth exiles our enemies to Terra Nova. The primarily obligation of the Sentries is to ensure that their memories of our world do not return and that they seamlessly integrate into the fabric of Terra Nova's cultures and societies.

"For centuries, a member of the Heartland Royals would be assigned as the mentor to the next Sentry of the Enderby family. There were certain 'secrets of the trade', so to speak, that only the members of the royal family were privy to, with respect to how any Earthly matters were to be handled. This learning could only be passed on through this pre-selected mentorship, and so, long ago it was decided between King Zahar and George's father, Lord Samuel Enderby, that Clara would be the mentor and trainer of the next Enderby Sentry. Though, never have these mentorships ended up the way it did this time around – with Clara and George falling in love with each other, that is. After years of training and mentoring, George Enderby, being the oldest child of the Enderby family was set to take on the role that was to be his destiny. However, that all changed the day Maggie was born. But, I'm getting a bit ahead of myself, here.

"The Sentry training was conducted via special portals connecting our two worlds. Think of it as a two-way mirror that allowed Clara and George do all the necessary training. There is one thing that has never been possible to explain by anyone in Heartland, nor any Gate Keeper or Sentry on Terra Nova for that matter. Time passes differently in each of our worlds. Depending on the cycle of our moons…a day in Heartland usually lasts about… well, approximately a year in Terra Nova. Why is this so important? Well, for George, this training took four whole years. For Clara, on the other hand, this training technically only lasted four days. However, with the help of some magic and advanced Terra Nova technology, Clara was able to practically pause time on her side of the Gates and stretch out those seconds into hours. So, as George connected with Clara every day for four years, he did not see much of a change in her appearance. But Clara, in that time got to see George grow up from a teenage boy to a fully-grown man. By the time George completed his training, they were the same age, but still aging at different speeds.

"Just before George was to complete his final stages of the training and start his post as the Gate Keeper Sentry, he asked for an audience with King Zahar. He knew that for him to stop aging at a much, much faster rate than Clara because of how time worked between our worlds there must be something that the King could do. He needed his time imprint to be synchronized with Clara's. He knew he had nothing to lose by simply asking for the improbable.

"Wait a minute, what does that mean?" asked Molly.

"You mean synchronizing the time imprints?"

"Yes. How does it work?" Molly was very confused about the whole 'time imprint' thing.

"Well...time is precious, no matter which side of the Gates you find yourself on. And so, there were rumors floating around amongst the Gate Keepers of Terra Nova, that there was a slight possibility to manually set one's time imprint, so they would age at the same rate as someone in Heartland. Think of it this way - one could potentially spend a whole year in Terra Nova, but physiologically only age one day. Talk about a possibility for a nearly eternal life on that side of the Gates."

"Wow, that would be incredible," said Molly in amazement.

"Yes, that would be. However, no one really knew how it could be done. Or whether the rumors were true in the first place. Some speculated that a potion prepared of secret ingredients from all the Heartland segments when taken at a certain time of night would do the trick; and others figured a mere bath in the purest pool of water would do it.

"And, if anyone was able to confirm whether it was possible, it was King Zahar. Luckily for George and Clara, the rumors were true and it was possible to synchronize the time imprints. Although this was one of the most sacred and secret ceremonies, it was actually much simpler than anyone over the centuries

271

would have thought. The only two requirements were the presence of an Oracle – someone who can summon Azusa the almighty, and a sponsor – someone who's time imprint the subject was to adopt.

"George crossed to Heartland and then flew on the back of a mighty dragon until he reached the Heartland castle at the edge of the Capital. He ran through the castle gates as fast as his feet could carry him, for he knew he only had a few hours before he had to return to Earth. When he arrived, George found Clara in the garden. George was completely oblivious to anyone present, except for Clara. He didn't notice King Zahar standing there, or Regina watching from the window of the castle library. She knew why George was at the castle and was not pleased by it one bit.

"There she was...looking not much different than she did when George last saw her, but as beautiful as always. Although to him a few months had gone by, to her, merely a few hours. You see, it is never easy for anyone on the other side of the gate. A whole month is a very long time. A whole month without the one you love, seems like an eternity. To George, every day, although filled with purpose and importance, seemed to last forever. They kissed passionately. Their bond was so strong that no one or nothing could stand between them. Not even the distance of time. King Zahar was also well aware of that.

"After a moment, as if George regained some sort of normal

consciousness and was no longer blinded by the sheer need to see and hold Clara in his arms, he realized that King Zahar was standing next to them. George explained that as rewarding of an experience these past years were for him, it was not easy. Right there, in front of him, he professed his love for Clara."

"I vividly remember your father telling me this," said Astoria, "Aecus, why don't you let me continue?" she sighed as she started recalling this romantic moment. "George turned to Clara. He pressed his forehead against hers and said with a gentle whisper, 'I'm yours, if you'll be mine.' He started to cry. He missed her very much and the fact that he could once again see her, touch her, embrace her, even if only for this brief moment, left him very emotional. Clara had always dreamt of this moment and softly replied, 'yes, I will'. After a moment, George turned to the King and asked for that very sacred and secret ceremony. A ceremony that would bind their two souls together, syncing their timelines for eternity. The King looked at them both. He looked at them very hard, trying to find something that would make his mind guide the decision against this union, for he knew it would be a difficult one. After a few moments with a gentle smile he replied, 'I believe that is truly what must be done'.

"The sacred promise ceremony can only take place in the presence of Azusa, the divine creator of all life in Heartland. She is inside every living being, guiding our souls, protecting us.

Some say she is the voice of reason within us. However, only a select few have the ability to summon her. This magical ceremony can only be performed by the purest of souls, and so, summoning Azusa is not to be taken lightly. She chooses the purest souls and gives them the ability to connect with her. These purest souls are called Oracles. King Zahar was one of the seven living Oracles. When the Oracle summons Azusa, she speaks directly through them. They become her voice as the Oracle enters a state of trance that allows them to channel her. However, this summoning can only take place at the most sacred place of Heartland – the Forest of Inkhans."

"Wow. That is so fascinating," said Molly.

"Just wait until you hear about the ceremony," said Astoria in excitement. "King Zahar, George and Clara headed straight to the ancient forest. Their dragons were already waiting for them at the edge of the castle garden. This is not a place that can be visited by just anyone. Only Oracles have the ability to unlock this sacred place that is buried deep below the roots of the ancient forest. To get there, they had to make their way through the main gates of the Tree of Life located in the center of the ancient forest, then head down through the endless underground tunnels, past the Chambers, which are…"

Aecus, all flustered, suddenly interrupted Astoria. "Yes, Astoria, let's just get to the main part," Aecus knew very well that now was definitely not the time to talk about the Chambers.

"Right," said Astoria as she quickly regained her focus. "King Zahar led them down the ancient underground passages, tunnels and bridges across cavernous spaces until they arrived at the exact spot – the Locus of Antecedents. According to the King's recollections, this was a beautiful place hidden in the heart of an underground world, unlike any he had ever seen. Nobody really knew how it was possible, but this world seemed to have its own unique ecosystem, full of lush greenery, streams and lakes filled with the clearest water, with the most unique birds and animals that called it their home." Aecus let out a small grunt, suggesting Astoria was once again letting her thoughts trail off. She did that often. She would get lost in the narrative which tended to make her stories drag. Molly picked up on this instantly and smiled. No matter what shape these two took, their personalities and mannerisms remained the same. For a moment she felt as if she were back at the mansion, watching them passively interacting with one another, which she could not help but find charming.

"Okay...okay...I'll stick to the 'important' parts of the story," said Astoria with a slight eye roll. "After a moment, King Zahar closed his eyes and the ground around them started to shake. Glass walls started to rise all around and suddenly Clara and George found themselves standing on a white marble floor that just seemed to have emerged from the ground. The glass ceiling sealed overhead, forming a glittering dome above. A bright light formed from the center where the King was standing. It expanded until it covered the entire space, as if it swallowed them all. Moments later, the bright light cleared. Clara and George found themselves standing opposite each other, dressed in white.

"The sacred promise ceremony is an irreversible process in which two beings promise themselves to each other, for eternity. It is a magical ceremony in which the two souls intertwine, leaving a piece in one another, connecting each other forever, whilst their time imprints synchronize in perfect unison. This ceremony would initiate a time imprint change procedure, which would change George's Earthly time imprint to the one of Heartland's.

"King Zahar opened his eyes and looked straight at them, and to their surprise, a female voice came out of him. Though his lips were not moving, it was a voice that had both power and presence. It was the voice of Azusa.

" 'Rise,' said Azusa. She started the enchantment as Clara and George elevated off the ground. As they were rising, a string of white light emitted from their chests. The strings started to make their way around the glass dome, as if searching for something. With each beat of their hearts the light pushed forward and forward as if propelled with a jolt of wondrous energy, until that very moment when the two strings found each other directly above Clara and George. The strings of light started to intertwine, making their way down towards them until finally the ends connected. The room was once again filled with a bright light. When the ceremony was over, Clara and George found themselves standing on the ground wearing the same clothes they came in."

"That must've been quite something," said Molly.

"I know," replied Astoria with a smile.

"There was something you said earlier about Regina. Why was she so obsessed with my father?" asked Molly.

"Well, love is a strange thing that makes one do unexplainable things," said Aecus. "For several months following the ceremony, Regina tirelessly tried to do everything in her power to make George fall in love with her. I'm getting ahead of myself again…a little backstory.

"Regina was the eldest daughter of King of Nubilus of Shadowland. And was once-upon a time Clara's best friend. In the final stages of George's training, Clara and Regina spent a significant amount of time on Terra Nova. By the time his training was almost complete, George and Clara were head over heels in love with one another, and Regina found herself the third wheel every time the three of them spent time together. Regina yearned to have the kind of relationship Clara had with George. Over time,

Regina's jealousy turned into a strong obsession, that eventually brought out the worst in her.

"So now we're back to Regina's motive. In order to put her plan into action she needed to spend time with George without Clara's presence because when she was around, he noticed nobody else. The problem was, that unless accompanied by a member of the Heartland Royal Family, crossing the gates was strictly prohibited to almost everyone. Often times Regina begged Clara to just get her across the gate so she could 'explore' more of Terra Nova, then Clara could return back to her duties on Heartland. Which worked for a while. But as Regina's obsession grew, so did her desire to get to Terra Nova more often, so she needed to come up with a plan that didn't involve Clara. She pretended to be an Attendant. Attendants are the health authority of Heartland. Their primary job is to ensure that Gate Keepers and their families remain in good health during and after their assignments on Terra Nova. They were one of the few that had the ability to travel freely between our two worlds. Surprisingly clever, Regina never found trouble crossing any gate. With each crossing she became more skilled. One thing she quickly discovered was that on Terra Nova, one of her special abilities was transfiguration. She could take on any form she wanted to. With each stay on Terra Nova she became more comfortable adapting to the life around her in her various forms.

With each visit, however, the purpose was always the same – to seduce George. She failed at every attempt, no matter how hard she tried. She could be the most beautiful woman with gorgeous hair, body and appearance; or highly intelligent; a singer; an aggressive martial arts sensei; a dark, tall and handsome, well-built man; a coffee barista. None of these personas worked. It was as if George was de-sensitized to feeling any desires or deep feelings towards another human being besides Clara. The only form Regina refused to ever take, even though it would have undoubtedly brought her success, was the form of Clara. She needed George to desire her in whatever form she chose.

"This would probably be a good time to mention - just as Clara was mentor to George, Regina was mentor to Corcoran. They were both troubled from the start, let's be honest. And one day, they started to dabble in some very dark and forbidden magic. Since nothing else seemed to be working for her, Regina turned to dark magic to try to win George's heart. And then, she did the unthinkable.

"Due to some security breaches, the rules around Attendants crossing tightened, Regina found herself without the ability to cross the Gates. Although Clara was extremely occupied with her duties at Heartland, Regina persuaded her to go and visit George for a few days. She tried to convince her that it was best that the two of them went over there to help him prepare for the final exams and his inauguration ceremony as the Sentry of the Terra Nova Gate Keepers. Clara could not stay for the entire duration, so the night she returned to Heartland, Regina put her newly acquired dark magic skills to the test.

"When George was asleep that night, Regina put a spell on him that made him instantly fall in love with her. She hoped that one night together was all she needed to make sure his love for her would never fade. After that fateful night, as luck would have it, Regina became pregnant. The combination of the use of dark magic, Regina's Heartland time imprint and George's modified time imprint caused irreversible and unforeseeable consequences. The baby's evolution inside Regina's womb sped up to an unimaginable rate. The pregnancy lasted less than one day, Regina went into labor and the baby was born the following night."

"That was Maggie, wasn't it?" Molly asked.

"Yes, it was little Maggie indeed," said Astoria.

Molly looked at her puzzled, "Then Maggie is my half-sister?" Molly just now realized that no matter how much her mind was trying to ignore what the Grimoire of The Gate Keepers showed her earlier, it was in fact true.

"Yes. Yes, she is," replied Astoria. "It's quite a shock, I know and was equally so for George. The second night into their 'black magic romance' George was sleeping soundly one moment, the next he was awakened by Regina screaming in agony. At that moment, the curse that Regina had cast over him, had been broken. Then little Maggie was born. The birth took all of Regina's strength and at the end she ended up losing consciousness. George was left alone, trying to figure out what to do with this newborn baby that wouldn't stop crying, while trying to make sure Regina was still breathing and alive.

"He cleaned up little Maggie, wrapped her in some blankets and just held her. There she was, this tiny little baby in George's arms. After a while, little Maggie finally fell asleep. He didn't know what to do. The only thing he was sure of was that he needed Clara, so he activated a free-form portal and called for her. He was not authorized to initiate these, but he knew he had no choice. When Clara arrived, she saw George holding little Maggie with Regina still unconscious on the bed.

"They stood there silently. Both of them looking at little Maggie until Clara spoke up. She asked George how it all happened. He didn't understand any of it. One minute he was asleep, and next Regina was giving birth. It didn't make any sense to either of them. But Clara could sense that something was really wrong here.

"She knew exactly what needed to be done. Clara turned to the front door, activated a free-form portal, then summoned Fon and Dorn and sent them to get her father immediately.

"A few moments later, the portal lit up and through it walked in King Zahar, followed by Asgoth and Thana. Regina was slowly waking up. King Zahar could instantly sense the betrayal. He examined the baby and knew right away who her parents were. He looked at Regina with a stern look and ordered Asgoth and Thana to take her back through the portal. That night, King Zahar left without a word leaving George, Clara and the baby behind. He returned three days later and told them that Regina was held captive in Shadowland for not only breaking the sacred bond between them, but also for meddling in dark magic. It was up to her father, King Nubilus to decide upon her fate.

"He then ordered Clara to return to Heartland, George to get back to his Gate Keeper duties, and that I was to raise little Maggie on Terra Nova. You see, keeping Maggie there, while Regina was being strictly monitored in Heartland was the only way to ensure everyone's safety.

"Maggie had a wonderful childhood. But magic was too strong within her, and so soon it was evident that in order to harness her magical power, she needed to understand the world she was part of and learn all about that part of her heritage. Remember that little device Clara used to stretch out those precious minutes into hours. Well, Maggie used it, too, every time she visited Heartland. And did she ever take advantage of every borrowed second. She was a quick learner, she was smart, brave, and very opinionated. But we love her very much, despite that." Astoria added with a gentle smile before continuing. "She was able to spend a lot of time here in Heartland without losing much of it on the Terra Nova side of the Gates."

Molly was slowly processing all of this. It was far too difficult to take it all in. She couldn't believe she had a sister, somewhere out there. A girl that looked just like her.

"Maggie. I can't believe she's my sister!" said Molly. "But why did Regina think I was Maggie?" Molly was so confused about all of this. None of it made sense to her. "Does she not know I'm not her?"

Molly had so many questions but was suddenly distracted by the beautiful music coming from the enchanted merry-go-round. It started to slowly transform into a Ferris wheel with magical winged horses flying around it. She could see her friends in all their bliss, happily riding the majestic ride without a care in the world.

In that precise moment, a flash of blinding light emitted from the center of the Ferris wheel. Out of this force of light an image emerged. A massive image of the most feared wizard in all of Heartland.

"Nice celebration we...are...having!" said Corcoran very slowly, followed by a malicious laugh. "Don't try to block this transmission, I'll be brief. I promise!

"When the night is young, and the two moons pass as one," started Corcoran, obviously reading this from a note someone just handed to him, "the diary of the chosen you shall bring. If, by chance, you disobey, when the clock strikes each hour, the fate of a Skylandian will be grey. Argh...who wrote this garbage?" he said turning to his side, addressing someone who wasn't visible in the image. "Argh...enough of these stupid riddles. Meet me at the edge of the Skyland segment at witching hour. Bring me the diary. I'll...be...waiting."

And with those final words, the image of Corcoran vanished causing a massive explosion that sent the winged horses shooting out like fireworks. The beautiful ornate wings instantly breaking off one by one. The entire merry-go-round started to fall apart mid-air, sending the magical creatures that were moments ago enjoying the majestic ride, tumbling to the ground.

# CHAPTER 30

## *She's finally back!*

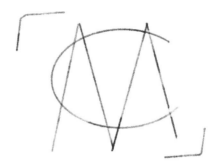

Maeve walked through the door of Dr. Claremore's office and plopped herself on the love seat without saying a word.

"She's back!" said Dorn excitedly. "Maggie!!! She's here!"

"Welcome," said Maggie as she walked into the room holding a cup of tea. "Would you like a cup?"

"Spare me the niceties," Maeve shot back at her.

"How have you been, Maeve?" asked Maggie. Maeve didn't reply.

"I guess she's not in the mood to talk," said Fon.

"Okay, then. I'll start," said Maggie. "It has been a very pleasant day. I got up at eight am..."

"Please stop. I'm not interested in a play-by-play of your boring day," said Maeve. "Can we just sit here and quietly wait for your billable hour to be up?"

"We certainly could," replied Maggie. "But I have always been a proponent of spending my time productively."

"Suit yourself!" said Maeve.

"What can we do to get her to start talking?" wondered Fon. "We need to get her engaged in conversation, otherwise we will have no chance in getting her to see the story through another lens, so to speak. I am sensing something. I think she is conflicted about what she read and wants to get it off her chest, but just doesn't know how to go about it. She's not mouthing-off as usual, which I find to be a good sign. It's not like her to just sit there quietly."

"Naturally, we need to earn her trust, somehow," said Dorn. "Hopefully then she'll open up to us. That is the only way." Maggie looked at the fairy brothers suggesting that she had it all under control.

"I see that you have been reading the book," started Maggie. "You know me, I like to get to the point right away, so let's talk about it."

"There's nothing to talk about. It's a stupid story about a stupid boring girl," spouted off Maeve. "Nothing of importance or significance happens in that story. Why anyone would read it is beyond me."

*"Well, I believe that a book is a precious gift that deserves to be read," said Maggie. "Giving a book a chance is the first step towards discovering a world of infinite possibilities. If you are lucky, through reading a book you may discover something about your own self as well." Maggie paused for a moment trying to gauge Maeve's reaction before continuing. "Books have the power to shape the world we live in. I do believe, that more important than anything else in one's existence, that a book has the power to change lives. That is, if the reader allows it to happen."*

*"Well...let me tell you that the only thing I 'discovered' about myself was how impatient I get when reading a stupid teenage fantasy-fiction novel," said Maeve.*

*"So, then you agree with the general statement that books can help shape our minds, our thoughts. Obviously, after reading this book you have some opinions. Meaning the book shaped the way you think about what you read, correct?" said Maggie.*

*"Certainly!" replied Maeve with such attitude, it made Fon raise is eyebrows instantly. "If one could agree that shaping one's mind to become angrier by the minute while reading this book is also a possible outcome of that theory, then I absolutely and whole-heartedly agree with you."*

*"Clever girl," said Fon with a smirk.*

*"Ok, let's unpack that anger, if you don't mind," said Maggie.*

287

*"Why do you think that happened?"*

*"Why did I think it? Well, first of all, every story has two sides. But sadly, no writer ever allows enough time to develop the backstory of their villain character or characters. Or characters that are perceived or painted to be villains when they are perhaps the unfortunate casualty here. Why is that? They deserve to be known by the reader at a much deeper level. They deserve to tell their own story, share their own feelings, and show the readers why they ended up where they did. Something must have led them to become who they are. We often only see the final outcome of the long journey that got them where they're at, and if we, as readers, don't get to experience that full journey, we develop a skewed perspective of them as characters. We are wired to then simply accept the fact that they are evil and bad. Our perception of them is based on the narrative written by the writer or the reactions the other characters have towards them. That is certainly a disadvantage to any villain character to help, even for a tiny bit, justify the reason why they are the way they are. Putting aside the morality of her decisions, think, just think for one moment how different the story would be if it were told from Regina's perspective."*

*"Mic drop!" said Dorn. "She is totally right, if you ask me."*

*Maggie sat there, not being able to articulate what she was thinking. Dorn was right. He was absolutely right. Maeve was onto* something here. "*I see your point,*" she said with honesty.

"*What hurt me the most was King Nubilus' declaration. 'And believe me when I say, that given the chance, she would end our lives with no hesitation.' How dare he makes such awful statement about his own daughter. He was obviously so far removed emotionally from his relationship with Regina that he completely gave up on understanding her actions. I'm sure he gave her no chance to explain.*" Maeve seemed very affected by this.

One thing Maggie wasn't expecting from any of these sessions with Maeve or the girls that came before her, was for one of them to shine a completely different light on her own story.

"*Funny how a story, when told through a different perspective, could potentially shape someone else's reality, their perception of the world and their own self,*" said Fon looking at Maggie.

For many Earthly years, through the work Maggie was doing here, she was focused on changing Regina. She desperately wanted to change her to accept her wrong doings. Maggie just realized one thing. That approach was altogether wrong. If Maggie were to save Regina, she, too, needed to understand the story from Regina's perspective.

"*Do you mind if we continue reading the story of Zonks together?*" asked Maggie, "*I'd very much like to start a dialog with you, to understand how you see it all.*"

"We can give it a try, I suppose," said Maeve.

"Good. I'm happy to hear that," said Maggie. "I'd like to take a different approach going forward, if that is alright with you. Rather than continuing with the tried-and-true approach, and by that, I mean reading the story, I'd like us to experience it together using virtual reality."

Maggie had a plan. If this were to work at all, they both needed to experience this story in a different way. The power of VR visual story telling is often underrated. It is a powerful but dangerous tool. This was Maggie's last chance to save Regina.

"Oh, my goodness," said Fon and Dorn at the same time.

"Prepare to have your mind blown, brother," said Fon. "We get to live through it all again. It'll feel like watching a movie for the first time but knowing what was going to happen next."

"Alright, let's stand," said Maggie, "I'm ready, if you are."

Maeve simply nodded, as she rose from her chair.

Maggie entered a series of keystrokes on her tablet and within a split second, the entire room transformed. They found themselves standing right in the heart of the Capital, looking at Molly, Aecus and Astoria. From here on, they were the invisible observers watching the story unfold in front of their eyes.

# CHAPTER 31

## *Who's with me?*

**M**olly rushed towards the rubble of the merry-go-around and started to dig her way to where Aiken and Eyya were buried amongst the debris.

"Aiken! Eyya...are you alright?" she asked.

"Yes, we are alright," replied Eyya as she clumsily stood up, dusting herself off and checking for any sign of injury. Aiken's shirt was torn to shreds, but otherwise he seemed to be alright.

"Ritana? Maya?" yelled Molly as loud as she could. "Where are you?" Molly was panicking. She searched the piles of rubble, throwing pieces of broken horses aside. "This can't be happening. This thing with Corcoran has got to end. Ritana!!!! Maya!!!"

"It'll be alright, Molly," said Eyya comforting her. "We will find them. Maya!!!" Eyya ran off towards a pile of rubble to the left of them, searching desperately. There were dozens of magical creatures crawling out from under the broken wood, gasping for clear air.

"They are here!" said Aecus as he moved a piece of rubble with his head off Ritana's body. "Ritana, are you alright? Can you hear me?"

"I don't know…" scraped and bruised with her sleeve half ripped off, she pushed a piece of wood off her legs. Molly rushed over to her and helped her up.

"Can you walk?" asked Molly.

"Yes, I can. I think I'm okay," replied Ritana as she limped out of the wreckage and onto the cobblestone street, holding her gashed forearm.

"Help! Help me!" Molly heard a cry from a short distance away.

"It's Maya!" Molly cried out. "She's stuck under this horse. Aecus, help!" Together, they pushed the broken horse off Maya, who seemed to be in worse shape than the rest. Blood gashing from her forehead was turning her beautiful white hair many shades of ruby.

"Ah, well, I always thought I'd look good as a red head," said Maya with a laugh as she put her crooked glasses back on.

Astoria walked closer, lifted her front paw and placed it on

Maya's gouged forehead.

"This will stop the bleeding, but unfortunately won't help the headache. Voco Potentia de Tus," she chanted. Within a few seconds, the wound instantly sealed itself.

Molly helped Maya off the ground, and they walked over to join the rest of the gang. She looked them over, one by one. They were all torn and bruised, and she realized this was all her fault. She was desperately trying to clear her mind to be able to focus on what needed to be done next. But her emotions were quickly starting to take over.

"I'm so sorry," she said as tears ran down her cheeks. "This is all because of me. I'll never forgive myself for this."

"Molly, none of this is your fault," said Astoria trying to comfort her. "You shouldn't blame yourself for this. Corcoran is an evil man who will do whatever it takes to get what he wants, that is for sure. Even if it means killing innocent people along the way to get to you." Astoria's heart was breaking. How could this have happened. How could she have let it happen?

"Astoria, now is not the time to be scaring the kids! Everything will be alright, now let's go!" said Aecus.

She could not believe the words that were coming out of his mouth. "Scaring the kids?!? I am not trying to scare anyone! They need to know the truth, Aecus. They need to know that their lives, just as ours, are in danger! This is serious stuff! And not talking about it and pretending that everything is alright...is...not...right! I have waited long enough, watched you and the Councilors talk about matters like these with little to no emotional attachment, treating every death as a price that needed to be paid. And, yes, that includes the death of King Zahar. Enough already! Let's speak plainly and say exactly what needs to be said. Because the truth is, we should never have agreed to any of this, Aecus!" Astoria was angry. Not with Aecus, but with herself. Because she was fully to be blamed for all of this. Had she never agreed to Maggie's plan, then none of this would have happened.

"You are correct, my love. I'm sorry to have upset you. But, you must all go back to the Grand Hall at once," said Aecus.

"But how could this happen? Is Corcoran coming?" Eyya was freaking out.

"I am not sure," replied Aecus. "Astoria and I will find out as much as we can but go now. You need to get off the streets, and to safety."

"Come everyone, let's go," said Ritana as she started heading towards the Grand Hall.

They ran down the cobblestone street past crowds of magical creatures, among which were dozens of Attendants ready to help the wounded.

"I don't understand," started Molly. "How could this have happened?"

"Let's see, the merry-go-round served as an apparatus of some sorts," said Ritana, "one that transmitted a signal coming from Corcoran."

"But I don't understand how," added Maya. "Aren't there spells that protect the city from this kind of invasion?"

"We have to hurry," Aiken rushed them. "We have to get to the Grand Hall. This chatter is just slowing us down!"

"He said he wanted someone's diary? But why?" asked Eyya all confused.

"He wants my diary," said Molly after a moment. She decided it was best they know everything, before it was too late.

"YOU ARE THE CHOSEN ONE?" said Eyya with her voice increasing in pitch, as she grabbed Molly's arm and stopped her in the middle of the street. "I wasn't sure at first..." she added, but instantly cutting herself short for Ritana shot her a glance indicating for her to stop blabbering before she said anything more.

Molly took a deep breath, and simply replied, "yes. I never wanted it to be, but yes - it seems that I am."

"It all makes sense now," said Eyya as they continued towards the Grand Hall. "That is why we are going off to the Forest of Inkhans. I was wondering why they would allow a...no offence...a 'mixed blood' to enter the ancient forest."

"A mixed blood? Stop it!" mouthed Ritana. She really needed

Eyya to stop blabbering.

"According to the prophecy I'm supposed to lead some sort of a revolution that will unite Heartland and ensure the safety of Terra Nova forever." She ended there, knowing that they had to keep moving, even though she wanted to let them know that she now knew about Maggie.

"I think the merry-go-round served as a signal receiver of some sort," continued Ritana, trying to change the subject as they hurried down the street. Terra Nova technology was her specialty.

"A what?" asked Eyya.

"It's technology that was invented on Terra Nova. No magic is strong enough to transmit an image of someone from that far away and be displayed with such clarity. We are quite far away from Skyland, so there must've also been a signal booster placed somewhere along the away," Ritana paused, the only sound heard was the echo of their footsteps on the deserted street. "Unless..." she continued, "unless someone placed one at Junction Manor! It is just the right spot, the halfway mark between here and Skyland."

"We are here!" said Aiken. "Molly, you are the only one who has the key to get us in."

"I know," said Molly hesitantly, "let me handle this." Molly opened the main door into the building, finding herself facing the tall desk at which sat the same goblin they met when they first arrived. He was looking sternly down at them. Her heart was beating faster than ever, for Molly, the thought of being in charge, being the leader...being the one counted on to make decisions and keep everyone safe at the same time caused her quite a bit of anxiety. At times, it felt crippling. She had no idea what lay ahead, but she promised herself to take things one at a time. 'Little by little,' as Madame de la Fleur would always say, 'one step at a time'.

"My name is Molly. Daughter of Lord Enderby and..." Molly paused for a moment, took a deep breath, then continued, "Clara, the Queen of Heartland."

Eyya and Ritana looked at each other in shock.

"Did you tell her?" whispered Ritana.

"No!" Eyya whispered back. "Why would you even assume it was me?"

"Place your wrist in the circle," said the goblin in a low, growly voice. And just as before, the desk and chair were swallowed into the ground, and then the goblin proceeded to open the pathway through the painting of the winged lion.

They made their way down the stairs and straight towards the elevators. "If he wants my diary so bad, he can have it," said Molly. "We have to see the Councilors and tell them right away."

"You can't hand over your diary, Molly," protested Eyya. "We

297

will have absolutely no hope in defeating him then."

"You're right," said Molly realizing that handing over her diary would be the wrong move. One by one, they all piled into the elevator.

"Where to?" asked the handsome elevator attendant elf.

"To The Oval Room," replied Molly.

"I'm afraid I can't do that," said the elf.

"But I have authorization," said Molly showing off her new tattoo.

"Ah, yes. The Councilors are not in session presently and we do not have any tours scheduled, therefore The Oval Room is closed," replied the elf.

"Let me handle this," whispered Ritana as she moved to the front of the group. "Hiii-eee, Jude. Is that your name?" she said as she gently touched his name tag on his lapel.

"Yes...it...is," stuttered the shy elevator attendant. He was certainly a bit intimidated by Ritana's advances and her beauty, even though she looked a bit disheveled from the accident.

"Forgive my appearance. I don't always look like this," said Ritana in a flirty manner. "We had a bit of an accident earlier – the whole merry-go-around exploded around us, and we fell to the ground. I'm sure you heard all about it by now. It was such a shocking experience." Ritana was batting her eyelashes hoping to gain some extra points, while she pulled little Maya in front of

left. It was the one belonging to the Woodland Councilor.

"What do you suppose we should do about it?" asked the Woodland Councilor. "This whole situation is getting out of hand. She is more of a liability now than ever."

"I agree," said the Winterland Councilor.

"Closing one Gate only has the potential to cause severe consequences," added the Waterland Councilor. "It is certainly not something we were counting on."

"What options do we have? Can we even trust Lord Enderby to know what he's doing?" asked the Barrenland Councilor.

"On a positive note," started the Shadowland Councilor, "I have a good feeling that Queen Clara will stay out of the Capital. Getting her out of here will certainly help our plan."

"But what about Theseus?" asked the Woodland Councilor.

"Leave him to me," replied the Shadowland Councilor.

Molly was about to reach the handle of the door, when suddenly stopped by a strange sound. A light flickered and soon it dimly illuminated the room.

"Is anyone there?" asked a strange voice. "Is anyone receiving this? Please, someone?"

Aiken ran towards the sound. "What do you want?" he whispered nervously, recognizing the boy in the mirror.

They all rushed towards the Skyland mirror. It was activated. In it, stood the image of a cloaked young man.

"What's going on?" asked Molly as they all cramped in between the mirror and the chair below.

"Who is this?" asked Eyya.

"Shhh, someone will hear you," the boy said as he took off his hood. "I'm Bevan. I don't have much time. Corcoran is going to attack Waterland at first dawn. You have to tell someone, please! Corcoran's army is going to move out at midnight. He's taking most of his armed guards with him. I have to go. Someone is coming!" said Bevan quickly pulling the hood of his cloak before he disappeared.

"We have to do something!" said Molly. "We have to tell the Councilors! They have to alert Waterland so they are prepared for the attack." Molly headed straight up the stairs and towards the private room of the Woodland Councilor.

"We need to hold off on closing the Skyland Gate until we can come up with a more solid plan," said the Woodland Councilor.

"Excuse us!" said Molly as she barged in on the conversation. All the Councilors turned towards her. "You have to alert Waterland. You have to tell them that he is coming. We have to send our armies."

"What are you talking about?" asked the Woodland Councilor.

"We just received news that Corcoran is going to attack Waterland at first dawn. Please, you have to do something."

"Nonsense," said the Waterland Councilor with a stern look. "It is highly improbable that Corcoran would do such a thing. Who did you hear this news from?"

"We received a message from a boy named Bevan just now, through the Skyland mirror," said Molly, shaking. She wanted them to get up off their feet and do something. Do something immediately. Lives were at stake, innocent lives of mermen and mermaids. Including her friend Caspian.

"Well, please do not worry," said the Shadowland Councilor as he proceeded to walk them out of the private room, down the stairs and towards the main door. "Everything is as it should be. I am certain that everything is under control and the patrols at each segment's border will alert us of any activities. Please, return to your dorms and rest. You have a long journey ahead of you."

The Councilor proceeded to push them gently through the door before shutting it behind them.

"I can't believe they are so daft," said Ritana angrily. "Also, I don't trust that guy. This is ridiculous, I hate adults! They never listen to anything we say."

"We can't just sit here and do nothing," said Eyya.

"This scares me very much," said Molly as she started walking down the hallway. "We have to do something. I just don't know what. But first we have to tell Clara and my father. I hope they are still in the library. Follow me!" she said before stopping and turning towards them. "There is only one slight problem. How to get to the library without being spotted. We'd have to risk using the elevator, and for that we have to have authorization to do so. Even if we somehow manage to get that far, someone would certainly question what business we had there."

"Perhaps Ritana's new boyfriend could help us out again," said Eyya with a smile.

"I'm ready to charm that little elf with my beauty and sophistication," said Ritana striking a pose.

Molly paused for a moment. "Let's not cash in another favor with him just yet," she said before continuing. "I can't believe I'm about to break a solemn promise. Argh...I hate how it makes me feel. You all have to promise me that you will forget about everything you're about to see the moment we get to the library." They all leaned in, full of excitement, for they knew Molly was about to reveal something. "We'll have to use the secret passageways!"

"Secret passageways?" said Eyya with her eyes widening in amazement. "I knew it! I always knew there were secret passageways here! But inquiring minds want to know. How do you know about them?"

Molly recalled the fun she had playing hide and seek, moving through the secret hallways of the Grand Hall. There were many times she raced Aecus from one room to the next. She had the most fun finding her way through the vast mazes of the hidden hallways and rooms while Aecus took the normal route of elevators and stairs.

"A long time ago, when I was around ten years old, Aecus showed me these secret passages, so I could easily move around without having to obtain approvals, or to explain myself to the elevator attendants or to anyone else. Even I," said Molly pointing at herself, "require authorization to move about this place. Follow me!"

Molly led them down the hallway until they reached a walk-through lounge with a few chairs, small tables with lamps and a cozy looking fireplace. Through this room hurriedly passed dozens of witches and wizards carrying stacks of papers, briefcases or gizmos that resembled a cross between a vintage typewriter and an abacus. None of them even noticed the state the kids were in - disheveled, with torn clothes and bruises on their faces. Eyya kept trying every little knob and lamp switch hoping to uncover a secret passageway.

"Eyya, what are you doing?" whispered Molly as she pulled her by the arm, and quickly hopped in front of a painting that was hanging on the wall pretending to admire it. "Do you want everyone to know our business? Please just act like everything is normal."

"Gotcha!" whispered Eyya with a wink. "Isn't this a lovely evening?" asked Eyya in a voice that would raise suspicion in an instant, "evening good sir. We are just admiring this wonderful artwork. Won't you look at this..."

"Eyya, my dear Eyya, isn't this painting just glorious?" asked Molly as she dragged her along to another piece of art hanging on the wall. "You're not helping with that voice of yours" she whispered. "You're really bad at this." Molly added with a smile. "Just stay quiet and follow my lead, okay?"

"Emphasis on 'quiet'," added Maya.

"Look at shy little Maya, cracking jokes," said Ritana with a smile as she punched Maya's shoulder. Maya blushed a little. She was the youngest of the bunch and often felt like she was more of a nuisance or a burden to all of them. In her mind they were all older, wiser, and cooler than she was, and she was just happy to be able to tag along with them every chance she got.

"Gotcha!" said Eyya enthusiastically.

"Ok Eyya, my investigative friend," said Molly once the lounge cleared, "can you find the buttons that open the secret door? I'll give you a hint – they are somewhere around the fireplace. Also, you have five seconds. The rest of you keep an eye out."

"What? That's not a fair time allotment," replied Eyya with a frown on her face. She tried to push a couple little protruding stone pieces on the fireplace, raised a candelabra, even a few books that were on the mantle. Nothing. "Dagnabbit, it's not working," said Eyya frustrated.

"Alright, time's up, my friend. Let me at it!" said Molly and she gently shoved Eyya aside.

"Oh, shrapnel," said Eyya disappointed.

"Hurry, someone's coming," said Aiken.

"There is a definite trick to this," started Molly, "each fireplace leads to the secret passageways, and each lock opens the exact same way, with the exception of one unique step that is specific to each fireplace. I think this one, just needs a little tap at the end," said Molly as she examined the fireplace.

"There's also a little rhyme I modified to remember these steps. It goes like this. Super-cauliflower-istic-expect-the-unexpected," as Molly recited this little rhyme, which was a fun little variation of the longest made-up word in the English language, she started the sequence to reveal the secret passage. First, she pressed a little stone, which unlocked a carving of a flower on the mantel that she pulled out and turned clockwise, then pressed it back into its original position. Then she pulled the lever that opened the chimney damper, then kicked the base part of the fireplace, and lastly tapped underneath the mantel. And with that final magic touch, the fireplace insert parted, revealing an opening to the secret hallways.

"That's a cool little rhyme," said Maya.

"Well, it's a good thing, there's no fire burning in this fireplace," said Ritana with a smirk.

"Alright everyone, hurry," said Molly as she crawled through, followed by the rest of the gang. She had barely enough time to close the fireplace before a witch pulling a cart full of files and boxes appeared from around the corner.

"That was close," said Maya.

"Wow, look at this," said Ritana in amazement. "This is incredible. But how does this work?" she continued as she tried to examine the wall for any sign of mechanics.

"I'll tell you all about it later, but right now we have no time to lose. Follow me! The hallways won't be lit well, so be careful!" ordered Molly, as she headed down a short narrow hallway that led to a metal spiral staircase. One-by-one, up they went for what seemed like a very long time.

"How far is it?" asked Eyya. "My legs are hurting. Guys, I'm so out of shape! I'm also getting dizzy going round and round and round up this spiral staircase."

"Not far," replied Molly. "The good news is, The Oval Room is in the same wing as the library, separated by six floors. We should be there shortly."

They made it up to the top of the spiral staircase, then followed Molly down a maze of hallways. "It's this way!" she said with ever-growing confidence. With each turn Molly gently brushed one of the stone bricks, as if to familiarize herself with the direction.

"I think we're here," said Molly as she reached out and pressed one of the stones on the wall at the end of a dead-end hallway. A secret door opened, revealing an entrance way through one of the bookcases on the main floor of the Library.

"Dad? Mom! You need to hear this!" said Molly as she ran into the room. The rest of them rushed in behind her. "They're not here!" Molly started to panic.

"Don't worry, Molly, I'm sure they are around somewhere," said Ritana.

"I don't think they are. Look, Molly! There is a folded card that reads *Astoria, please ensure Zonks gets this letter,*" said Eyya as she handed her a wax sealed envelope addressed 'Dear Zonks'.

Molly opened the letter and started to read it as her friends gathered around her. "They left for the Forest of Inkhans. Clara needed to retrieve some ancient protocols that my dad had to take back with him to Terra Nova. Well, that's that," said Molly. "We have no time to go after them. We have to go on a rescue mission."

"On a rescue mission?" asked Eyya bewildered. "What do you mean? Who are we rescuing? We certainly can't save the whole Waterland all by ourselves."

"That we can't," said Molly with solemn realization. "But we have to save Caspian. We have to at least try! Who's with me?"

"I am!" said Aiken without hesitation.

"I am!" said Maya.

"I am!" said Eyya.

"I am…" said Ritana. "We are the A team, after all. Aren't we?"

"Yeah, as-scared-as-a-scarecrow team," added Eyya. They all laughed and came to the sudden realization that as scary as the prospect of rescuing Caspian was, it was what had to be done.

"The only problem is we can't just grab a couple dragons and fly over to the shores without being seen," said Ritana, the logical one. She was really good at thinking a problem through fully, taking all the angles into account.

"That's true, I hadn't thought of that," said Eyya scratching her head. "Using the fast-moving spell is out, too. It would take us forever."

"And we can't apparate either. The Council imposed rules against that earlier this year," added Maya. "They said those in transit are most vulnerable to be attacked by Overlanders."

"There might be a quicker way," said Molly with a sparkle in her eye.

"Is it dangerous?" asked Maya.

"Not nearly as dangerous as what we've been through thus far," replied Molly. "The only problem is, I need to access my diary. In it, I remember writing a code for the elevators. An elevator capsule can take us straight to the shores of Waterland safely.

"What? That seems impossible," said Eyya in amazement.

"Remember the tracks we took from Junction Manor, and then the ones from the inside of the waterfall to The Tipsy Shrew?" asked Molly. "Well, they are both part of a network of abandoned railway tracks. The only way to use them is by using special codes. This may be our only chance." Everyone just stared at her. "What, you didn't know about this?" They all shook their heads. "I know, I know...my brain is full of garbage information."

"More like useful information," said Eyya with a giggle.

"Where is your diary now?" asked Aiken.

"It's filed over there," replied Molly pointing towards the bookcase at the top of the staircase. "Follow me. But please! Please do not touch any of the diaries inside!" Molly pleaded.

"Why is that?" asked Ritana.

"Their contents tend to erase when touched by anyone other than the Gate Keepers, unless permission is given."

"Oh, that is some serious stuff!" said Maya.

"Well, why are we just standing around?" said Molly excitedly. "Let's find my diary!"

They all ran up the stairs to the second level of the library. The books at the top of the stairs leading up to the balcony came to life and revealed an opening as Molly outstretched her right arm in front of the bookcase. Everyone followed Molly inside, albeit a bit hesitantly.

"Wow, I have never seen anything like this," said Eyya in awe.

"Look at all these books," said Ritana, as she was about to run her fingers along their spines.

"Remember," said Molly quickly, "don't touch any of the books. Stay right behind me."

Molly arrived at the forcefield separating the entrance tunnel with the main chamber. She touched it with her right hand. A beam of light around her hand expanded to the very edges of the tunnel, then instantly reversed direction causing the force field to shrink until it reached her spread out fingers. And with that, the forcefield completely disappeared.

"Uhm...what kind of magic is this?" asked Maya apprehensively.

"You don't have to worry, Maya. It is an ancient spell that protects the Chamber of the Gate Keepers," started Molly. "This is where the diaries of all the Gate Keepers are stored. Come this way, I think mine is in this area."

They followed Molly close behind. So close that Maya was practically touching Molly's back and jumped instantly when she heard the eerie sound of shuffling and ruffling.

"What was that?" asked Maya as she clung to Molly.

"Oh that," said Molly with a smile. "Yeah, it scared me too at first. It's just the books, shuffling around. I find the sound quite soothing, actually."

"Well, I think it's creepy," said Maya.

"My diary should be here, somewhere," said Molly as she walked down the hallway where she left her diary earlier that evening. "I'm quite certain this is where I put it, but it doesn't appear to be here anymore. Aiken, can you push that ladder over here?"

Molly climbed the ladder but still could not find her diary. "I can't believe it, it's gone!" The books started to shift around, switching places, moving about the entire bookcase, as if being shuffled like a deck of cards.

"Argh! Now what?" asked Molly frustrated. "We don't have time for this! At this rate, I'll never find my diary, we'll never be able to figure out the coordinates we need, and we'll never be able to save Caspian in time. This is hopeless!"

"Never say that, Molly," said Eyya. "I'm sure we'll find it."

Molly climbed down the ladder and headed straight out into the open circular room. The kids followed right behind her. She was determined to leave the Library at once and find another way to get to Caspian. The grimoire in the middle lit up as Molly passed by it.

"Look, Molly!" said Aiken excitedly. "Look at this book!"

Zonks and The Gate Keepers

Molly rushed towards the center platform where the illuminated grimoire rested atop the old podium. 'Numbers!' she thought to herself. "I hate numbers!" she said out loud. "I'm great at other things, but not figuring out what to do with numbers!" In each of the six circles that previously showed the names of the Heartland segments was a single digit number. But the number kept changing every couple of seconds.

"What do these numbers mean?" asked Eyya as she came closer.

"I don't know," said Molly, sweat dripping from her brow. "Numbers stress me out big time! I'm bad with numbers. I'm bad at math and I'm bad at figuring out any logic around numbers!" Molly's anxiety started to creep up. Her heartbeat increased, her breathing doubled its speed. A bright light appeared in the seventh circle, which was previously empty. That circle was slightly bigger than the rest.

"Now what is this supposed to mean?" said Molly with frustration in her voice. The rest of the kids gathered around the podium.

"Ok, Molly. Don't stress," said Ritana, trying to comfort her. "I'm sure we'll figure this out. Concentrate. We just have to concentrate."

Molly closed her eyes, took a couple of deep breaths and tried to clear her mind. To her surprise, it was working. She was getting better and better at this and that gave her some level of comfort. "Ok, there are two sets of three circles on either side of the words Grimoire of the Gate Keepers. Then there's this bigger circle, all lit up like a star on top of the Christmas tree. What does this mean? I don't have time for this. Just reveal the location of my diary and we'll be out of here!" said Molly, angrily kicking the podium. The calm and focus she found moments earlier had gone.

"Molly," Aiken stepped in, "it'll be alright. Five heads are better than one. I just know we'll come up with something."

"I think I might have something," stuttered Maya in amazement. "I think I got it! First take a look at the circles with the numbers. Yes, there are three on either side of the title. You see!" Everyone leaned in to take a closer look. "The numbers keep changing. I think what we need to figure out first is how to stop them from changing." Maya tapped each circle, but nothing happened. "Well, that didn't work."

"Let me try," said Molly, energized by a sliver of hope thinking that perhaps it would only respond to a Gate Keeper. She started tapping each circle, but again nothing happened. "Show me where my diary is you stupid book!" The numbers just kept changing. It also seemed they were changing faster than before.

"Wait!" said Maya. "Give me your right hand." Maya grabbed

Molly's hand and gently placed it on top of the circle with the light coming out of it.

"Yes! Something is happening!" said Maya as the numbers in the first circle from the left started to change at much slower rate until it stopped. "Number three."

One of the hallways to the left of them illuminated a tiny bit. It was a barely noticeable change in the level of light, but Maya's eye certainly caught it.

"Yes. That makes sense now! Look up." Everyone looked up. "Not at the ceiling, you dummies. Look straight ahead. What do you see?" Maya added with a smile.

"A painting of what looks like Aecus and Astoria heading into the sunset?" said Eyya.

"Do you see anything else?" prodded Maya.

"Yes, curtains, books, shelves, stone floor. I'm not exactly sure what you are getting at," said Ritana barely containing her impatience with Maya.

"Look at how these numbers are laid out compared to the layout of the room," said Maya excitedly. "You see how on either side of the grimoire's name there are circles with changing numbers. On either side of the painting, there are three long hallways lined with bookshelves full of diaries. Now, I'm not exactly sure where your diary shuffled off to, but I think it is in hallway number three over there." Maya pointed toward the

315

hallway that had a number three on top of its entrance.

"That number wasn't there before," said Ritana excitedly. "We are onto something. What's next."

"Ok, now what?" asked Molly, her anxiousness starting to ease a bit, as she slowly caressed the circle with number 3 in it.

"I think you figured it out," said Maya. The number in another circle started to slow down. "Look! Number one. It looks like each time you tap the circle where the number stopped changing, it causes the numbers in another circle to stop changing. That's how it works! Now that we figured out how to stop the numbers from changing, we have to figure out what those numbers mean."

"You're so smart, Maya! I don't know what we would do without you!" smiled Molly. "Thank you. We'll find this beast of a diary, even if I have to tear apart this entire place myself." Molly couldn't believe the words that were coming out of her mouth, but now was not the time to contemplate her temper. "The numbers will give us the location of my diary. We have number three and number one. We know that the diary is located somewhere in hallway number three."

"Alright!" said Maya excitedly as she ran down towards the hallway with the number three above its entrance. "Each hallway is lined with bookshelves as far as the eye can see," she continued. "The second number may just represent the left or right side. What's the next number, Molly?"

Molly touched the circle with the number one in it, which caused the next circle to stop changing numbers, until the number five was displayed. "It's five. The number is five!" shouted Molly.

"This is really exciting!" said Eyya.

"Tell me about it. I feel like I'm in a bingo hall, calling out numbers," said Molly with a laugh. Eyya just looked at her puzzled, obviously not knowing what a bingo hall was.

"I think..." shouted Maya as she looked down the long hallway, examining every possibility for what this number may represent, "...I see a light down the hallway on the left side. Yes!!! The number one represents the left side of the hallway and the number five..." Maya started running down the hallway counting from one to five. "Yes, it's the fifth stone column that partitions these bookshelves."

"What did you say?" shouted Molly. At this point, Maya was quite a way down the hallway, and Molly had a hard time hearing her.

"I have an idea. Eyya, come with me," said Ritana as she grabbed Eyya's arm, leading her to the entrance of hallway number three. "I'll run down to the halfway mark between the hallway entrance and where Maya is. You stay here, and we can pass the messages back-and-forth. It'll be much easier this way."

"That's a great idea," shouted Molly as Ritana started to run.

"Alright, I'm in place," shouted Ritana. "Maya, what did you say?" "I said, the third number represents the number of stone pillars separating the sections of these big bookshelves. The small lamp on fifth one was lit up. What's the next number?"

"Maya figured out the third number," shouted Ritana. "What's the next number?"

"What's the next number?" shouted Eyya.

Molly went to work. She tapped the circle with the number five in it, until the next circle stopped changing numbers, revealing number seven.

"It's seven. The next number is seven!" shouted Molly.

Both Eyya and Ritana repeated the number.

"There seem to be about a dozen individual bookshelves side by side between each stone pillar!" shouted Maya. "Ah, I found it. It is the seventh bookshelf. There is a small light that just lit up. What's the next number?"

"What's the next number?" shouted Ritana back to Eyya.

"We're ready for the next number, Molly!" shouted Eyya.

"It's 12. The number is 12!" shouted Molly.

Once again, both Eyya and Ritana repeated the number, as their voices echoed down the long hallway. Up until now Aiken just stood there next to Molly, watching quietly.

Molly could not wait any longer, she ran her fingers over the circle with the number 12, revealing the final number. She then jumped off the platform and ran straight towards hallway number three.

"I've got the final number," said Molly as she ran past Eyya, who followed right behind her. "Come on Aiken, what are you waiting for?" she shouted.

They all ran down the hallway towards Maya. It only now occurred to Molly how long these hallways were. She was out of breath by the time she got to Maya.

"What's the last number?" asked Maya once everyone got there.

"It's 22," replied Molly.

"So, the last two numbers are 12 and 22," said Maya looking up, trying to see any sign of a clue.

"Alright, what do you need?" whispered Molly to herself. "You stupid little book, where are you!"

"I'm sure we'll figure out what's next, Molly," said Maya turning towards her.

"Don't get discouraged," said Eyya, trying to comfort her.

While the girls tried to comfort Molly, Aiken dragged over a ladder and started climbing it. With each step, the ladder begun to vibrate.

"Something is happening!" he shouted. He almost reached the half-way point as the vibration became stronger and stronger.

"Aiken, what are you doing?" shouted Eyya, but he did not

hear her. As if in a trance, he was climbing the ladder one step at a time. Light illuminated from behind each book on the 12th shelf. Aiken was about to reach for one of them when Molly shouted.

"Don't touch it, Aiken!" Aiken was shot back and off the ladder, falling down to the floor and landing on his back. He seemed to have regained consciousness, and quickly realized what he was trying to do.

"Are you alright?" asked Molly looking over at him.

"I'm okay, I think. I don't know what just happened. I don't know what got into me," he replied.

"Molly, I think I know what the other two numbers mean," said Maya. "I think that your diary is on the 12th shelf. Once you get up that high, count out 22 books from the left."

As Molly reached the 12th shelf, the shuffling of the books stopped immediately.

"It's happening. We found it," said Eyya, jumping in excitement.

A bright light illuminated the entire row, until it slowly shrunk around one book. That was it. That was Molly's diary. She grabbed it off the shelf as everyone cheered.

"Alright, where is it? Where is it?" said Molly as she flipped through the pages of her diary. "I know it's here, somewhere. Ah, yes! Here!" Everyone leaned in to have a closer look. "The elevator code is 44-79-23-1. Can somebody remember that?"

"44-79-23-1. Got it!" said Maya.

"Thanks, girl," said Molly.

"What do all those numbers mean?" asked Ritana.

"It is far too complicated to explain right now," said Molly. "It has to do with the placement of each destination - both geographically as well as in time and space. I don't really understand it fully myself."

"The elevator will take us to an abandoned train platform, like the one at Junction Manor," said Molly. "I just hope there will be some train cars left in there so we can borrow one of them and head straight to the shores of Waterland. Maya, can you remember another number?"

"Yes!" Maya replied eagerly.

"Here it is," said Molly after flipping through a few pages in her diary. "This is the code for the train, so it can find the platform by the seashore. It is 33-87-65-2." Maya nodded.

"Alright," continued Molly as she put her diary back on the shelf in the exact spot where she found it, before making her way back down the ladder. "Once we get out of the library, you have to act as if nothing is out of the ordinary." Molly looked sternly at Eyya. "No more shenanigans. We have to make our way back to the elevator lobby without raising any suspicion. Let's go."

They all began to head down hallway number three towards

the exit with Aiken trailing at the back. He swiftly turned around, pulled out a thin grey glove from his bag and placed it on his right hand. He then used the fast-moving spell to make his way back up the ladder and reached with his gloved hand for Molly's diary before it had a chance to be shuffled away. He forcefully shoved the diary into his messenger bag, removed the glove and put it in his pocket. He ran to catch up with the gang just as they reached the entrance to the chamber. Nobody seemed to notice he hadn't been with them for that brief moment. As the books behind them closed the entrance shut, he gently touched the bag where the book lay inside and whispered, "I'm sorry, Molly," he whispered to himself.

to be continued

# Book 2, CHAPTER 1

*Time to go.*

Theseus led Clara and George through the beautiful gardens of the Grand Hall. "Your Majesty; Lord Enderby, this way," he said. Meticulously kept ornate hedges and bushes lined the cobblestone pathways that continued across stone bridges, leading the way over calm creeks of water spilling into small ponds, until they found their way towards the cliffs and disappeared into the depths below. They reached what seemed to be a partial ruin of an old house. Most of it was gone, except for a section of the front façade with partial window casings, a doorway and the remnants of some old marble flooring. This small mansion once proudly overlooked the ancient Forest of Inkhans that stretched below the cliff. Theseus led them through the doorway opening, where three majestic dragons waited on what remained of the marble floor of the entrance hall of the mansion; saddled and ready to go.

They mounted their dragons and flew off and over the cliff towards the vast forests below. It was a very long time since Clara felt the wind in her hair, riding so freely. Ever since the death of her father she had felt lost. No matter how hard she tried, she could not shake that dreadful feeling of spinning out of control, faster and faster with each minute with nothing in sight to grab onto. She was losing control over Heartland. She could not help but feel if she were a better leader, had she been stronger - none of this would have happened. She could have prevented all of this. Her family was together yet torn apart again. She promised herself she would be strong. She needed to be. For herself, for Maggie, Molly, George and for Heartland.

They flew over the gorgeous landscape of woods and clearings, rivers and creeks, until they reached the tall dark green trees of the ancient forest.

Theseus pointed towards the direction of the largest tree. This was it, George thought. This was the ancient Forest of Inkhans, with the oldest tree in all of Heartland - the Tree of Life nestled right in the middle of it. As if a hundred tree trunks were fused together, with their massive crown stretching towards the sky, the tree stood tall above the rest of Woodland.

The dragons hovered briefly over top of the Tree of Life. The wind from their wings caused the branches to open up, allowing them to slowly disappear amongst the leaves. As if the ancient tree swallowed them in whole. The dragons gently landed, causing the dust to stir off the ground.

As they dismounted their dragons, George looked up to see the massive crown of the Tree of Life above them, like a canopy. Ahead of them was a long bridge crossing the body of water surrounding the island that housed the massive tree.

Eyya's father, King Silva of Woodland was waiting for them. "Welcome, Queen Clara of Heartland and Lord Enderby. We have been awaiting your arrival."

"Thank you," said Clara. "Have Fon and Dorn had the chance to brief you."

"Yes, they just left," said the King. "We don't have much time. Allow me to introduce you to Corbus Damwich, our Oracle. Your Majesty, he will guide you to the sacred place where the ancient scrolls are hidden."

This woodland elf must have been a few centuries old, with only a few strands of long, thin, white hair left on his head. His white-bearded face looked weathered and wrinkled. In his hand he held a staff that curved at the top where a leaf gently circled inside a swirl of green mist.

"Lord Enderby," King Silva continued. "I wish we had the

chance to meet under much more pleasant circumstances, but none-the-less, I am delighted to welcome you to our land. It will be my honor to guide you to the Woodland Gate."

"Thank you," said George.

"Theseus, please return to the Capital and ensure everything is ready for the children's journey," said Clara. "Please assist Aecus and Astoria in any way you can. I will see you tomorrow."

"Yes, your Majesty," replied Theseus. He mounted his dragon and flew off.

"George, I will see you at the Gate," said Clara. She kissed him and then they went on their separate ways.

## ABOUT THE AUTHOR

As a child growing up in Slovakia, Martin's story telling journey started at the age of three, when he would learn and recite short poems to anyone who would listen. That love transitioned into almost three decades of performing on stage and in film both in Slovakia and then in Canada after immigrating here in 2000.

The journey of being a writer started in the fall of 2009 in the form of bedtime stories Martin would conjure up for his daughter Cassidy, who was the true inspiration for this book. Cassidy's nickname had always been Zonks because she would often fall asleep, or 'zonk out' before finishing her bottles.

As the story started to grow, Martin began writing down the elements of the story and after over ten years of molding and shaping the text, the story of **Zonks and the Gate Keepers** was born. This story is a true family collaboration – with chapter heading illustrations created by Cassidy and editing by his wife Stephanie. A big thank you goes out to Corina Pospisil for her insights and inputs.

The book you are holding in your hands is part of a much larger story called **The Chronicles of Heartland** – which consist of the three-part series of **Zonks and The Gatekeepers** and seven novellas dedicated to each of the Heartland segments. Martin was honored for his significant contribution to the arts in Canada and is the distinguished recipient of the Queen's Diamond Jubilee Medal.

*"I hope you will enjoy reading the story of Molly and Maggie just as much as I enjoyed writing it. At its core, this is a complicated family story that teaches us that we can't always forget the unintentional pain caused by others, but perhaps we can find a way to at least understand why they acted the way they did and ultimately seek a path towards forgiveness."*

*~ Martin Galba*
www.martin-galba.com

Made in the USA
Monee, IL
16 September 2021